Praise for
Jenny Hal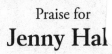

Christmas Wishes and Mistletoe Kisses

"[A] tender treat that can be savored in any season."

—*Publishers Weekly* (Starred Review)

"[Jenny] Hale's impeccably executed contemporary romance is the perfect gift for readers who love sweetly romantic love stories imbued with all the warmth and joy of the holiday season."

—*Booklist*

It Started with Christmas

"This sweet small-town romance will leave readers feeling warm all the way through."   —*Publishers Weekly*

The Summer House

"Hale's rich and slow-building romance is enhanced by the allure of the North Carolina coast...North Carolina's beautiful Outer Banks are the perfect setting for this sweet, poignant romance, and authentic characters and a riveting story make it a keeper worth savoring."

—*Publishers Weekly* (Starred Review)

"Like a paper and ink version of a chick-flick...gives you the butterflies and leaves you happy and hopeful."   —*Due South*

a Christmas
to remember

ALSO BY JENNY HALE

a Christmas to remember

JENNY HALE

FOREVER

NEW YORK   BOSTON

Copyright © 2014, 2019 by Jenny Hale

Cover design by Emma Graves. Cover images © Shuttershock. Cover copyright © 2020 by Hachette Book Group, Inc.

Forever
Hachette Book Group
1290 Avenue of the Americas, New York, NY 10104
read-forever.com
twitter.com/readforeverpub

Originally published in 2014 and 2019 by Bookouture, an imprint of StoryFire Ltd.
First Forever Edition: October 2020

Forever is an imprint of Grand Central Publishing. The Forever name and logo are trademarks of Hachette Book Group, Inc.

The publisher is not responsible for websites (or their content) that are not owned by the publisher.

The Hachette Speakers Bureau provides a wide range of authors for speaking events. To find out more, go to www.hachettespeakersbureau.com or call (866) 376-6591.

LCCN: 2020938828

ISBN 978-1-5387-5368-2 (trade paperback)

Printed in the United States of America

LSC-C

10 9 8 7 6 5 4 3 2

For Tia,
who has been there for me since childhood.

Chapter One

People under stress can benefit from doing something familiar.

Carrie highlighted the passage in her book and closed it. With a deep breath, she set it on the passenger seat of the car next to a half-empty box of candy canes she'd bought at a border store between North Carolina and Virginia on her way to her new nanny position.

Growing up in a small town in North Carolina, Carrie's life had been very predictable. She'd gone to school with friends in her neighborhood, and every afternoon—even on the coldest days—her mother had waited on the swing of their long front porch for her to get off the bus. When it was snowing—like it was now—she and her parents went sleigh riding down the big hill in her front yard, and afterward, her father brought in logs from the back porch and started a fire in their stone fireplace to warm them up. She and her friends would sit in front of the flickering flames, legs stretched out, their fuzzy socks all in a row while her mother divvied out mugs of hot cocoa. She never tired of it. She relished the warm memories.

And now Carrie sat in her car, far away from all that was familiar. She'd taken this job in Virginia because her new boss, Adam Fletcher, had offered her a job she couldn't refuse. And the position was temporary, only lasting through New Year's. Even though she hadn't planned to continue on as a caregiver, Carrie had decided that this would be her last nanny job before moving on to something else.

The snow was coming down all around her, and she could feel the chill of winter slipping into the car. The sky was a seamless white, blurring with the snow-covered ground. All the houses on this street were brick, their red and brown surfaces the only color against the blank canvas of snow. Even the street was covered, and snowflakes were falling so quickly that they hid the tire tracks nearly as fast as passing cars could create them. Carrie allowed the white expanse through her windshield and the quiet scene outside to calm her, just as her cell phone lit up on the seat, the ringtone shrill against the surrounding silence. She grabbed it before she'd even looked at the number.

"Hello?" she said, closing her eyes and cringing because she'd been impulsive in answering—she only had a few minutes left before she had to be on the Fletchers' doorstep. Trying to rush someone off the phone would only frazzle her, and she didn't want to be frazzled on day one.

"Hi. Is this Carrie Blake?"

"Yes."

"It's Adam Fletcher."

She sat up straight, every inch of her body on high alert. Adam, her new boss, had an authoritative voice, the kind that made her want to put her best foot forward, the kind that made her over-analyze every single word that came out of her mouth just to be sure she'd made a good impression. He was also in the house right beside her.

"Hello," she said, not knowing what to say next.

"Is that you outside, sitting in your car?"

She didn't want to look over at the house for fear that she'd make eye contact with him through a window. She'd been sitting outside for the last five minutes, waiting for her watch to tick over to four thirty, when he'd asked her to come by. She'd driven there in enough time to give herself a few minutes to spare. She'd sat in her car, reading her most recent purchase: *How to Overcome Life's Little Worries*.

"I was waiting for four thirty," she said honestly.

"Well, it's freezing. Please hang up and come in."

"Okay . . . Bye." She clicked off her phone and dropped it into her handbag. How ridiculous must she look sitting outside in the car? Had he seen her reading, catching the drips on her coffee cup with her bottom lip as they slid underneath the lid?

The snow was falling so hard that it was coming down sideways, landing the size of quarters onto her car, and collecting in large quantities at the base of her windshield. Carrie pulled her coat up around her chin and turned the engine off. With her hands wrapped around her coffee cup, she drank the last sip as she looked across the wide, snow-filled yard to the house that would be her residence for the upcoming weeks.

The Fletcher house was easily in the multimillion-dollar range. Houses in this part of Richmond weren't cheap, and this one had to be somewhere at the top of the list. The whole thing was painted brick—white like the snow—which set it apart from the other homes nearby. It had wings on each side, and, as she squinted to see through the precipitation, it looked like an original slate roof. The house was in the city, but outside of the downtown area enough that it had a yard and sidewalks lined with trees. The road snaked alongside the James River like an old friend, bending and turning just the same. She'd never worked in a home this grand before.

Adam Fletcher had seemed a bit formal when they'd spoken, but pleasant, and had given her no indication that he was so wealthy. *Why would he, though*? she thought. She wasn't even inside yet and her hands were jittering.

Getting coffee had been her "something familiar" that her book had suggested would ease her nerves. Since she'd arrived in Richmond earlier than expected, she'd driven through the city, squeezing down narrow side streets and following the small city blocks until she'd found a coffee shop. Even with the time she'd spent trying to get a parking spot, when half the parallel spots were full of plowed snow, she'd been able to stop for a cup of coffee. It was an unfussy little shop with burlap bags of coffee against the counter, the whole place smelling of roasted beans. There were a few quaint wooden tables and chairs nestled in the corner against a chalkboard full of pastel lettering. Noticing the time, she'd taken her coffee to go. The coffee hadn't helped to calm her, though. Perhaps she hadn't picked the right familiar thing to do.

When it came to her personal life, Carrie felt as though she could never quite get it right. And this time of year was always the worst. At Christmas, when everyone spent time with their families, she either spent her days working, or she went home to her mother and father. While she loved her parents dearly, she longed to have her own family to come home to. She wanted children, a loving husband—a family with whom she could make new memories as perfect as those of her childhood. She wanted a giant Christmas tree and stockings on the fireplace, to make cookies for Santa, and catch her kids peeking at the presents under the tree. But as the years went by, she just didn't know how to achieve what she wanted.

Ten years ago, when she was twenty-three, Carrie had graduated with an early childhood degree and jumped right into her first job quickly. She found that she was fairly successful as a live-in nanny, and she enjoyed it, so that was what she'd spent the past decade doing. She'd taken the kids to the park in the summer, eating picnic lunches on blankets, flying kites in the breeze. She'd taken them ice skating at the outdoor rinks, laughing with them as they attempted to stand, looking like Bambi on ice, their little legs slipping out from under them. She'd made muffins for breakfast with the children and homemade bread for dinner. She'd painted, constructed, colored, and cut—each creation so unique and perfect that she struggled to take it off the refrigerator when it got old. She loved being a nanny. But because of the job she hadn't dated anyone seriously, and she hadn't been able to learn who she wanted to be.

Carrie had read enough self-help books to know that she wasn't happy, but she wasn't sure exactly how to change that. What she did know was that if she ever wanted to have her own life, and the possibility of her own family, she'd have to eventually find a job that had regular hours, where she could work with people over the age of five and come home at a decent time. She'd gotten college course catalogs from some of the colleges back home, and she'd leafed through a few of them, but she hadn't found what she wanted to do.

There wasn't anyone she could talk to about her predicament. Her parents, while supportive, just told her to choose something else and do it. Neither of them had jobs they loved, and they said that she may have to *settle* on something like they had. But she didn't want to settle. She moved around so much as she changed jobs that she lost touch with a lot of her college friends and she hadn't really made any new friends. It all left her feeling lost.

This was to be her last job, and then, if she didn't find something else she really wanted to do, she would just have to choose something. But right now, it was time to face her new family. She opened the door and stepped into the frigid air. The wind blew at her in frosty gusts, slithering down her coat collar despite her new striped scarf. She lumped a few things into her handbag, pulled it close to her body for extra warmth, and trudged across the yard, her head down to keep the snow out of her face.

She clomped her way through the snow until she reached the landing. Sitting at the top of three very wide brick steps was a black door as shiny as the house's shutters, with a brass knocker in the center. On either side, a row of single windowpanes stretched from the top of the door all the way down to the porch. The light was on inside. Before she could even ring the bell, she could make out a shadow behind the curtain and she heard footsteps getting closer.

The door opened.

Carrie blinked over and over to steady herself as she stood in front of Adam Fletcher.

He was definitely easy on the eyes. His dark blond hair looked as though he'd just run his fingers through it, and he was wearing a thick sweater with a collar, jeans, and loafers, a watch the size of Texas that looked more expensive than any she'd ever seen in real life peeking out from under his sleeve. His lips were pressed into a pleasant expression, and his eyes, as blue as ocean waves, were looking straight at her... Waiting for her to say something? Should she speak first?

"Hello," he said, before she could get her thoughts straight. He reached out for a handshake. "Adam. Adam Fletcher. Nice to meet you."

"Hi," she said, clasping his hand. She could feel the warmth through her glove. She'd never read up on how to handle a handsome boss before. As she was mentally adding it to her list of books to find, she realized that she hadn't said anything more than "hi," so she quickly added "I'm Carrie Blake. It's nice to meet you." *He just said "Nice to meet you." Ugh!* she thought. She squared her shoulders, smiled, and nodded like her book had said.

Chapter Two

It's often helpful to find healthy distractions.

Somehow, she didn't think that Adam Fletcher was the kind of distraction her book had in mind but this situation was definitely occupying her thoughts. In her past positions, Carrie had usually dealt with mothers. They'd all fit a general description: working mother, trying to meet the demands of business while also raising children, pulling long hours. She was used to walking around in her pajamas in the mornings and getting herself breakfast before she'd even gotten ready for the day. What would it be like sharing a house with a man? He'd said on the phone that he was a single dad, but it hadn't sunk in until now. She had a feeling that this may take her a bit of getting used to.

Adam ushered her inside, shutting the door behind her, and Carrie took in the entryway. The floor was some sort of marble that stretched up the curving staircase. She gazed up the dark wood banister all the way to the balcony, where she reached an enormous chandelier, two stories up. It was an explosion of wrought iron in the shape of leaves and branches that stretched up to teardrop-shaped light bulbs, their light most likely on a dimmer switch because they were almost flickering. Back on the first floor, an entryway table stood against the side of the staircase, and on it was an iron lamp that sent a buttery yellow light around the room. And beside the lamp, sat a heavy silver frame, containing a photo of two babies with wispy hair and milky skin, both dressed in white linen outfits. One was a bibbed overall and the other was a little dress with white smocking across the front.

"Ah," he said, causing her to shift her focus over to him. "Those are the twins, David and Olivia. They're older now—four—as I mentioned when we spoke on the phone."

She turned back to the picture. Looking at their little faces, the dimple on the boy's right cheek, the blue of the girl's eyes behind her long eyelashes, it melted her nerves away. As she took in the photos, it occurred to her that there weren't any Christmas decorations in the house, and she wondered if they didn't celebrate.

Carrie couldn't imagine not celebrating Christmas with kids—it was her favorite holiday. Nothing compared to their faces lighting up with the magic of the season. Seeing them under the lights of the Christmas tree, reading stories in their pajamas, and leaving cookies on a plate with a cup of milk for Santa Claus, watching them unwrap presents in a wild, ripping frenzy, as if they couldn't get to the inside fast enough. She loved the Christmases she could spend with children, and she always felt a little cheated when she was given time off. Suddenly, Carrie wanted to see the Fletcher kids right away; she could hardly wait to introduce herself.

"The children are in the playroom. Would you like to meet them?" Adam said as if reading her mind. "Then we can chat about the specifics of the position." He opened a door in the hallway and pulled out a wooden hanger that matched all the others in the closet. "May I take your coat?"

Carrie shrugged it off and handed it to him along with her scarf and gloves. She caught herself wondering if her outfit was professional enough. Did she have scuffs on her shoes? They were surely wet and discolored from the snow outside. What must her hair look like covered in melting snow? She tucked it behind her ear. She'd never worried about how she looked before. Usually, she was covered in spit-up, cloth diapers draped on her shoulders, sock feet.

Adam's demeanor dripped with confidence. He had a way about him that seemed strong and self-assured—she didn't know if it was his walk or the way he held his shoulders, but she could sense it just by looking at him.

"The playroom is this way." He pointed down the hallway. "It's Natalie's last day with us. She's found a full-time position," he said, smiling cordially in Carrie's direction. "You'll be taking over tomorrow." He looked down at her, causing a little flutter.

They arrived at the door, and Carrie had to stifle a gasp as she peered inside. It looked like something out of a storybook. Every toy was neatly displayed on dark wood library shelves that stretched the height of the ceiling, a rolling ladder poised on a track that circled the room. There were rocking horses that resembled the ones on a carousel, enormous foam blocks in one corner, an art table bigger than her car. A young woman she assumed was Natalie sat on the floor beside the kids as she delicately balanced a wooden cube on the top of a tower of multicolored blocks. Her dark, shiny hair was pulled back into a perfect ponytail at the back of her neck, every strand in place. She had a gentle but controlled expression.

Next to her, a little boy was dressed in a tiny pair of jeans, with socks that matched the red of his sweater. His hair was dark blond like his daddy's, and curled around his ears. He had big gray eyes and a round face. His brows were furrowed in concentration as he steadied a wobbling block. He tried to keep it from falling, and by accident knocked it off. Carrie could see the tension in his shoulders as he blew air out of his thin pink lips. He picked the block up off the floor and studied the tower to find a better spot. Carrie noticed the tight grip he had around the block, the way his toes moved inside his socks as he focused on the tower, and she thought that the little boy seemed to be carrying a lot of worry. She understood about worry.

The little girl walked over to Carrie, grabbed her hands and smiled, revealing a row of white, perfectly shaped teeth. Then, as quickly as she'd come over, she went back to the tower. Her hair was slightly lighter than her brother's, the golden strands bringing out the blue of her eyes. She had a heart-shaped face and a little pout that twitched as she balanced her block. When the blocks were all placed on their tower, the little girl turned to Carrie. "Hello," she said in a high-pitched voice, as she played with the hem of her dress, showing her tights underneath. "I'm Olivia."

"Hi," Carrie said to her, unable to control her smile. Olivia's hair had been pulled into a ponytail, tufts of curls escaping it, sending little flyaways toward her face. She pushed them out of her eyes with the palms of her hands, her little nails painted a sparkly pink. Olivia's dress was navy blue with an embroidery pattern at the top like the one in the picture downstairs, but this pattern was the same light blue as her tights. Her navy shoes had petite silver buckles that shone as her feet pattered along the rug.

Natalie looked up too and smiled. "Hello," she said. "You must be Carrie." She stood to greet her.

"I'll leave you now," Adam said, stepping back through the doorway. "Natalie, if you don't mind, just lead Carrie to my office when you're done showing her around the playroom." As he walked out,

Carrie wished he would stay. It was such a surprising feeling to have, but he had a quality about him that made her want to know more. With his quiet nature, he came off a little mysterious.

Just before Adam left, Carrie saw him smile at his children, but she noticed they hadn't run to him. They hadn't lit up when they'd seen him, and there was something distant about their encounter. In fact, as he exited, they stood quietly, their faces still and calm, their hands unmoving, their tiny feet planted in that spot. It rattled her. She'd never witnessed children who were so reserved, so careful about how they interacted with their own parent. While he was direct and no-nonsense, Adam didn't seem scary or worrying at all, so it was strange to her that the children would act that way toward him.

He shut the door, and the children continued to watch her, as Carrie sat down cross-legged on the giant burgundy and spruce-colored rug. "What are you playing?" she asked the kids but instead of answering, the children looked at Natalie.

"Blocks." Natalie smiled.

"What's the game?"

"Oh, there wasn't a game. We were just building."

The lone towers of single blocks stood in the center of the rug, all the other toys tucked away in their places. It was clear that Natalie's style of child rearing was different than hers. Natalie had a quietness about her, a rigidity that was clear just by watching the way she interacted with the children. She seemed pleasant and caring, but by the look of the tower and the toys surrounding them, she wasn't the type to get down on her hands and knees and ride them around on her back or toss them into the air just to make them laugh. Carrie wondered if her style of child care would fit in this house. There were more blocks in the bucket, so she reached in and pulled one out.

"Where should I put it?" she asked the little boy, David. What she wanted to do was pull out the bin of cars, build a parking garage, perhaps make a drive-in theater, and act out a story. Or she could see if the kids could build towers as tall as themselves and then pretend to be monsters and knock them down. She had all kinds of ideas, but she had to tread lightly. This wasn't her job yet. She turned to David, who was clearly shy in her presence, and handed him the block. "Why don't you do it for me? Do you think you can balance it?"

He seemed unsure. Olivia leaned over to him, her fingernails glittering in the lamplight, and whispered, "Put it there, David," pointing to an open spot next to the tallest tower. He took a quick look in Carrie's direction and then placed the block where his sister had said to put it.

"It's nearly dinnertime," Natalie said. "Can we start to clean up?"

Carrie assessed the tiny pile of blocks. It was certainly different than the cleanup times she'd had with children. David picked up the bucket and started dropping blocks into it. Olivia was spinning circles and watching her dress puff out like the sail of a ship.

"Olivia, can you help David, please?" Natalie said.

Olivia continued to spin, seemingly too engrossed in her twirling to hear Natalie.

"I'll count to three, and then it's a time-out," she said gently but firmly.

Carrie, not wanting to step on Natalie's toes but feeling there may be a better way, said, "Do you mind if I try, just to get a feel for the children?"

"Not at all."

"Olivia!" Carrie said in a dramatic whisper. "Olivia!" she called again.

The girl stopped and looked at Carrie. "I'm dizzy!" she giggled, which made Carrie smile. She wobbled over to Carrie and cocked her head to the side, her ponytail dropping onto her shoulder. The little girl looked up through her light, delicate eyelashes as she blinked her eyes, presumably to clear the dizziness from her vision.

"Olivia. I have my eye on one block, and if you find the one I'm looking for, I have something special for you, but it won't count unless you've put it in the bucket. Do you want to play my game?"

"What do you have for me?"

"Something red and white and minty-sweet!"

"Oh yes!" she said, her little eyebrows rising in excitement.

"May I play?" David called, dumping all the blocks back out onto the floor, the multicolored shapes tumbling onto the carpet.

Carrie laughed. "Yes. You may play."

One by one, the kids picked up blocks, saying, "Is this it?" and putting them into the bucket.

"I can't tell you until they're all in!" Carrie said.

Before long, the two children were hopping around, grabbing blocks and running over to Carrie, smiles spread across their faces. Carrie delighted in the curiosity in their expressions, the excitement they had, their small hands as they grabbed each block, and it warmed her. There was nothing better than this. The children hurriedly put the blocks into the bin until the floor was completely empty.

Carrie walked over to the bucket and peered inside. "Hmmm," she said, digging around. The kids were still bouncing with excitement, their eyes on her. She reached in and pulled out a red square block. "Who picked this one up? I can't remember," she said, and both children threw their hands in the air.

"Me! Me!" they called.

"I think it was Olivia…" Carrie said, a mock look of confusion on her face. David's face fell in disappointment. "Wait. Was it David?" David's eyes widened, and he looked up from the floor. Olivia was spinning again with her arms out like an airplane, every few seconds stopping to look at Carrie.

"I can't remember! You two picked them up so quickly that I couldn't keep up! I suppose I'll have to give you *both* a treat." She reached into her handbag and pulled out two red and white mini candy canes that she'd put in her bag at the last minute before she came. "Keep them in your pockets for after dinner," she said. Both kids grinned, their bright eyes glistening in the lamplight.

"That was a good trick," Natalie said, smiling at her. "I think you'll enjoy these two. I sure did. Adam works a lot, so you'll be on call twenty-four hours a day, but it's a lovely family. As much as I love them, I've found a full-time position that only requires me to work during regular daytime hours."

Carrie could relate. While she couldn't deny the excitement of being with the kids, she felt a tiny yearning to have an opportunity like Natalie was describing. But it sounded like Carrie was the perfect person for this job. With nobody to come home to, there was nothing keeping her from spending every single minute with the Fletcher family.

Chapter Three

Take five minutes per day and do something that makes you happy.

That's what Carrie had read in her book, *Finding Your Inner Happiness: Live Strong and Happy*. Only five minutes? She should be deliriously happy then, she tried to convince herself. She was happy being with children twenty-four hours a day. That was one thousand, four hundred, forty minutes every day. She should be cartwheels-and-dancing-in-the-streets happy.

As Natalie left her at Adam's office door, she thought about the commitment she was making. Natalie had said herself that Adam Fletcher was never home, and she'd have to provide round-the-clock care for the children. So she decided to really enjoy her last job, to take in every moment. She knocked on the office door.

"Come in, please," she heard from the other side.

Carrie opened the door to find him sitting behind a shiny wooden desk, stained dark like everything else in the house. The entire back wall was covered in wood shelving like the playroom, and filled with books. Had he read them all? She wanted to walk closer and inspect the titles. One can learn a lot about a person by what books they read. A floor lamp that reached upward and then curved toward the workspace cast a glow onto the surface of his desk. On his desk was a single picture frame but the back was to her, and she wondered if it had a photo of his kids. There was a soufflé ramekin next to it and a fork.

Carrie knew her dishes, and soufflés were one of her favorites. She could make sweet ones, spicy ones, savory ones...It didn't matter, she loved them all.

Adam stood up. He had clearly noticed her eyeing the dish. "I tried to make a soufflé." He looked embarrassed. "I absolutely love them, but I can't seem to get it right."

Upon closer inspection, she realized that he hadn't *eaten* the soufflé; it was a withered, yellow spot baked into the bottom of the ramekin. The thought of such a successful person trying *un*successfully to cook gave her a little punch of amusement, and she had to bite her lip to keep from smiling. "They aren't as fussy as you'd imagine," she said after recovering. "It's all about getting enough air in the egg whites, that's all. I'll bet you did everything else right."

For the first time, with a little huff of laughter preceding it, he smiled at her—a big, warm smile—and she reached for the nearest chair to steady herself. Just seeing that smile made her wonder what it would be like to come home to someone in the evenings, have another adult to talk to, to ask about her day.

"Maybe you can show me how sometime."

She swallowed so she could get words to come out of her mouth. "I'd love to," she said.

"Have a seat." He pointed to the chair across from his desk. "Natalie's staying with the children until they're in bed tonight. You won't officially start until tomorrow. So, let's go over your duties."

Carrie was glad to sit down because her legs were becoming jellylike from their little soufflé moment. From what she'd seen so far, Adam was kind and warm, but there was something about him that was extremely intimidating. She could tell just by how he held himself, how smart he was and how fierce he probably was at his job. Carrie had worked for wealthy people before, but never anyone this wealthy. Her own upbringing was a world away from this lifestyle, and she feared she may do or say something to draw attention to it.

"Shall we jump right in?" he said, forcing her to make eye contact.

"Yes." She smiled nervously.

His expression was softer all of a sudden, as if he were taking her in. It only made her feel more tense. "Oh, I'm so sorry," he said. "I haven't even given you a moment to get settled. Would you like something to drink?"

Glass of wine? she thought with amusement. She needed something to settle her nerves. If he gave her a glass to hold, she'd probably spill it all over her lap. "I'm fine, thank you," she said, keeping her hands on her thighs.

"Okay then. Well…" He leaned on his desk with his forearms. It reminded her of something she'd read about how waiters should squat down by tables to take people's orders in restaurants. Their proximity was supposed to put the patrons at ease. Was Adam trying to put her at ease? Could he sense her nervousness?

"I have a cleaning lady. Name's Rose. So, you won't have to clean while you're here. Your entire focus should be the children. You'll be moving into Natalie's bedroom upstairs," he said. "It's closest to the kids' rooms. I had her change the sheets today and clean up after herself, so it's ready for you. Do you have your bags with you?"

"Yes. I left them in the car."

"No problem, I'll help you get them in. It's snowing quite a bit outside. We'd better do that soon."

"Okay."

"Basically, the house is yours—whatever you need, feel free to use it. You're in charge of the children the entire time they're here. I have them until January, when they'll return to their mother after Christmas break. You come highly recommended, so I trust you to use whatever techniques you feel appropriate, and I'll let you know if I disagree with any of your strategies."

"Do the children have any special requirements, any allergies or anything that I should be made aware of?" she asked, trying to get her mind back on the job. She was glad to be talking about the children. It was easing her anxiety a bit. Children, she knew.

"Nope. None that I'm aware of."

"Excellent. How about naptimes and bedtimes?"

Adam had looked so assertive, so strong, but with that question, she saw uncertainty on his face—it was subtle, but she'd caught it.

He jotted something onto a pad of paper. "I'll make a note to ask Natalie to leave you a list of specifics regarding times, food preferences, and the like." He continued to write, and she was glad for the break in eye contact. "Let's talk about Christmas," he said.

Christmas! She was so happy he'd mentioned it. "Do you celebrate it?" she asked carefully, surprised that he'd brought it up, given that there wasn't a single decoration in the house.

"Of course!" He smiled again, sending her stomach into a whirl. "I've taken four days off over the holidays. My family is coming here since this is my first Christmas with the kids—they usually stay with their mother, but she's off to Italy, the Amalfi Coast." Did Carrie detect a wounded quality to his voice at the mention of his ex-wife? He cleared his throat. "My mother insists on coming, so you'll have a house full of my relatives. Do not feel in the slightest that you need to entertain them. Your only duties are regarding the children's needs."

Again, she'd be put in a situation that she'd never experienced: having to watch the children under the eye of Adam's family. She looked at the man across from her and tried to envision what his parents would be like. Who had raised this wealthy man who worked all but four days at Christmas? Had he built quiet block towers in a museum of a toy room or had he sunk his hands up to his elbows in paint to see what all the colors mixed together might look like? She imagined that he was probably the block type.

"Are they staying through Christmas Day?" she asked.

"Yes."

"So... Were you planning to..." She didn't want to offend him on day one, but she had to ask. After all, they were into the month of December. "Were you going to get a tree or anything?"

"Ye-es," he said slowly, with thought behind it. It was clear that the idea had only just occurred to him. "I'm sorry. I haven't had anyone here at Christmas before, and with the kids always at their mother's, I never did anything special for the holiday. I was going to give you a credit card to order a few gifts for the kids online. From me..."

Her eyes wanted to pop out of their sockets, her mouth wanted to hang down to the floor in exasperation, but she kept it all inside. What about Santa Claus? What about tree decorating and cookie baking? Didn't he realize how important those experiences were? And didn't he know what to buy his own children? She hoped to goodness the kids got all those experiences at their mother's.

"May I have a small allowance for holiday activities?" she asked.

"Absolutely. Buy whatever you'd like. And you can decorate the house however you see fit. It would make my mother easier to live with." So, he wasn't completely closed off to the idea. Carrie wondered if, like the kids, he too just needed to get his hands in some paint to loosen up. She thought of his sleeves rolled up, his fingers covered in primary colors, the children beside him, that smile on his face... Then, quickly, she cleared her mind of it.

"David and Olivia have a Christmas pageant on December twenty-first." His eyes were already trusting as he looked at her. "The family may want to attend, but just to be sure I've got all my ducks in a row, I'd like you to be in charge of getting the kids there. It's at five o'clock."

She pulled out her cell phone and keyed in the date and time. As she did, she wondered if he was asking her to take them because he wasn't planning on going. Wouldn't he want to see his children dressed as little angels or the baby Jesus? Didn't he realize that he only had a blip in his life to see them like that, and then they'd be too old?

"I'm sure you're ready to have some supper. Shall we get your bags?" he asked.

"Okay," she said, wondering how this holiday would go.

Chapter Four

Speak confidently. Confidence is key in making favorable first impressions.

"Let me just grab a few beers on the way in." Adam closed the garage door, shutting out the drifting snow, and set her suitcases down. "Do you like beer, by chance?" he asked. He led her to a stainless steel refrigerator on the far wall of the garage. With a tug on the handle, the door opened, revealing rows upon rows of brown, long-necked bottles. They had trendy yellow and red labels that read *Salty Shockoe*. Carrie followed the curly S's with her eyes, noting the detail in the lettering.

The truth was she actually did like beer. Back in college, she'd been the only one of her friends who really, truly preferred it to other drinks. She would come home on the weekends and watch football with her dad. He always let her pick the beer, and their visits to the supermarket to get snacks before games were fond memories. As they sat on the sofa together, her mother would plop down beside them, wrinkle her nose at their bottles, watch a few minutes of the game and then busy herself with something else, but Carrie could stay there all day. She hadn't recalled a memory like that in quite a while. It made her feel nostalgic and lonely at the same time.

"I do like beer," she said, wondering why Adam had so many bottles.

She'd never seen this particular brand before, but Carrie had heard how Richmond was known for its craft beers and microbrews. It had been featured on a travel show she'd seen on TV once.

"You *do* like beer?" He seemed surprised. Then she thought about what he probably saw when he looked at her: her light brown hair tucked behind her ears, her colorless lip-gloss, her frumpy sweater. She probably didn't look like she ever went out a day in her life. It had been so long since she'd had any opportunity to, she'd sort of forgotten about herself.

With children, she didn't have to worry about how she looked or what she said. With adults, she had to be more careful, think more about how they may view her, and it made her uneasy. Compounding her apprehension was the fact that she knew once she found a different career and actually had the time to go out, she didn't feel comfortable having drinks with strangers or going to bars to meet people. She just wanted that one person who would love her in her frumpy sweater and bunchy socks. Finding that person, though, seemed exhausting.

Adam shut the door to the refrigerator. "Follow me. I'll get you some supper and you can try this." He held up one of the bottles. Was he going to have a drink with her? How could she make conversation? She'd been out of the game too long to know how to talk to a man with no children pulling on her attention. Perhaps they could talk about David and Olivia, she thought. But what would she say once that conversation had died down? She didn't know much about the area or anything about him. A prickle of nervousness pelted her skin. She'd only just gotten there, she kept telling herself, so it would take a little while for her to become comfortable and assertive. But she would eventually relax. Right?

Carrie followed Adam down the hallway until they reached the kitchen. The smell of something cooking in the oven made her tummy rumble. Natalie and the children weren't there. She guessed that the children must have already finished supper and were on their way to their baths, and she felt a little sad that she couldn't share her meal with them. Meals were the best time to talk to each other.

Adam popped the top off one of the bottles and poured out a small amount. "It's more flavorful in a glass the first time you try it. You can taste it better," he said, handing it to her.

When the froth had fizzled, she took a sip. The flavor of it took her right back to all those weekends with her dad: the team jerseys they wore on game day, tossing footballs in the backyard after the game, the smell of burgers on the grill. Those memories were so rich, so happy. Would she ever have her own family to make memories like those?

"What do you think?" he asked, taking a sip from his own bottle.

"It's delicious," she said. Her memories and the beer had calmed her significantly. *Familiar*, she thought with a grin. *I'll bet that's what my book meant.* She turned the bottle around in her hand and peered down at the label. "I've never had this brand before. I like the label," she said out loud by accident. This was why she shouldn't go out and try to meet people, she thought, because she ended up talking about beer labels. Her skills in being alluring and interesting were horrifying.

Politely, Adam looked down at his bottle, studying it. "I don't know. I'm not sure about all the white space there," he said.

He was clearly trying to make her stupid comment seem relevant, but she knew good and well what a ridiculous topic she'd started. She should have known better. But he didn't really seem that bothered by the conversation, so she continued. "Wouldn't it look nice with some green on the white background? Maybe for Christmas." She smiled.

Adam pursed his lips and nodded as if contemplating her suggestion. *Either he's great at hiding boredom, or he's really into this beer*, she thought.

"I think you're right. I'll let my graphics guy know. Maybe we'll make you a special bottle."

"Sorry?" The whole time she was talking, was she giving opinions on a label that he'd designed? She mentally scrambled to recall her exact words. What had she said to him? Thank God she hadn't said it was terrible!

"I own Shockoe Brewery downtown. This is my beer."

He didn't design the labels. He owned the whole thing. She was putting it together now. That explained all the beer in his garage. She'd seen an ad on a billboard for Shockoe Brewery on her way into Richmond. It had had a picture of the inside of the facility. It was massive, with a stainless steel brew kettle behind glass and, in the center, a fancy-looking restaurant. Getting a beer there would be a very different experience from the grocery store trips she'd made with her dad. As she looked at Adam now, in his sweater and jeans, holding his beer in the dim evening light of his kitchen, she felt like she'd just seen him for the first time.

With a pair of poth olders, he retrieved a steaming dish of lasagna from the top of a stainless steel double oven and set it down on the counter. "I'm not a great cook. Normally I have someone do it for me, but occasionally I try." He grinned at her and she enjoyed the bit of personality he was allowing to show. "I thought you'd like something for supper, so I made this. Since my soufflé didn't turn out, I may have some with you, if that's all right." He set a serving spoon onto the counter and slid it toward her.

Carrie loved to cook. She didn't have a lot of time to do it, but it was one of her most favorite things to do. When she was young, she experimented in her kitchen, and her mother would just shake her head at the mess of bowls and utensils that she'd piled into the sink. But her mom never got upset with Carrie. She'd even bought her cookbooks one year for her birthday.

She stepped beside him and picked up the spoon while he put two plates down next to her. The lasagna looked delicious, and her stomach was rumbling. The steam rose into the air when she scooped out a serving and lumped it onto the first plate.

"So you like to cook?" she asked.

"I do, although I don't have a lot of time these days," he said.

"I understand." She took her plate and followed him over to the kitchen table. It was a long, rectangular table nearly as large as one meant for a dining room, but it was more casual, made of oak with straight lines and minimal details. She wondered if it was ever full of people or if it always sat empty. She lowered herself down and scooted her chair under the table.

Adam poured more beer, tipping her glass at a slant to reduce the amount of froth at the top. She watched the amber liquid slide past the rim and down the side of the glass until it was sparkling and fizzing. "Work has me busy around the clock."

"Mine too." She grinned.

There it was again—that little exhale of amusement just before a big, warm smile that sent her nerves into a frenzy. There was something undeniably kind about Adam. She caught his gaze, unsure of what to do with it, so she looked out the substantial kitchen window at the snow falling. It drifted to the ground like feathers.

She didn't have to consult her books to know why she was nervous. It was because Adam looked only a few years older than her, and he had millions. He owned his own company. He'd married, had kids, and bought a home. Carrie had nothing material to show for her adult years, she'd never been married or even dated long-term. It made her feel like she'd made all the wrong choices in life.

"Tell me about your kids," she said, trying to find familiar ground to which she could add and fill the silence.

He chewed a bite of his lasagna and swallowed. "What do you want to know?" he asked.

Carrie pushed her fork around her plate, scooping up a bite. "What are they like?"

"Well, David's quiet, like me." He smiled again, causing her stomach to knot up. "And Olivia's the chatty one. She'll talk to anybody."

Carrie grinned at the memory of Olivia spinning her circles. "What does she like to talk about?"

Adam took a sip of his beer, the skin between his eyes creasing slightly. He set the glass down onto the table slowly, his face showing contemplation. He was silent for a minute before he said, "Oh, little-girl things, I suppose." Then, with an awkward look, he broke eye contact.

Her thoughts went back to that moment in the playroom when he'd popped in on them and they hadn't run to him. It occurred to Carrie that perhaps Adam didn't know his children very well. He'd asked *her* to buy their presents, and he wasn't even tucking them into bed at that very moment; he was sitting here having supper with Carrie. He seemed like such a nice person, so why was he so standoffish with them? She didn't press him any further.

Carrie had spent the last hour in the early morning tossing between the starched sheets on her new bed. The kids weren't up yet, nor was the sun, but she was. She was thinking. Adam hadn't stayed at the table very long last night at supper, but she didn't blame him. He'd said he had work to do. She hoped she hadn't bored him to death. She ran through the handful of things she'd said, her gestures, wondering what he thought of her. The bed creaked as she rolled over, clicked on the lamp, and grabbed her book off her nightstand. She opened to the spot where she'd marked her place and read. *Trust yourself. Believe in your intuition. Go with your instincts. These are traits of confident people...*

Those words were easier said than done. Adam's family was coming into town in three days. She was about as worried as she'd ever been about getting things right. How could she be confident with all of that going on? Then she thought about the one area of her life where she was the most comfortable, the most successful: children. She decided, right then and there, that she was going to focus on David and Olivia. Everything else—she hoped—would fall into place.

She crawled out of bed and peeked through the window. The snow was still falling, the streets so covered that she couldn't tell where the yards ended and the road began. The trees were topped with snow, their branches like black sketch marks on a white canvas. The frigid air made the panes of the window so cold that just standing there she had made them foggy from her breath. It had been a long time since she'd seen snow like this. As the gray clouds had lightened with the day, she decided she'd better get ready. The children would be up soon.

Her room had an en-suite bathroom with a closet full of huge, fluffy white towels. She turned on the water in the shower, the steam filling the room, and got in. As the water sheeted over her, she thought about the day ahead. She pictured David and Olivia standing by their block tower. Had they ever gotten dirty? Had they ever been allowed to let their creativity run wild? She hoped that they had, but after watching them yesterday, she wondered. Carrie decided that today they should play in the snow. What children don't like to play in the snow? And there was certainly enough of it.

When she got out of the shower, she dressed, got herself ready, and grabbed the food-coloring bottles from her suitcase. She hadn't heard from the kids yet. Were they with their father? Maybe she had been wrong about him. Perhaps they were all downstairs and he was making them pancakes or something. Wouldn't that be wonderful?

She walked quietly down the hall until she reached their rooms, and checked on David first. He was in his bed, playing with a stuffed dinosaur.

"Hello, David," she said with a smile. "Have you been up very long?" He looked over at her shyly, his eyes darting down to his dinosaur. He didn't say anything, so she asked, "When did your dinosaur wake up?"

"When the clock said six-oh-oh," he said.

Six o'clock? she thought. *That was an hour ago.* "Have you really been up that long?" she asked. He nodded. She didn't know what rules Natalie had put in place, but the last thing Carrie wanted was to have the children sitting alone in their beds for an hour. They were probably starving. "David, as soon as you wake up in the mornings, will you come and get me in Natalie's room? Even if I'm asleep. Would you do that for me?" He nodded again. "Why don't we check on Olivia?"

David rolled over onto his belly and swung his feet off the side of his bed, hopping down. He grabbed his dinosaur and stood next to Carrie. His curly hair was bunched in haphazard clumps on his head and his pajama bottoms were twisted, but he didn't seem fazed as he darted over to the corner to grab his slippers. They were big, puffy things in the shape of lambs. He struggled to hold his dinosaur and get his heel into the slipper, but after a few tugs, he got it on and stood up.

"Ready?"

He looked up at her and she led the way.

As they walked down the hallway, she asked, "Have you seen your daddy yet this morning?"

David shook his head. "He goes to work."

"Did he leave already?"

"I don't know."

That sadness that she'd felt earlier was back in full force. Why didn't Adam's own son know if he was in the house or not? Why hadn't David felt that he could get up and go see his father? And why hadn't Adam even checked on his children before he left? It was all a stark contrast to the warmth that she'd seen in Adam's face last night. It didn't make any sense.

She opened Olivia's door, and when she did, the little girl sat up in bed and looked at them with groggy eyes. Her hair was in a braid, loose strands puffed out around it, falling down along the sides of her face. She rubbed her eyes. "Can we get up?" she asked.

"You can always get up on the mornings when I'm here. Just come and wake me up. I'll get up with you whenever you're ready to start the day."

Olivia looked at David then back at Carrie, her face showing uncertainty. "Okay," she said quietly.

These were the facts that she had: One, there were two children in front of her who clearly had not ever played or acted the way she expected children to. Two, Adam didn't seem to have prepared in the slightest for Christmas. And three, Adam had put her in charge. Time to work some magic.

"Kids, what do you want for breakfast?" she asked. They continued to look back and forth at each other. "What do you usually have?"

"Oatmeal and fruit," Olivia said.

"Do you like oatmeal and fruit?"

Olivia didn't answer.

"What would you rather have?" Carrie stopped in the hallway and kneeled down to their level. "It's okay. Tell me."

Neither of them answered. They were only four. Perhaps they genuinely didn't know what they wanted to eat.

"Would you rather have pancakes?" she asked.

Their eyes were as big as saucers. "Yes!" Olivia answered.

"With chocolate chips or bananas? Or both?"

David finally spoke. "Both."

"Yes, both!" Olivia said, hopping on her toes.

"Perfect. Let's go make pancakes. After that"—she pulled out the small bottles of food coloring that she'd brought from her last job—"I'd like to take these out into the snow and make a rainbow volcano. Would you like to join me?"

She hadn't heard such noise come from these two since she'd gotten there. They were whooping and stomping and giggling all at once.

"*That's* the answer I wanted to hear." She smiled and stood back up. "Now let's go make those pancakes."

When they got to the kitchen, Carrie pulled two chairs over to the sink. "Wash your hands, please. We need clean hands to make our breakfast. Hold them out." She squirted foamy soap into each of their hands, piling it up as if they were holding a fistful of whipped cream. When they started to laugh, she squirted more until their little fingers were lost in the suds. "Hang on. I don't think I've put enough on. Rub them together," she said, hiding her own laughter at seeing their expressions, and squirting more. The children looked at each other, clearly trying to decide if she was serious. Then she turned on the water and asked them to rinse.

After hand washing was complete, Carrie scooted their chairs over to the island in the center of the kitchen. It was a large slab of granite with cherrywood cabinets underneath and sleek chrome drawer-pulls and handles. "Hop up," she told the kids, and they climbed onto the chairs again. Olivia was on one side of the island and David on the other. All they were doing was standing on chairs, but they were giggling like crazy. Olivia's chest rose and fell with every giggle, her eyes darting from side to side, and David's smile was wide and jovial, his dimple showing on his cheek just like his baby picture.

"Why are you laughing?" Carrie asked.

"I'm very tall," Olivia said with a grin that spread across her entire face. She put her hands on the counter and leaned on it, hopping up and down in her chair. Carrie laughed. She'd missed this age. She set the flour, baking powder, salt, and sugar in front of her and began measuring out the amounts into a bowl she'd found in the cabinet beside the sink.

"Let's make sure your hands are dry," she said, wiping Olivia's fingers with a towel. "You're in charge of mixing."

"What do I do?" she asked.

"Put your hands in the bowl. Then, wiggle your fingers until it's all mixed up."

Olivia put her hands into the bowl of dry ingredients. "Oh!" she said. "It's soft!" She moved her hands around in it, sending a cloud of flour into the air.

"Perfect. You're doing great! Keep going!"

"But what will *I* do?" David said, his lips twitching downward in disappointment.

"Not to worry, you get to be the river maker."

"The what?" he asked, his face lighting up.

Carrie set the milk down in front of David, along with an egg and some butter. "You're going to make a river in Olivia's mountain of flour. A milk and egg river. Have you ever cracked an egg before?" she asked him.

He shook his head.

"Okay then. We'll need to practice." She pulled out another bowl and three more eggs from the fridge, setting them in front of David. "Still mixing over there, Olivia?"

Olivia had so much flour in her hair that it looked like cotton candy. "Yes!" she said as a clump of flour sailed overboard onto the counter.

"Excellent. Now, David. Here's an egg. Tap it along the side of this bowl until you see a crack in it. Give it a good whack."

David tapped. Then harder. And harder, his little toes pressing against the chair in concentration, until he yelped, the yolk drooling down the side of the bowl. His fingers were yellow and dripping, and she handed him another egg.

"Try one more time. You've almost got it."

Once they got the wet ingredients all into David's bowl, she showed him how to spoon them in, making his river. David was a serious little boy, but this made him laugh. As they mixed the batter, Carrie asked, "What would you like for Christmas, Olivia?"

"I'd like Daddy to take us ice skating."

David seemed to perk up at the mention of his father.

"Has he taken you before?" Carrie had taken kids ice skating quite a bit in the winter, and she'd seen a Richmond outdoor rink online when she'd researched the area.

"One time he said he would, but his work called, and he forgot."

Carrie felt the disappointment that Olivia had probably experienced that day. She couldn't imagine not keeping her word with a child. How would they ever grow up to be trustworthy adults if they weren't taught what trust was? She hoped that something out of his control had pulled Adam away from her request, and he really hadn't forgotten, because that would just be terrible. "Would you want to go with me?" she asked.

Olivia seemed to be contemplating the question, her lips pressed together in thought. "I want to go with Daddy because he can skate with David. I want to skate with Snow White."

"Oh!" Carrie chuckled. "I didn't realize that Snow White was part of your Christmas wish."

"Yes," Olivia said, her face serious as if her request were completely feasible. "I want to go ice skating with Daddy and Snow White."

"And I want to skate with Daddy," David said.

"Well that would be a lot of fun," Carrie said.

The counter was covered in bowls, raw egg, and flour, the children wrist-deep in it all, their faces so intent on their tasks, smiles on their lips. Carrie stopped for just a moment to take it all in.

How could these children have been denied experiences like these? It was clear that they'd never done anything like this in their lives. This—right here—was what she was meant to do with her life. It didn't make her feel important or overly successful in a business sort of way, but it made her feel like she was doing something real. Something meaningful. And she didn't want to give it up, as much as she knew she'd have to if she ever wanted anything more.

"Good morning."

Carrie nearly jumped out of her skin at the sound of another adult voice in the room. Once she'd recovered, she looked toward the double doorway to the kitchen where Adam was standing. She took in the shape of his strong shoulders through his pressed shirt, the masculine quality of his hands as he fiddled with the cuff, pulling it over his watch. There was something about him that was so magnetic, so handsome, that she couldn't look away. She smiled instead.

"Did you sleep well?" he asked, looking at her in a way that she swore made him seem like he wanted to say something other than just that. His face was curious, as if he were surveying the entire scene around him without having to take his eyes off her. She nodded, trying to ignore her assumptions and take the question at face value. Carrie wondered if he ever let himself go. Did he ever walk around the house in socks, scruff on his face, flannel pajama bottoms? She wished he would. It would make her feel more at ease around him.

"I did, thank you."

Adam finally looked at his children, the edges of his mouth turned up just slightly. Then his gaze moved along the mess on the island. "Is everything all right?" he asked.

Carrie wiped a runaway strand of hair off her forehead with the back of her wrist, wondering if she'd put a streak of flour across her face, trying to make out what he was thinking. What if he didn't believe that making pancakes at the age of four was an appropriate activity?

"Yes, everything's fine," she said a little nervously. "We're just making breakfast."

He nodded slowly. "Well, I'm off to work."

She waited for the children to say, "Bye, Daddy!" and try to hug him with their dirty hands, but they just watched him with blank faces. Finally, David offered a little wave. Adam held up his hand to say goodbye then turned around and headed down the hallway. Her worst fears were confirmed. These children didn't have a bond with their father at all. They were missing out on such a warm, kind man, and he was missing out, too. He was missing seeing their faces light up with joy, their sweet giggles, and all the tiny moments that were slipping away. Why didn't he make an effort? What was keeping him from getting to know his children? Carrie looked at their perfect, little faces, and she couldn't fathom how he could live with them day in and day out when they were here, and not spend every single minute with them.

"Say, 'Bye, Daddy,'" she coaxed the children in a whisper.

"Bye, Daddy," they said in unison.

"Have a good day!" she called down the hallway as the front door shut, and he was gone.

Chapter Five

Surround yourself with positive energy.

Carrie had read that once, and she believed it did help. How could the children enjoy the season when there wasn't the first shred of Christmas in the house? With the kids finally in bed for the night, she opened her laptop on the kitchen table, holding Adam's credit card in her hand. With only a few clicks, she'd put a wreath for the front door, window candles for every window, greenery and ribbon for the banisters, more white lights than she could count, and seven boxes of ornaments into her virtual shopping basket. She hit the *Purchase Now* button, making sure to choose the most expedient shipping options. On a pad of paper, she jotted down the amount she'd spent and took it into his office for his review. It was time to get this house ready for Christmas.

There were a few things, however, that she hadn't purchased on purpose. One was the tree and the other were the presents that Adam had asked her to buy. Holding on to her own memories of her father as he loaded the tree they'd chosen together onto the top of their car while they held paper cups of hot cocoa with cold hands, she felt very strongly that Adam should be the one to get those things for his kids. She wasn't quite sure how she would change his mind about it, but she was going to try. She looked at the clock on the oven. It was nearly eight o'clock, and he wasn't home yet. She pulled out the dish of lasagna and put it into the oven to reheat.

As she sat in the silent kitchen, now clean with no trace of the pancake making, she felt very alone. She'd had a fantastic day with the children. They'd really enjoyed the pancakes and, after, they'd played in the snow and made the rainbow volcano with her food coloring. When, begrudgingly, they'd had to admit that they were too cold to stay out any longer, they'd come inside and had a bath. The rest of the day, she'd spent playing games. By the time they'd had dinner, she could see the exhaustion on their faces—their drooping eyelids, their rosy cheeks. They'd fallen asleep by ten minutes to seven, leaving her an hour with her thoughts.

Carrie wondered if Adam had any idea how lucky he was. He had an amazing home and two wonderful children who were capable of so much love. As she was putting them to bed, David reached up and kissed her cheek. "I had lots of fun today," he'd told her, his eyes blinking from fatigue. She'd only known him a day, and he'd given her a kiss. She saw the way he'd looked at Adam this morning, as if he wanted him to stay, his hand raised in the air to say goodbye, his eyes following Adam so intently. How much David could learn from his father.

And Olivia—had Adam ever watched her as she danced? Why hadn't he ever grabbed her hands and spun her around? It would be so easy to do. One day he'd wake up and they'd be teenagers, leaving home to go off to some college far away—and he'd never get this time back. She'd barely met this family, but the reality of that fact weighed heavily on her shoulders.

The black of night was on the other side of the three large windows by the kitchen table, with not a star in the sky. The large room was well heated, but she still caught the odd draft from the freezing weather outside. The wind blew the snow sideways, causing it to stick against the bottom of the window.

Suddenly, breaking the silence, she heard the hum of the electric garage door. Adam was finally home. To mask the fizzle of energy that had sprung up inside, she busied herself with getting the lasagna out of the oven and pulling out cutlery. She'd planned to make him a plate, since he was probably hungry having worked so late.

He walked in and set his laptop case down against the wall by the hallway. "Hello," he said, looking around. She could see the slight shadow of stubble on his face, the fatigue in his eyes that reminded her of Olivia's, the way his hair had begun to curl like David's just slightly from a day's work. "The kitchen looks considerably better than when I left it this morning," he said, a grin playing at his lips. "Where are the children?"

"In bed." Carrie pulled a serving spoon from the drawer she'd found earlier when she was making pancakes and dished some lasagna onto a plate for Adam. "I heated up some supper. Are you hungry?"

"You don't have to make me supper each night. I don't always come home in time to eat it, and I don't want you going to any trouble on my account, but thank you for making it tonight. I'm starving," he said as he slipped his coat off and draped it on a chair.

She dished out a scoop of lasagna for herself and put the plates across from each other on the kitchen table. Adam poured some wine from the fridge into two glasses and joined her.

"The kids are in bed already? Natalie was usually wrestling with them to go to sleep whenever I came home at this hour." He placed a glass of wine by her plate.

Carrie smiled. "If you tire them out enough, you don't have to wrestle with them. David actually asked if he could go to bed." She took a sip of wine. "Thank you for the wine." She wasn't quite as nervous around him tonight, she'd noticed. "I bought some Christmas decorations on your credit card," she said. "I opted for one-day shipping," she said cautiously. "I put the amount that I spent down on a sticky note on your desk."

There it was again—that smile. He was so attractive that she could hardly manage to look him in the eye. It made her head feel like she'd had more than just a sip of her wine. She took a big drink.

His entire focus was on her, fondness in his eyes, the silence surrounding them offering no distractions. "Thank you. I trust that you won't spend my life's savings, and I'll get the bill, so you don't have to write it on a sticky note for me." He picked up his glass of wine and took a drink. This little moment between them sent her head spinning against her will.

She wondered about what kind of women he dated. But as quickly as her thoughts had come, she reined them in. He was a kind person with a friendly smile—that was it. And she loved his children already. Other than that, she didn't need to entertain any further thoughts about Adam Fletcher.

His phone went off next to his plate and, with an apologetic nod, he answered. "Hello," he said. The skin between his eyes puckered and his gaze fell onto the table, seemingly not registering what was in front of him—he was thinking, listening. He nodded and then with hardly a breath, set down his fork and said, "Andy, we're talking *ten* states here. That's nearly the entire East Coast. Distribution will be interrupted unless we can get them on board…" He stood up, walked across the room, and pulled a file of papers from his laptop case. "I don't care what they say. You know as well as I do…Have you settled the deal on the facility with Robert?…Call Robert and find out what's going on. This expansion can't happen without those two things going off without a hitch." His voice faded out as he left the room.

Carrie found herself alone again for quite some time. She finally decided to eat without him before her supper got cold. When she'd finished her food and the glass of wine, Adam still hadn't returned. His plate sat untouched. Carrie couldn't help but feel insignificant. Whatever he had to talk about—whoever this Robert person was— was clearly more important than having supper. She knew that he'd said not to worry about his meals, but it didn't make her feel any better. He'd just spent an entire day at work. Surely, he could make enough time to eat, if only not to appear as rude as he did at that moment. Fear swept through her as she thought about how many times he might have done something like that to the children. She hoped, when and if he had, he'd at least have been discreet about it.

After she'd cleared the dishes, Carrie made her way to her room to turn in for the night, noticing a light on in the office as she passed by. As she dressed for bed and settled in under her covers, she wondered what could possibly be so important that it couldn't wait until the next day when he was so clearly tired and hungry. He'd said that some nights he came home even later than he had tonight. He'd gone out this morning shortly after the children had gotten up and he came back after they were in bed. How could he cope with that?

She'd had to put his entire supper back in the fridge. Exasperation slinked through her slowly until she could feel it harden her expression. There was no reason to work like that. It wasn't right. She didn't know anything about what it took to run a business, but she knew what it was like to have responsibilities, and Adam had more responsibilities than just that brewery. He had two children and a life, and she feared that he was choosing work over both.

If tonight was any indication of how he spent his days, it was clear that he wasn't around enough to know them. Part of her wanted to get out of bed, go into his office and talk about all the things she was thinking, but she knew it wasn't her place. It made her feel helpless as she saw the faces of David and Olivia in her mind. They had so much joy to offer, if he'd let them.

She remembered the ramekin on his desk and wondered if he ate most of his meals in his office. He hadn't had supper, and, adding to her frustration, she couldn't sleep thinking about it, knowing that he probably hadn't eaten since lunchtime. So that she could have peace of mind, she slipped on her jeans and a sweater and went down to the kitchen. It was still dark and clean the way she'd left it. She opened the fridge, sending the only light into the room, and pulled out some sandwich fixings, wanting to at least put something light in his belly at this late hour. She fixed him a sandwich and glass of water and headed upstairs.

As she neared the office, she could hear the sound of keys clicking. The clicking increased to a frantic pace and subsided, then more. Carrie walked through the door, and he looked up.

"I brought you a sandwich," she said.

Adam's face dropped from expectant to serious, and he looked contemplative and even a bit regretful, as if he'd only then realized he'd left her in the kitchen tonight without even an apology. She set the sandwich on his desk and turned to leave. He was clearly busy, and she didn't want to interrupt him. If she did, he'd probably never go to bed.

"Carrie," he said quietly.

She turned around.

"Thank you."

"You're welcome," she returned, leaving his office and walking back to her room through that lovely house and past the children's rooms. It was all there on the other side of his office door, just waiting for him to make memories, and it seemed that he didn't even realize it.

Chapter Six

Know your strengths and use them.

"Let's decorate for Christmas!" she said to the children, the front door wide open and the brick landing full of the boxes of decorations that she'd ordered. She pulled them inside one by one, dropping snow onto the wide oriental runner that ran the length of the entryway. David tried to get one of the boxes open while Olivia hopped up and down in excitement. Olivia had dressed herself today, and she had on her fairy tutu, a green and white striped shirt, and her bunny slippers.

"I can't get it," David said, his face full of concern. Carrie smiled, thinking how much he looked like Adam. He was just like him in so many ways—the way his eyebrows pulled together, the pout of his lips when he was thinking, his serious personality. Unlike his sister, David had asked Carrie to pick out his clothes, ensuring that they were meant to go together.

"It's okay. I'll get some scissors from the office. Do you want to come with me?"

"Yes!" Olivia bounced up and down, and Carrie laughed. The personalities of these two twins were like night and day.

The children followed her to get the scissors, and, when Carrie entered the office, she noticed that Adam must have taken care of the sandwich plate from last night. She wondered what time he'd finally gone to bed. He was already gone when the kids woke her up this morning, and the coffee was cold in the coffeepot, so he seemed to have left quite early. She opened the drawer and retrieved the scissors.

"Which one should we open first?" she asked Olivia when she returned.

Olivia stood, playing with the tulle of her tutu. "This one," she said, pointing at the largest of the boxes.

Carrie dragged the scissors along the taped seam and popped open the top flaps of the box, revealing the Christmas greenery she'd ordered. She pulled it out, cut off the cardboard wrapping and allowed it to fall loose in her hand. Then, like an enormous spruce-colored feather boa, she tossed it around Olivia's shoulders.

"Oh!" Olivia said, spinning around and rustling the greenery with her fingers. "I love this! What's it for, Carrie?" She unwrapped it from her neck and spread it out on the floor, her hands getting lost in the bunches of greenery.

"It's going to go on the stairway banister," she said, unable to hide her grin.

"Can I keep some of it?"

"If we have any left, you may."

David reached in and pulled out a set of window candles. "Where do these go?" he asked, opening their packaging and inspecting the plug at the end.

"David, see if you can find any little light bulbs in the box. You'll need those for what you have in your hand. That's a pair of window candles. Does your mommy put up window candles?"

"No." He shook his head and reached into the box again. "Is this it?"

"Hmm, that looks like it may be a set of ornaments. Try again."

"I miss Mommy," Olivia said, suddenly very still. Her hands were by her sides, her face somber. "When can we go home?"

Carrie kneeled down in front of Olivia. "I'm sure you do miss your mommy. You'll get to see her in a few weeks." She smiled for Olivia's benefit. David walked over, still holding the window candle, and stood next to Olivia. His actions were almost protective, as if he were trying to shield his sister from her own worry.

"I miss it when she tucks us in at night," Olivia said. David nodded in agreement.

"Well, you're being very brave," Carrie acknowledged.

It must be hard for them, she thought, having to spend Christmas with a virtual stranger, their father too busy to spend any time with them, their mother away. She wondered what their mother was like. Did she play with them? Did she do things, take them places? Quietly, still thinking about the children, she helped David unpack the rest of the Christmas decorations. Carrie was glad that she could be there for them so that she could try to ease their fears if they needed her. *They shouldn't be worrying*, she thought. *They should be enjoying Christmas.*

A few minutes had passed when she looked back at Olivia. She'd covered the post of the banister with the greenery, using almost all of it, and wrapping it so tightly that the post wasn't even visible.

"I'll help you get the rest up in a minute, Olivia. You're doing great."

"Is this right?" she asked.

"You know, it looks lovely, but I may have to use some of it to do the rest of the balcony. The store didn't send enough to make it as nice as you're doing it. I'll help you thin it out in just a second. Let me get David some light bulbs so he can test these lights for me." She pulled the light bulbs out of the box. "Here we go," she said, screwing one into the candle that David was holding. "Let me plug it in for you and then you test the switch. How about that?"

David puffed his chest and looked around, obviously happy with the task he'd been given. With a very focused expression, he held a candle, setting down the other, and turned the switch. "This one works," he said in his best grown-up voice. "Let me try this one now." His little fingers fumbled a bit with the switch but he got it on. "This one works too."

"Fantastic. Maybe you can start standing them up against the wall there." Carrie pointed to the wall closest to him. "We'll know that those are the ones that light up just fine. Good work, David." He gave her a solemn nod and went back to unwrapping more window candles.

"You know, your grandma and grandpa will be coming in a few days. We'll have to get the house all Christmassy for them," Carrie said, trying to make a little conversation as she carefully unwound Olivia's greenery.

"Is there a Christmas tree in that box?" Olivia asked. "It'll be awfully small."

"No." Carrie chuckled. "I thought maybe we'd take your daddy with us to get a tree."

"Why?" she asked.

"Well, because he may want to help us pick it out."

"He won't want to."

"How do you know?"

"Because, silly, he has to work!" Olivia giggled, but Carrie felt the impact of her words. Adam had shown his kids that he'd rather work than be with them. They didn't even believe that he was capable of wanting to get a Christmas tree.

"David, don't you think your daddy would like to get a Christmas tree with us?"

"He'll probably tell us to get it. That's what he does when we need things—he tells Natalie to do it."

"Well, I think we should try to persuade him to go. Let's explain to him how wonderful it will be and maybe it will make him want to go with us. It would be fun." The children's looks to one another told her they weren't convinced. She may have some more persuading to do.

It was after eight o'clock again when Adam got home. He entered the kitchen, talking on his cell phone, his eyes darting to Carrie and then away.

"What's the printing cost if we switched printers?" he said.

The excitement she felt at seeing him mixed with the frustration she had for the way he ignored everyone, giving her a headache. She rubbed the bridge of her nose, trying to ease the pinch there but stopped quickly when Adam turned toward her. But he didn't make eye contact.

"While you're with the team," he said, still not looking at Carrie, "let them know that I've signed off on the Westwood building with Robert. I'm so glad we had him on our side."

Carrie sat down at the table with a bowl of stew she'd cooked during the day and two cards made by Olivia and David.

"…And I'll need a cost proposal for the printing." Adam shrugged off his coat and set his shoes neatly by the door to the hallway.

Carrie got up and dished Adam a bowl of stew from the pot that she had warming on the stove. Then she poured two glasses of the wine from the bottle that he had used last night.

He seemed to finally notice that she'd prepared supper and said, "Okay. Let me chew on the rest for a while. I'll call you back." He set his phone onto the counter and turned toward the table.

She took her place, picked up her glass of wine, and waited.

"I thought I told you that you didn't have to make me supper," he said with a tired grin.

"I didn't. I made myself supper. You just benefitted from the large recipe," she teased, hoping she hadn't crossed any lines. She took a risk teasing him, but seeing his friendly grin, she felt like she could. "Wine?" She held up his glass.

He smiled that smile that could make her knees buckle. She felt as if she'd known him longer than she had—she was already invested in him and his family. Even when she was frustrated by his behavior, she was glad to have him around. And, when he finally stopped working for a second, it was nice to have his company. While she loved the children, she enjoyed having an adult around too. She wished he'd stay still, sit down, and talk to her.

"Have you been baking?" he asked.

"No. Just the stew. Why?"

"I smell peppermint."

"Oh, it's the Christmas candle." She pointed to a large red and white striped jar flickering on the island. It had been one of the purchases she'd made with his credit card.

"It's nice," he said. When he sat down, she slid the two cards toward him. "What's this?" he asked, taking a sip of wine.

"David and Olivia have written you a letter." She directed his attention to the front of each card. "Why You Should Get a Christmas Tree With Us," she read, looking up at him as uncertainty tickled her skin.

Carrie didn't know him very well, and she was pushing things to impose something like this on him. It made her a little worried that she'd offend him, but she'd already started the conversation, and she felt it in her heart to do this, so she'd better finish it.

She opened the cards. "Olivia said that you should get a Christmas tree because they are heavy, and you can help to carry it for us. See"—she tapped a circle with eyes on the paper—"this is you carrying the tree." She took David's card and read it aloud. "David says you should get a Christmas tree with us because you could help us pay for it. That's his money there." She set the cards down on the table. "Olivia thinks you're strong and David thinks you can provide for the family." She didn't want to point out the obvious—that neither child said they *wanted* to be with their daddy to get a tree. She was hopeful that Adam would make that connection and realize that he needed to be with them sometimes if he ever planned on having any kind of bond with them.

Adam studied the cards for quite some time, and Carrie wondered if he understood her message. Then he cleared his throat and looked up. "When would we buy this Christmas tree?"

"How about Saturday?"

He studied her face, but it was clear that he was thinking, not waiting. "I was planning on going into the office this weekend. I need to get a few things done, and there's no way I'll get them finished by Friday." He shook his head. "Things are very busy right now."

"Maybe one evening?"

"They're asleep when I get home."

In every other part of her life, she was unsure of her choices, but when it came to the needs of children, she just knew what they needed and this time was no different. She couldn't bring herself to back down. Carrie mustered all her strength and said, "Maybe you can find some time when you can come home while they're awake."

"Easier said than done."

Even though she'd known him only a short time, she felt that she needed to be honest with him. "From what I've seen so far, you seem pretty good at getting things done. Perhaps you can get this done as well."

At first, he looked at her indignantly—it was just for a moment—and she wondered if he'd ever been spoken to that directly before. She hadn't meant to be rude, just honest. His children needed him. Their well-being was her number one priority—he'd said that himself.

"Look, I have things to deal with that are more important than a *tree*."

"This isn't about a tree. It's about being with your children," she said, the words coming out gently. She wasn't trying to upset him. But she couldn't just sit by and see such a wonderful family not enjoy themselves because work was getting in the way. It seemed like such a waste.

"You're making this bigger than it is. The kids spelled it out for you. They need strength and money to get that tree. There's someone at the lot who will tie it to your car for you, and you have my credit card."

"I remember getting a tree with my dad," she said, still careful in her approach. "I remember each year specifically. Those were great memories, Adam. Your kids aren't going to have any memories of you except the ones where you're absent."

His jaw clenched, but his eyes looked as though he were considering. She watched him, a glimmer of hope swelling up inside her. "Please," she said, capitalizing on that possible moment of deliberation.

He took in a deep breath and let it out slowly, his eyes still on her. "You are definitely not shy about your thoughts," he said, still studying her face. "I can't do Saturday…" he said more to himself than to her and shook his head. The way he looked at her wound her stomach into knots, but she held her ground, nearly pleading with her eyes.

The silence between them was deafening as Carrie waited for the outcome of her forward comment. She was willing to bet that demanding things from a boss on day two was not something that any of her books would have recommended, but it felt like the right thing to do. Perhaps she'd made a mistake in asking him to get a tree. She was out of her comfort zone.

Adam took a sip of his wine, set down the glass, and started eating his stew, leaving her hanging on that last thought. She'd been waiting so patiently, hoping to hear his answer, and he'd completely abandoned the conversation. She wondered if he was still mulling it over at all. She watched him eating, wanting to shake him by the shoulders.

"The Christmas decorations looked very nice when I drove up," he said at last. "I like what you've done with the white lights outside and the window candles."

"Thank you," she said, her voice so quiet it was almost a whisper. She didn't know what else to say. His reaction puzzled her. She couldn't tell what he was thinking. Was he angry? Should she have just left well enough alone? It was only the second day of her employment; she had a long way to go. She'd never faced this situation before.

She looked down at her stew and ate a spoonful. It was still hot enough that the steam was rising in front of her. She stirred it around, the vegetables spinning in the broth. The more she sat there, the more she thought she might have been wrong making such a bold suggestion. No matter what she thought about Adam Fletcher, she barely knew him, and she worried that she'd overstepped her bounds. What had she been thinking to pry into his life and speak to him like that? She was the nanny, and he was her employer. Guilt settled in her stomach, making it difficult to eat another bite.

Adam picked up his phone and started scrolling through something, that serious face of his returning—the pursed lips, the crease between his eyes. Was he just going to leave the conversation at that? Never even address the fact that she'd asked him to get a Christmas tree with his own children? Was he going to make a call, get involved with his work again, and walk out not to return until the next morning? She felt so helpless in that moment because it was clear from only a few days with them that what the kids needed was time with their father, and Adam needed to show them love. They were all missing so much.

"I can try to meet you at ten o'clock tomorrow. Can we do it in an hour?" he asked, typing on his phone. He *was* mulling it over. She could see now that he'd been scrolling through his calendar. She was so excited that she could've jumped up and hugged him. Instead, she focused on his face, how he pressed his lips together, the way he blinked slowly to fight fatigue, the strength in his cheekbones. He was good-looking, certainly, but the fact that he'd listened to her, paid attention to her request, and honored it, made him more attractive than any good looks could. She had to work to keep the smile from spreading across her face. Adam Fletcher was getting a Christmas tree. She'd done it, and the success of it felt so good. She'd gone with her gut, and she'd been right. The kids would be able to say that they bought a tree with their father. How wonderful.

"Yes," she said. "We can do it in an hour."

Chapter Seven

Deep breathing can evoke calm.

Carrie tried unsuccessfully to control her excitement as she got the children ready. She took in a big breath and let it out slowly. It was nearly nine forty-five, and they were meeting Adam at the Christmas tree farm down the road in fifteen minutes. She tucked Olivia's scarf into her coat. "I've got the car running, but it will take me some time to clear it. Would anyone like to help me get the snow off the car?"

"Me!" Olivia jumped up and down. "Oh, I'm hot," she said suddenly, pulling at her scarf.

Carrie smiled down at her. Only Olivia's dark blue eyes and pink cheeks were visible. The rest of her was so bundled that her entire body was lost underneath.

"I can help too," David said quietly, tugging on the wrist of his mittens to pull them on. His face was contorted in concentration as he struggled to get his fingers in. His stocking cap fell a little lower than it should be, and he kept trying to push it out of his eyes.

"I'm hot," Olivia said again.

Carrie opened the front door, letting in a gust of freezing air. "This should help," she said, ushering the kids outside into the snow. The sun had come out, casting golden light on the white expanse around them. All they could see was the bright blue of the sky and the glitter of snow. Carrie couldn't help but be excited about this trip. It was a tiny step in the right direction. If she could get Adam to spend an hour with the kids on her third day of work, what could she accomplish with more time?

She handed David a little brush she'd found in the garage, and passed a scraper to Olivia. "David, can you be sure all the lights on the car are brushed clean, please? And Olivia, you can scrape the mirrors on the outside for me." The children, eager to assist, got right to work. Carrie had already brushed the snow off the windshield, and the heat from the defrost inside had done the rest of the work, but she wanted the car to be warm enough. So, to keep the kids busy and to make them feel like they'd done something grownup, she'd had them help. By the time their interest was dwindling, it was a few minutes before ten o'clock, so she buckled them into the car and headed for the Christmas tree lot.

She arrived right on time and had to stifle a smile as she saw Adam standing at the front of the lot, his coat pulled up around his chin, his breath billowing out in front of him, talking on his cell phone. *One step at a time*, she thought.

He looked like something out of a magazine, and she couldn't believe how in the world, looking like he did, he was still single. As she parked the car, she thought how similar they were. He wasn't dating anyone seriously for the same reason that she wasn't—they both worked all the time.

"There's your daddy," she said, turning off the engine.

"I can't wait to get a tree!" Olivia said. David sat quietly, his eyes on his father. His face was curious, watching, as if he were taking in every one of Adam's movements. Carrie could tell that David was like a little adult himself, and if he were just given the opportunity, he'd probably want to spend every minute with his daddy. Her mind was spinning with ways to facilitate that scenario.

She opened the car door and helped the kids unbuckle themselves. They hopped out, and she quickly assessed the parking lot, worried they'd run to Adam, but they didn't. They stood right with her, and she noticed again what little bond they had with their father. Adam had looked their way and finished his call, sliding his phone into his pocket. He put up a hand and waved at them. In the sunlight, she noticed that his hair had strands of bronze like Olivia's, and his face was even more striking when he wasn't exhausted. She took the children's hands on either side of her and walked across the parking lot.

"Hi," she said as they neared Adam.

"Hello." He had his hands in the pockets of his coat.

He had a quality about him that made her want to walk with him, take her time, get to know him better, but she was there for one purpose: to get the children together with their father. "There are a lot of trees here," she said for the kids' benefit. "We may want to split up. David, why don't you go with your daddy, and Olivia and I will go to the other side. We'll each find a tree and compare them. How does that sound?"

David was still watching his father, a hesitant look on his face. Then, without warning, he leaned toward Carrie and whispered, "I want to go with you too." He moved closer to Carrie, putting a giant gap between the three of them and Adam.

Carrie had made the suggestion, hoping to give David a little time with his dad, to give them a chance to enjoy each other, and it had just backfired terribly. A wave of uneasiness washed over her as she looked over at Adam. How must it feel to have a son who would rather be with his nanny than with his own father? Even given the situation, it had to hurt at least a little. She searched his face, however, if it had upset him, he hid it well. His smile was gone, but his face was pleasant.

"Why don't we go together?" he suggested. "We have enough time to find a tree, even if we don't split up. Plus, Carrie knows what would look best in the house."

"Okay," she said, glad that the atmosphere was still friendly and happy for the most part. They started walking into the rows of spruce trees, all tied to posts, their branches dusted with snow. Big, buzzing white light bulbs hung from tree post to tree post, their light masked by the bright sun. Despite the clear weather, the temperature outside was so cold that the snow hadn't moved. It still blanketed the field, contrasting with the green of the Christmas trees and the blue of the sky. Carrie ran her hand down one of the evergreens, its short needles springing into place from under her palm, sending a tiny puff of snow down to the ground.

"Do you want a fat tree or a skinny one?" she asked David.

"A big fat one," he smiled, his dimple showing on his cheek. "That will give us room for more presents!" He giggled.

Carrie thought about this comment. As of now, David didn't have any presents because Adam hadn't bought any—and unbeknownst to him, she wasn't going to do it. Did Adam even know what his children liked? Did he know what would make them gasp and squeal with joy on Christmas morning? She had a lot of work ahead of her if she was going to get him to buy the presents. At this point, it seemed daunting, and she felt a twinge of worry that she wouldn't be able to accomplish such a task. She worried, too, about the children.

What would their Christmas be like if they opened a bunch of gifts that they hadn't asked for or if Santa didn't come? Adam only had a handful of years where the wonder was present in his children's faces. And then it would be gone. Forever. He'd never get that magic back. If she didn't work fast, his children would grow up and look back on their childhood never knowing that kind of joy.

She remembered Christmases with her own parents, how it felt to unwrap that one gift that had been at the top of her list. She held fondly the security in the knowledge that her parents had known exactly what to get her. Her parents had looked long and hard to find the very things—down to the right color or model—that she'd put on her list. They'd done it because they loved her. If Carrie bought the children gifts, what would that tell them about Adam?

Adam was kind and gentle, and she knew that deep down he loved his kids too. If he didn't, he wouldn't have worked so hard to get a top nanny, and he wouldn't have met them today. Perhaps he just didn't know how to show that love. Clearly, being the Founder and CEO of Shockoe Brewery—she'd noticed on his letterhead—he knew how to run things. She'd read on the Internet last night how his beer was shipped statewide, and he had a very successful restaurant and brewery. By the ease in which he offered his credit card, things were unquestionably going well for him. Maybe he was like her in that he stuck to what he did best—running the brewery—and let everything else flounder.

"What presents would you like for Christmas, David?" she asked.

Olivia had run ahead, and was bent over, her scarf now out of her jacket, dragging along the ground as she peered under a tree. "There's not much room under this one," she called back to them and then ran a little farther up the lot to check another.

"I'd like a race car set," David said.

Carrie took a mental note.

"Oh, that sounds fun, David. If you get one, may I play with it too?" Olivia asked.

David nodded, a grin emerging through his serious expression. Carrie stopped in front of a perfectly shaped Christmas tree that stood taller than Adam, and looked it up and down. "What about this one?" she asked, looking at Adam for his opinion.

He shrugged. "I'm sure you're better at knowing what would work in the house than I am," he said. "Get whatever you like."

His cheeks were pink from the cold. Carrie wanted to put her hands on them and warm them up. The thought surprised her, and she quickly turned away from him, focusing on the tree. Handsome as he was, she hadn't until that very moment contemplated what it would be like to comfort him or touch him. She couldn't be having thoughts like that. When she had finally cleared the notion from her mind, she looked back at him, and his eyes met hers. He regarded her almost curiously, and she worried that he could read her mind.

Adam's phone rang in his pocket, slashing through the moment. He turned to answer it, and Carrie finally managed to take a breath. The children were hiding behind trees, giggling, knocking into their branches, and causing snow to puff out in the sunlight, falling to the ground like glitter.

"Andy…" he said, taking a step away, his back to her. He was quiet, listening, striding back and forth, spots of wetness beginning to show on his high-dollar shoes. "If we go that route, I'm going to need a cost analysis. I can't make that type of decision without some sort of discussion. Have you asked the team?" His back was still to her, but his pacing had brought him closer, and she tried to occupy herself with looking at the tree so as not to eavesdrop. "Shall we meet tonight and discuss it over a drink?"

She immediately thought about how late that would put Adam getting home tonight, and the disappointment of it hit her harder than it should. She found herself becoming oddly envious of this Andy, wishing she, too, could go for a drink and have a night out with adults.

Andy. What if Andy was a woman? Adam was having drinks to discuss work, but it was still drinks he was having. She imagined a tall, striking woman in heels and the kind of dress that Carrie had never owned, a cocktail in her hand, her head tipping back in laughter at something Adam said. Yes, that would most likely be the type of person he'd go out with. She looked down at her jeans and coat, her striped gloves and scarf, thinking how casual she looked.

Carrie shifted her thoughts to the tree she'd found. It was perfect in every way. Her focus should be on making the Fletcher home an inviting Christmas atmosphere for the twins and giving them the best Christmas they could have. What Adam Fletcher chose to do with his time was not what she needed to be thinking about. She needed to finish this job well and take a good look at the college brochures she had so she could sort something out for after Christmas. As much as she wanted to be with children and remain a nanny, Carrie needed to move forward with her life. She knew that now more than ever.

The cold had made its way through her layers, and she was certain that the kids were probably chilly too. As soon as Adam was off the phone, she was going to tell him to just buy the tree in front of her without looking at any of the others. It was a fine tree, and, clearly, he needed to get back to work.

Adam let out a long sigh as he continued his phone conversation. "I'm going to be working late anyway to make up for the time I've lost today," he said quietly into the phone. "Let's just make it a night, shall we? You pick the place." Still talking on the phone, he pulled out his wallet and handed Carrie his credit card, barely making eye contact.

With that one gesture, she felt in the way, and she wished that she hadn't bothered to ask him to help them get a tree. She imagined that this was how David and Olivia must feel. Again, he'd dismissed her actions as if they meant nothing, and that was probably true. Last time, she'd been frustrated, irritated by his behavior, but this time, he'd disappointed her. She'd only been trying to include him and feel the Christmas spirit a little, but it was apparent that her decision to involve him had been wrong. Who was she kidding? She wasn't going to fix his family. She wasn't going to get him to know what presents to get his kids. She took the card from his hand and went to gather the children.

Chapter Eight

Label your bad habits and eliminate them.

Carrie underlined the sentence and marked the page with a bookmark. In her journal, she listed her first bad habit: meddling in people's business, her employer's family's business, to be precise. After the Christmas tree fiasco, there was no way she was ever going to put herself in that position again. Adam had made it quite clear by his actions where his family fell on his list of priorities.

Not to mention the way it had made her feel when he'd just dismissed her, handing out his credit card with barely a glance in her direction. He was missing out on so much. He had a lot of money and very nice things, but he didn't enjoy any of them. He came in after dark, ate, and went to bed alone. He never sat in his living room and enjoyed a good book or had a nice talk over a long dinner. He didn't sit back and watch his children play, knowing that every second was gone the moment it happened, and he'd never get it back. It seemed like he couldn't enjoy himself. The four days he'd taken off for Christmas should be interesting, she thought.

Carrie tried to see it from his side, and the more she thought about it, the more she realized that she hadn't gotten anywhere with him. He'd seen the trip to the tree lot as just another tick on his to-do list. It hadn't been about spending time with his children at all.

And the worst part was that their outing had given the kids yet one more occasion when their daddy hadn't made a difference in their lives. He was as absent standing there as he would've been at work. She had a sinking feeling, given the way the children acted around him, that it was always this way.

The trouble was that she genuinely liked Adam. He was friendly, usually, and seemed like a nice guy in general. She was rational enough to tell herself not to expect anything from him, but her instincts made her feel like he was capable of more, and that's what upset her. This problem was too big for her to solve, and while she wanted to fix it, she knew that wasn't her place.

And now, she sat at the kitchen table alone in this big house, with white lights glistening up the greenery on the banister at the front door, the glow of the tree she and the kids had decorated together today, and the peppermint scent in the air from the candle she'd bought—no one to enjoy it but her. It was nearly nine o'clock at night, and Adam wasn't home. He was probably still having drinks with Andy. She looked back toward the garage door. Silence.

Her supper plate sat empty in front of her, the food long gone. She'd eaten by herself, and she couldn't help but think how that had been her fault for asking him to get the tree. She'd pushed all his work back, and now he was doing business instead of being home. As annoyed as she was with him, she'd liked it when he'd come home the last two days. His quiet and controlled nature calmed her. She wondered if she could've done anything differently today.

With a deep breath, Carrie pushed away from the table, cleared her dishes, and cleaned up the kitchen. Before going upstairs, she dished Adam some food, put it in the refrigerator, and left him a note with directions for heating it up, just in case he hadn't eaten with Andy. Then she grabbed her book and went to bed.

Carrie peered out the front window at the enormous camper pulling in. The snow had melted considerably, revealing the black of the street and the aggregate driveway. It was definitely a different scene now than the one she'd encountered when she'd first arrived, but another storm was headed for them by the end of the day and, most likely, it would all be covered in snow and ice again by the morning.

"Is Grandma Joyce here?" Olivia asked, bouncing on her toes, the plastic of her pink and silver sparkle princess dress-up high heels causing a clacking sound against the hardwoods. Carrie looked down at the twins, just now noticing that they weren't perfectly dressed the way Natalie would have had them. Olivia was wearing her dress-up princess costume over the top of a pair of blue leggings and a green floral shirt. Her hair was bunched beneath her plastic crown, wisps falling around her face. David had jeans and a superhero T-shirt that he must have found in his summer clothes drawer when he'd dressed himself this morning.

The camper pulled forward and backward, making tracks in the snow, over and over in an attempt to park the gigantic vehicle in the driveway. The sky above it was a dark gray—the kind of sky that would dump snow at any moment—a far cry from yesterday's blue. Carrie wondered about the people in that camper. What were Adam's parents like? She'd never had extended family in the house while she was watching children before. It could make for a very difficult holiday if they didn't agree with her methods.

The camper finally came to a stop. The driver's side door opened, and a man got out. He was dressed in a pair of jeans and a wool coat. When he turned around, she bit her lip to keep from smiling. She knew exactly who he was just by his face, and she knew what Adam would look like in another twenty-five or so years. The man's hair was silver, and his stance wasn't as strong as Adam's, but he looked just like him. The door opened on the other side and a petite woman with a gentle expression got out. Her gray hair fell just above her shoulders, and she had it tucked behind her ears. Her giant coat nearly swallowed her, her dainty legs barely showing beneath it. She was rubbing her arms to keep warm as she walked around the camper. The man put his arm around her and tried to warm her up. He only let go of his wife to help an elderly man who was wobbling down the step of the camper, grabbing onto the side of the vehicle for support and barely getting down on his own. Her first inclination was to run out and help him—he looked very unsteady—but he seemed more stable once he was on the ground. The man pulled a walker out of the camper and placed it in front of him. Carrie wondered if he'd be able to get it through the snow outside, and she wished someone had shoveled the walk.

The family didn't look intimidating or even overly wealthy, which was surprising. After seeing Adam's huge house and all the expensive things in it, she'd just assumed that they would be. But the truth was, they looked a lot like her own parents. A sense of calm wrapped around her like a warm blanket as she saw their affection for one another. Then she had a jolt of excitement when she noted the license plate on the camper. It was from North Carolina—her home state. At least if she had to spend time with a family that wasn't her own, she could most likely relate to them.

The back door of the camper opened and two more people got out: a woman—Adam's sister? Then a man. When the group started walking toward the house, Olivia ran to open the door, David following behind her.

"Grandma Joyce!" Olivia called out, swinging the front door wide open and trying to step onto the snowy front steps with her princess heels.

"I'll come to you, Olivia," Joyce said with a grin that lit up her entire face. She darted around the two men as they made their way down the drive. As Joyce got closer, Carrie noticed that her eyes were the same blue as Adam's. "You're gonna slip if you come out here. I'm coming."

Carrie definitely recognized her North Carolina accent. It sent a soothing feeling through her. There was something unique about the accents in the Southern states; each one of them had their own slight differences. It was the way she said the word "I" and the drawl in the name "Olivia" that had given her away. It was the same drawl she'd heard when her mother had read her books at night all snuggled up in bed.

David—the ever protective and focused twin brother—reached out for Olivia's hand, helping awkwardly to get her off the snow and back into the house. "Come back in," he said, his face full of concern. "Hi, Grandpa Bruce!" he said, waving from the open door.

"Hey there, squirt!" Bruce said as he reached the front steps. The older man grabbed the railing and worked his way up. Bruce smiled like Adam too, but there was something wise about his smile that was different than his son's. Adam's was more affectionate, whereas this man's smile seemed to have years of understanding that one could only acquire from experience.

"Hello," Grandma Joyce said with a big smile when her gaze fell upon Carrie. She held out her hand in greeting. She had hardly a wrinkle. Just by looking at her, Carrie could tell so much about her character: the warmth in her eyes, her caring expression, her gentle but firm grip on Carrie's hand. Any worry that she still had about Adam's family melted away with that one introduction. "I hope Adam told you we were coming. I'm Adam's mother, Joyce, and this is his father, Bruce."

"Yes. He did tell me. It's nice to meet you," Carrie said, trying to look as professional as possible in her sock feet and jeans, though they didn't seem like the type of people to mind.

The others came up the steps.

"This is Adam's sister, Sharon, and her husband, Eric," Joyce said, moving out of the way so Carrie could meet them. Sharon was noticeably thin, even through her big coat, her long fingers peeking out from the sleeves. Her wedding ring looked gigantic on her skinny fingers, hanging loosely, the diamond sliding to the side. When her eyes met Carrie's, the corners of her mouth went up slightly to acknowledge their meeting, but that was all. Eric put his hand on her back, almost as if he were holding her up.

Carrie introduced herself and gestured for them to enter.

"They're leaving me out, but I'm Walter, Adam's grandfather," the elderly man said in a lighthearted way as he trailed behind them all on the way inside. Joyce was already shaking her head, an amused look on her face. She grabbed his walker as Walter held on to the door frame to help himself up the step into the house.

"It's nice to meet you," Carrie said. She already felt generally comfortable around them, which said a lot for their first impressions. Walter patted her on the shoulder and offered her a smile not unlike her own grandfather would have done, his legs becoming unsteady with the gesture, so he leaned back onto his walker for support.

"I'm glad Adam told you about us," Joyce said, closing the door after everyone had entered. "He failed, however, to mention *you*!"

"I'm so sorry—I thought he would have," she said, smiling back but feeling a twinge of disappointment that Adam had neglected to tell his family that he'd had a change in staff. However, how would he possibly have had any time to make a phone call to his family when he barely had time to eat? She had noticed last night's dinner dishes she'd prepared for him were rinsed out and set in the sink this morning. He'd gone before the kids had gotten her up, and she hadn't heard a peep from him all day. "I'm Carrie Blake."

Joyce picked Olivia up and gave her a squeeze. Olivia's shoes hung by the strap at her toes, the princess heels dangling from each foot. The little girl wrapped her arms around Joyce's neck. It was nice to see Olivia be so open and affectionate with her grandmother.

"Do you live here?" Joyce asked, glancing down at Carrie's sock feet. This was how she always dressed when watching children, but as she thought of Natalie, she considered the fact that not everyone followed the same dress code. Carrie needed clothing that was suitable for exploration, for learning, clothing that could get wrinkled, get paint on, get wet. There were so many opportunities for the children every day to learn and have fun. If they were dressed in their best clothes, they'd miss out on things like bathtub boat races or baking homemade pies.

Carrie led them down the hallway, where they could hang up their coats. "Yes, I live here," she said.

Joyce's eyes widened, a look of delighted surprise on her face. She scanned Carrie from her head to her toes. "Well, this is exciting news, Bruce!" Joyce turned to him. "It's good to see Adam moving forward." Joyce put Olivia down and wrapped her arms around David's shoulders. "Isn't it, Bruce?"

Carrie was so confused that she couldn't even hide it. She felt her face crumple with misunderstanding. Then the light bulb went off. "Oh! I'm the nanny," she said quickly, realizing that Joyce must have thought she was Adam's new girlfriend! "I just started. It's my fourth day."

"Oh dear!" Joyce laughed. "Sorry." She shook her head as if she couldn't believe her blunder. "It's just..." She shook her head again. When she looked back at Carrie, there were thoughts on her face, and it seemed as though her hopes had been dashed just a bit. She certainly had been excited at the idea of Adam dating.

Carrie busied herself with hanging up their coats in an attempt to change the focus of conversation. Then she led them into the living room. Walter grabbed on to Bruce's arm for support, leaving his walker in the hallway. When they sat down, the conversation quieted for a moment. Carrie turned toward the tree she'd decorated with the children.

The Christmas tree sent light across the polished hardwoods all the way up to the shaggy rug that sat under the furniture. It made the room feel cozy and complemented the oversized mantel around the fireplace that Carrie had draped greenery along—wide garlands of spruce with velvet cranberry-colored bows to match the tree skirt. David asked if he could go play in the playroom but Olivia stayed back.

"Forgive me, but I don't know why Adam needed a nanny," Joyce said, her Southern drawl strong and thick. "We could've just come up earlier. Or, heaven forbid, he take an extra few days off to do something non-work-related." Joyce's gaze settled on the Christmas tree. "At least he's decorated for Christmas, which is a delightful surprise."

"Carrie did our tree!" Olivia said. "And me! And David. We made that pretty tree ourselves!" Olivia leaned on the sofa, bouncing against it with her hands. Then she tipped her head toward Joyce, her face right next to her grandmother's. "Carrie made Daddy go with us to pick it out," she giggled.

Joyce listened intently, not breaking eye contact. "So Carrie made Daddy come, did she?" she said, a smile playing at her lips. "Nobody *makes* your daddy do anything. Perhaps he *wanted* to go," she said, letting the smile emerge for Olivia's benefit.

Carrie had never considered that. Even though he'd been distant and uninvolved the whole time, he *had* come with them to the tree lot. Had he wanted to go? Perhaps he just needed a little help with knowing what to do once he got there... Carrie couldn't deny the hope that bubbled up as she thought about it.

Chapter Nine

To improve your personal life, find ways to make connections with new people.

Carrie struggled with how to go about making new friendships when she was working around the clock. But tonight, while Adam was still at work, she had a chance to do just that. Walter had pulled her aside, making conversation just for the sake of something to do.

She'd told him where she was from when he'd asked, and he'd laughed—a jolly chuckle of a laugh—because he'd grown up quite close to her town. He'd asked about her family and whether she missed them at Christmas time, and of course she did.

"You're a very sweet girl," he said. "But I can tell something's on your mind. I can also tell that missing your family isn't what's bothering you." He shifted on the sofa, wiggling his right leg as if to get the circulation going. "But what do I know." He smiled. "I'm just an old man."

"I don't know anyone in Virginia," she admitted. "I'm new here."

"Ah." Walter didn't say anything else, but he kept looking at her as if he expected her to say more, so she kept going.

"I don't have any girlfriends to go out with…" she said.

"I had a girlfriend whom I liked to go out with once," he said, winking at her. There was something about Walter that drew her right in, as if she'd known him her entire life. It was like talking to her own grandfather. Carrie's grandfather, Pappy, had passed away almost a decade ago. That decade had seemed like a blip in time until she sat across from Walter. Being with him made the years without Pappy stretch into what seemed like a lifetime. Sitting there with him, she felt like she was with Pappy again.

"Her name was Beth," Walter said, pulling Carrie from her thoughts. "Beth was the only girl I ever wanted to go out with. She had a laugh like warm apple pie, and she smelled like roses. It took me a year to get up the courage to ask her to the picture show, and I worried that she wouldn't go, since it was dark in there, and she was quite the lady, but she went. I spent every day with her after that." Walter wiggled his leg again. "Every single day until the good Lord wanted to have her back." Walter's loss was evident even through his smile. "I know what you mean is all," he said. "I know what it's like not to have any *girlfriends* to go out with." He smiled a playful but knowing smile.

Carrie found out that the rest of Adam's family, too, wasn't much different than hers. They lived in a small town in rural North Carolina, and, like her, they enjoyed similar things. Walter kept a deck of cards in his back pocket for whenever he was bored. He pulled them out, and they played rummy all evening. As they played, she had a chance to chat since the kids were in bed. It turned out that Adam's sister, Sharon, had attended her college—they were two years apart—and she'd rented a beach house only a street over from the one where Carrie had vacationed with her parents as a kid.

She delighted in the banter between Walter and his son, Bruce. Walter chattered about the World Wars and politics—topics that generally didn't interest her—but he had a way of telling the stories that made her unable to pull herself away. Even when Joyce asked her to help cook supper, she found herself leaning toward the table to hear what he was saying. Whenever Bruce would question him on a fact, he could twist it into a joke and make everyone laugh—even Sharon, who sat quietly most of the time except when she leaned over to Eric to say something. Every so often, though, laughter would rise up in her, and a little amusement would escape. Carrie could tell how close this family was, and she felt a twinge of sadness that Adam wasn't there to share it.

She worried about him missing out on everything; it bothered her. Perhaps the upcoming snowstorm would keep him home...

Joyce, having heard about the impending storm, had stockpiled a ton of food in the camper, and Bruce had helped her unload it all earlier while Sharon and Eric took everyone's bags to their rooms. So, when it came to suppertime, Joyce set out cooking an extraordinary amount of food. Carrie was more than happy to help. She hadn't had a chance to cook like that since she'd lived at home with her parents.

A huge dish of bubbling macaroni and cheese baking in the oven sent a savory wave around the kitchen as they prepared the ingredients for the Brunswick stew. The garlic and onions were already in the pan with the butter, their flavors mixing in the air with the cheese. Carrie easily fell into the rhythm of cooking, the tasks coming easily to her after years of practice with her family. As Joyce pivoted between the island and the counter, just like her own mother had, Carrie couldn't help but feel excited. She was with people like her, which made her happy.

"When the timer goes off, Carrie, pull out the mac and cheese so we can get that cornbread cooking," Joyce said, her accent seeping out as thick as molasses the more relaxed she became. She added the ingredients to the pot she'd pulled from Adam's cabinet. It looked like it had never been used. This was the most comfortable that she could remember being in a long time. These people spoke her language: They played with the children, they enjoyed each other's company, and they liked good food. Cooking gave her something to do while she enjoyed these strangers. As she watched them all sitting at that giant table that had been so quiet with just her and Adam, she wondered why he'd only taken four days off.

At the kitchen table, Sharon set down a run of six cards and looked over at Eric under her lashes. "Top that," she challenged him quietly.

"Hold on," Bruce said. "I've got two hands here. I'm playing for Carrie while she helps Joyce. And Carrie has three sevens." He set them down, and winked in her direction.

"Thank you," Carrie said, smiling from across the kitchen, adding a little more cayenne to the Brunswick stew at Joyce's suggestion. The timer went off and, with mitted hands, she pulled out the macaroni and cheese casserole. It had a brown crust at the edges just like her mother's had. She set it on a mat on the island in the center of the kitchen and then put the cornbread in the oven.

Sharon had clicked on the light outside on the deck—an enormous wooden structure with levels and built-in seating. Carrie could only imagine the parties that Adam could have there in warmer weather. If he took the time.

"Carrie," Walter said. "I'm sure there's no shortage of beer in this house. Do you know where Adam keeps it? Bruce said he didn't see any in the fridge."

"He stores it in the garage. I'll just go and get some. How many?" She counted the show of hands. There were four. After she'd offered, it occurred to her: She had no idea if she was even allowed to take beers from his refrigerator in the garage. She'd never had the need before. Already, his family had made her feel so at ease that she'd just offered as if it were her house. She considered sending him a quick text just to ask.

But when she opened the door to the garage, she knocked into Adam, nearly toppling them both over. "Oh!" she said in stumbling back in surprise as Adam grabbed onto her to steady them both. "Hello," she said, her face only inches from his. She wriggled herself upright. The time she'd spent getting to know Adam's family made him look a little different to her tonight. It was almost as if she could see the boy that he'd have been; she could almost envision him in the big yard in North Carolina where he'd played as a child. A flutter rippled through her stomach, and she fought with everything she had not to feel it. She barely knew him.

"Hi," he said, the corners of his mouth turning upward. "I see the family's made it."

"Yes. They want to drink your beer. Are they allowed?" she whispered. She felt like some sort of prohibition agent, guarding his loot, her eyes darting around so as not to offend anyone who may be in earshot.

He let out a big "Ha!" that nearly sent her tumbling backward. "Why wouldn't they be able to? I think I would know where to get more," he chuckled. He backed up and walked with her to the refrigerator. His laughter was addictive—she wanted to hear more of it. She thought back to the way he looked sitting at his huge desk in the office upstairs, his brows puckered, his lips pressed together in a serious expression. His face now was a stark contrast to that. To see all that stress lifted off of his face gave him a kind of familiarity—he was more casual—and she liked that. "It's starting to snow again," he said.

All the cooking, the warm glow of the Christmas lights, and having him home—it all made the idea of more snow seem perfect. She wished selfishly that the storm would dump so much snow that he wouldn't be able to go into work. She was having such a lovely night with this family of strangers; she wanted him to be a part of it.

"Oh," he said. "I brought you something."

He'd brought *her* something? She smiled to conceal her surprise.

He reached into his briefcase and pulled out one Salty Shockoe bottle. The label was fancier with dark green holly and little red berries behind the words. "Since you were the designer, I thought I'd bring you your own bottle. No white space on this one." Her heart started to patter. Adam's gesture was so unexpected that it floored her. He'd thought enough of Carrie to take time out of his busy schedule and do something nice for her. As she looked at him now, his face was so attentive, so kind. She hadn't put her finger on it until then, but when he was in the present, he was really there.

"How many beers do we need?" he asked, his blue eyes on her. She took in a breath to try and get her thoughts straight.

"Four."

"I'll get one of the six-packs," he said, turning away and opening the fridge. Then he stopped and said, "You know what? Let me just take a case inside. With everyone here, we'll end up drinking it at some point." A ray of hope tickled her insides. Would he kick back and have a beer with them? Suddenly, she couldn't wait to get back in there. She followed him to the kitchen.

"Well look who decided to come home," Joyce said with a grin as Adam walked in with the case of beer. He set it down next to the refrigerator and gave her a hug.

"Hey, Mom," he said. "I warned you that I still have to work." He gave her a kiss on the cheek.

"I made supper. You'd better get that snowy coat off of ya and sit down and eat. The cornbread'll be coming out soon," she said with warmth behind her eyes. Carrie wondered if Joyce was thinking the same thing as she was: Don't go to your office and do work. Stay. Carrie hoped he wouldn't go.

"I'll open the beers," Eric said, clapping him on the back and squatting down to pick up the case of beer. When the two men made eye contact, there was an unsaid communication between them—she could feel it. Eric was friendly enough, but his eyes said something else too, something that they hadn't said when Carrie had met him. Eric carried the case over to the island and gently set it down.

Adam scooted out the chair and hung his coat on the back of it. When he took a seat, Carrie had to work to conceal her excitement. "Hey there, Gramps!" He threw up a hand to Walter.

He smiled at Sharon, but it wasn't his usual smile—there was something jagged and tense in their look to each other. They were both trying to hide it, but Carrie had caught it.

"How are you, Dad?" Adam asked.

"Can't complain." Bruce slid Carrie's hand of cards along the table toward Adam. "Here, play Carrie's cards for her while she helps your mother."

"What am I playing?" He scanned the game. "Oh. Rummy. I should have guessed." He grinned. "Whose go?"

"Yours."

After Carrie went back to the stove to help Joyce, she noticed that Adam was glancing over at her from behind his hand of cards while they played the game. It was subtle, his gaze not lingering for long, but she'd noticed it. An electric sort of energy shot through her. She'd never cared how she looked before or what people thought of her when she was working around the kitchen, but when his eyes were on her, she couldn't help but stand a little straighter, tuck her hair behind her ear when the loose strands fell down around her face.

She helped Joyce get the dishes out of the oven and off the stove, and she dished his plate first. Eric had popped the top off a few more beers and put one in front of Adam. She set Adam's plate down just as he took a swig from the bottle, and she had to stifle the fizz of attraction that ran though her seeing him in such a casual atmosphere. Being around him was easy, nice. Seeing him like that gave her hope that things could change for him. He had the ability to relax if she could just make him see that he needed to do it more often. Carrie went back over to the food to fix the others their plates.

Sharon stood up and shooed her away from the food. "Don't worry about us," she said, handing Carrie a plate. "You've done all the hard work. I'll get everyone's dishes served. There's an empty chair next to Adam." She smiled. "Why don't you relax and eat." The funny thing was that Carrie was more relaxed than she'd been in a long time.

"Want a beer?" Adam asked her as she sat down next to him. She nodded although she wanted to keep him there in that moment, with the snow coming down, the burning candle showing off the tiny gold flecks in his blue eyes. He got up, pulled one from the fridge, and popped off the top. "Want a glass?"

"I'm okay with the bottle," she said, the only reason being that he'd sit down. He handed it to her just as his phone rang in the pocket of his coat. *Don't answer*, she wanted to say but he already had. He put up a finger to hold everyone off for a second and then, with his head down, listening to the caller, he left the room, and her heart sank. Sharon caught her eye across the table. There were thoughts behind her eyes, and Carrie wondered if her disappointment showed on her face. She sat up a little straighter and stabbed a few macaroni noodles with her fork.

Joyce sat down, and everyone ate. Carrie watched Adam's plate of food getting cold at his empty spot. She felt terrible for Joyce and Bruce, and for his sister. They'd come all the way from North Carolina, and, as usual, he'd spent a few minutes in the moment, and then he was gone. She knew by their faces that they noticed and that it bothered them, but no one said anything. "Sorry," Adam said, startling Carrie. He addressed his family. "That was Andy, from the office." His eyes fluttered over to Carrie and then away. She guessed he could sense what everyone was thinking. "The number was my office number, so I was concerned it was something regarding work... Her car was stuck in the snow, and I thought I was going to have to go out and get her, but she got the car out."

Her. Andy *was* a woman. And he was contemplating running to her rescue in a snowstorm. Did he and Andy have some sort of relationship? Suddenly, Carrie's entire perspective changed. Andy wasn't just someone from the office. She was someone from the office who may be having a relationship with Adam. Someone who'd called from his own office phone. Someone who he'd gone for drinks with after work instead of coming straight home. The person he'd just left a few minutes before now. She didn't allow her mind to go any further than it had because she'd be jumping to conclusions, although it wouldn't be hard to do.

"I think I'm going to head up to bed," she said to the table, feeling uneasy. If Adam had a relationship with Andy that Carrie wasn't aware of, then she should probably only be present in professional situations. This was Adam's family time.

"But you haven't had any dessert. I've got a pie on ice. It won't take too long to heat it up," Joyce said, her face full of concern. Carrie prayed that Joyce couldn't read the revelations that were whirring inside her head right now.

"I'm very tired," she said, using the last of her mental energy to produce a genuine-looking smile. "Thank you for a lovely evening. I really enjoyed it." She turned away from them as quickly as she could, her face burning with embarrassment. Carrie needed a different working environment that had a clearer distinction between her duties and leisure time. She had better figure out what she was going to do soon because she certainly couldn't do this anymore.

Chapter Ten

When something worries you, examine your thoughts.

Carrie didn't need to examine her thoughts on this. She'd been pretty sure she needed to do something else career-wise for a while. The light coming through the window was nearly blinding—white and piercing. She squinted, trying to surface completely from her sleep. She pushed the covers off her legs, the chill of winter snaking around them, and got out of bed. Her book on positive thinking fell onto the floor, the bookmark sliding across the hardwoods. She picked it up and walked to the window.

A tiny break in the clouds had allowed the sun to peek through, but she could see more dark gray in the distance, which was good because with the amount of snow outside, the reflection of sunlight was so bright she could hardly enjoy it. She could make out the camper in the driveway, its roof piled with at least a foot of snow. The yard, the streets, and the driveway were all covered in a pristine blanket of white. Carrie loved the snow before anyone had walked in it, when it wasn't damaged by feet or muddied by cars. It reminded her of children—their innocence, their untainted little feelings—brand new, with no blemishes. She flipped through her book and tried to find the page where she'd stopped reading last night.

Once she'd marked her spot, she sat down on the four-poster bed in the room that Adam had given her. The walls were beige, the dark wood of the bedroom suite complementing them nicely. Just that one suite probably cost more money than she had in the bank. Adam was around her age, and he'd already accomplished so much. He had two beautiful children, a mansion of a house, and a successful business that he owned himself. She had her suitcases in the closet and her books. That was it. She worried that she'd gone too long, that she'd wasted too much time, and now she wouldn't be able to find that perfect person to create a life with. What if she never found that person? She equated a home and a family with growing up. Wasn't that what people did? They grew up, got married, and had a life. She didn't. Her life hadn't moved forward at all. She was stuck.

The sun slipped back behind the clouds, instantly shading the room in a gray light. She sat down on the bed, her book on her lap. Why did having the one job she loved most in life have to make her so miserable?

"Carrie?" a little voice whispered from the doorway of her room. "I'm awake."

Carrie turned around, producing the biggest smile she could muster. David was standing with his white and blue train pajamas and a blanket in his hand. His hair was disheveled and his feet were bare. She noticed his long eyelashes as he blinked, the soft pink on his cheeks from sleep, the crease mark on his forehead that his sheet had made, and she couldn't deny that she loved this. It wasn't his fault that her life was a mess. She'd only been with the children a few days and the thought of leaving them made her chest ache. She saw so much good in them, so much she could try to do to make their lives a little better. "Are we the first ones up?" she asked, consciously trying to keep the tone of her voice free of her thoughts.

"I think so," he said.

She stood and pulled three small bouncy balls that all fit in the palm of her hand and a cup from the case of toys that she brought with her to every job. They were perfect for moments like these. "I have a game you can play while I get ready. See if you can bounce the balls into the cup. You only get one try for each ball. If you don't get any in, you can start over." She grabbed a handful of clothes and wadded them into her arms. From the en-suite bathroom door, she said, "My guess is that you can get it into the cup five times before I'm done. What do you guess?"

"Seven," he said, smiling.

He was already bouncing when she went in to get ready for the day. She turned on the water at the sink and ran her toothbrush under the stream, thinking about her life, trying to weigh her options. Should she settle on another job? She imagined what it would be like to come home from work and have nothing to do in the evenings. As the thought entered her mind, she realized that she didn't know what to do with all that time. Where would she go? She hadn't thought about where she'd live or with whom she'd spend her free moments.

When Carrie was a little girl, she would dress up in her white dress and pretend she was getting married. All through her childhood, she imagined what life would be like as an adult. She thought about big family dinners, romantic evenings, sunsets on vacation, cozy days by the fire. She was realistic enough to know that those things wouldn't happen all the time, but she'd never fathomed that, for her, they wouldn't happen at all. The idea of not having them worried her beyond words.

The process of meeting someone and investing enough time in them to find out if they were worth spending her life with seemed daunting. She was already in her thirties. What if it took a lot of people before she found The One? Could she end up settling on more than just a job? She knew she never could, and so there was a real possibility that she would end up alone for the rest of her life. How empty she would feel.

When she'd finished getting ready, she emerged from the bathroom to find that Olivia had joined David in his bouncing game. Wearing her long flannel nightdress with little pink roses, Olivia had her hands on her hips and a pout on her face. They were in a disagreement over whose turn it was. "Good morning," she said to Olivia. "David, how many did you get?" she asked, trying to defuse their argument.

"Four," he said. He pursed his lips and looked at Olivia out of the corner of his eye. "It's my go."

"I have an idea. David, do you still have all three balls?" He nodded. "Let's all take one, last go—one ball each—and then we can get ready for the day. I have a special art project planned, and I'm going to need both of you to help."

That seemed to do the trick because they both perked up and David handed out the balls without a flinch. One more shot each, and they were running to their rooms to get dressed. She didn't even have to help them—they each went into their rooms faster than she could whisper, "I'll meet you downstairs."

When she turned to go down the stairs, she met Adam as he was coming up. "Good morning," she said, wishing she'd had a little more time to get ready for the day. She made a mental note to set her alarm for an hour earlier, now that she was getting used to the wake times of the children. She nervously tucked her hair behind her ears to hide any lack of style. She shouldn't want to impress him at all, but there was something about him that drew her in and made her want to bring out the best in him, just like she did with the kids.

"Good morning," he said, with a tiny inhale of breath.

She could tell it was an impulse to relieve some sort of stress. His shoulders were tight, his chest puffing out a bit with his breath. He smiled, but it wasn't his usual smile. It was the kind of smile that someone gives a stranger on the street, not a nanny who had just spent the night in his house.

"I'm going to be working from the home office this morning," he said. "The snow has blocked in my car. If you can please keep the noise down over my way, it would be appreciated." Funny—she remembered making that wish last night for him to get snowed in, but now, looking at how much stress it must be causing him, she wished that she hadn't.

"Oh. Okay. Is everything all right?" she asked.

"It's fine. I just needed to get into the office today. Oh, and Andy Simpson will be stopping by briefly to meet with me. She, thank God, can get her car out."

Carrie wanted to go back to her room and make herself more presentable.

The kids came barreling down the hallway, Olivia's giggles bouncing off the walls as they made their way to the staircase. When they got there, they both looked at Carrie, smiles on their faces. Although their welcome lifted her spirits, they'd barely acknowledged that Adam was standing there.

"Can you say hello to your daddy?" Carrie asked, glancing over at Adam with concern.

Both children looked up at him through their lashes bashfully, their chins down. Olivia offered a little smile as David said, "Hi, Daddy."

"Hello," he said back to them. Carrie could sense a lapse in confidence when he said it. It was subtle, as if he were trying not to show it, but it was there on his face. She could almost sense the thoughts in his head—how he didn't know the right words to say, how to react appropriately. He wanted to be good at it—he was so good at work—but he just didn't know how to be good at this. That's what she guessed, anyway.

"We have to be very quiet for your daddy today," she told them, trying to fill the silence that had fallen between them. "Olivia, do you think you can keep your grandma Joyce quiet?" Olivia giggled. "David, how about Grandpa Bruce? Think he can be quiet?" David's eyes darted around the floor, as if he were thinking of real ways to keep his grandfather quiet. "We'll do our best," she said to Adam with a smile.

"Thank you." There was something in his eyes as he said the words, almost as if he were taking in her methodology, learning how she spoke to the children. He had a curious expression, his face now soft and interested. There was something attractive about him when he looked at her like that. He walked past them, the children stepping closer to Carrie to let him by, and disappeared around the corner.

When they got downstairs, they had breakfast, and the house was completely quiet. It was still early, so they tiptoed to the playroom, where Carrie pulled out a bag she'd brought with her. On the drive between North Carolina and Virginia, she'd stopped at a few craft stores. She collected little things she could find at a reduced price—wooden boxes for painting, canvases that were two for a dollar, crayons, whatever was on sale.

"I have lots of Christmas paint," she said, pulling a pair of soft canvas stockings out of the bag and setting them on the art table. "I'll draw on some holly leaves if you'd like and you all can do the berries with your fingers. When they're dry, if the snow clears, we can take them to the candy shop and fill them up with Christmas candy. How does that sound?"

The children both nodded, their eyes the size of quarters and their mouths hanging open in surprise. Olivia was already reaching for the red paint. "It's sparkly!" she said, opening the top.

"Would you like some help getting it out of the container?"

"Yes, please," she said, raising her shoulders and grinning at David in anticipation. David sat with his hands in his lap, a small smile on his lips while Carrie squeezed the colors onto a paper plate.

"I have towels for you when you're finished."

As the kids painted, Carrie used a fine point bottle of green to outline the holly leaves around their tiny, red fingerprints. When they were all finished, she wrote their names in curly lettering at the top with a dark red.

"Oh, I like that, Carrie!" Olivia said, waving the rag and wiping her fingers clumsily as she attempted to get the paint from under her fingernails. Once his hands were clean, David inspected his stocking carefully, a satisfied expression on his face. He folded his arms and sat back in his chair, clearly happy with himself.

"We'll allow these to dry all day. Let's leave them on the table. Is everyone cleaned up?" Both children nodded.

"Hello," Joyce said, walking into the playroom. Carrie stopped talking and turned around. Joyce had her gray hair pinned back into a clip and a heather-blue sweater that came up to her neck, giving her creamy skin a rosy glow. Carrie hadn't noticed until then how much David favored her. "Good morning." She walked over and peered at the stockings. "These are beautiful."

"Carrie did the leaves," Olivia explained as she rummaged around in her dress-up box. She pulled out a pink boa and a flouncy hat and put them on.

"I did all the dots on mine," David said, looking up at her.

"It's lovely, David. You have perfect dots. I can see your fingerprints!"

Olivia called from across the room, "Grandma Joyce, will you stay and play with us?" She'd taken her hat off, and her hair was puffing out in untamed strands as the static took hold in the dry air.

"I'd love to."

"Want to play trains?" David asked, getting a bin full of track pieces from the shelf. Olivia slipped her feather boa off and let it shimmy to the floor. She lowered herself down onto her knees next to the train bin and pulled out two pieces of track.

"Certainly, we can play trains," Joyce said. "Your grandpa Bruce collects them. Do you remember his big tracks up in our attic?" The kids both shook their heads, and Joyce's face fell just a little, but she recovered well. She turned to Carrie. "It's been a long time since Adam's brought the kids to our house. I don't think they remember much at all about their visits."

Not knowing the best way to handle a comment like that, Carrie said simply, "He seems like a very busy man."

"Yes," Olivia answered. "Daddy is *very* busy."

Joyce snapped two pieces of track together and handed them to David. "Olivia's right." She patted Olivia's leg. "Adam works quite a bit. It's a tough job your daddy has, running that brewery. It takes all his time, doesn't it?" David handed Joyce two more pieces of track.

She clipped them together for him and attached them to the other pieces on the floor. "He wasn't always this way," she said. "But he found that he was quite successful at building this business, so he works very hard at it."

"He likes work," David said from the other side of the giant oval of track that they were building. "He said so, one time on the phone—that he loves his work and that's why he does it so much."

Carrie felt her stomach sour with that statement. *What does that tell the children?* They believed that Adam spent time on what he loved, and he never spent time with them. With his actions, every time he chose work, he was telling them that he loved work more than he loved them. Her heart broke for these kids. She'd promised herself that she wouldn't get involved, but she knew that she'd break that promise because she couldn't risk letting two beautiful children with a wonderful family believe that they weren't loved, that work was more important than they were. She'd only planned one art project today, but, suddenly, she changed her mind. Carrie got up and pulled a small canvas from her bag of crafts and set it on the art table. Then she turned to Joyce. "I actually need to speak to Adam. Would it be possible for me to slip out for just a moment?"

"Of course," Joyce said.

"Thank you." Without any further explanation, she walked down the hallway to the office.

Chapter Eleven

Look confident, even when you don't feel it.

Carrie repeated that line to herself. She had been toying with an idea for a craft for the kids that involved Adam, and she'd gone back and forth about it, not wanting to bother him, but she felt like it was the right thing to do. She just couldn't stand by and watch the children lose out on having fantastic memories with their father. She worried that her gesture may backfire like it had at the tree lot, but doing nothing wouldn't change the situation, so she pressed on. Nervously, she knocked on his door.

"Come in," he said, sounding preoccupied.

She opened the door all the way and walked in, her heart pattering.

"Everything all right?" he asked.

"Yes. I was wondering if you could stop your work for just a few minutes. It won't take long, I promise. I'm doing a craft with the children, and I'd like you to participate." She knew what he was probably thinking: *I've employed you to watch the children, not me. Why are you bothering me?* She could feel the question pelting her from all the way across the room.

Adam scratched his forehead, then rubbed his eyes. "I'm waiting on a call…"

"And what will happen if you miss it?" she questioned. She was being demanding, but she was willing to take her chances for the children.

His eyes narrowed and with a controlled, even voice, he said, "I *won't* miss the call."

"So that call is more important than your children?" There. She'd put it out there. It was completely not her place, but she felt so strong asking him. It was an important question to ask, and even if it cost her the job, he needed to hear it.

He stood up behind his desk, leaning on the surface of it with his hands, his fingers spread wide, his shoulders tense. "Pardon me?" She'd never seen him look at her with such a fierce expression, and it made her want to sink into the floor and hide there, but she wasn't backing down. "This call is *for* my children. If I fall down on the job, the whole thing will go under, and I won't be able to provide a thing for them. Your services certainly aren't free, are they? This house, their private schooling, everything they need is paid for by me." He took in a deep breath, let it out, and sat back down, clearly getting himself back under control. "Now, if you'll excuse me, I have a job to do. As do you."

She didn't let his anger ruffle her. She'd been insensitive with her question, and she should've approached things differently. "Do you know what Olivia wants for Christmas?" she asked, her tone kind and understanding.

His face didn't show a single change; he just waited for her to get out whatever it was she was going to say.

"She wants you to take her ice skating. That is what's most important to her. To Olivia, ice skating is as important as your call is to you. She told me that you were going to take her once, but you got involved with work and forgot. I sure would hate for the person who's calling you to forget to call. To drop the ball. To abandon whatever it is you are working on."

Carrie knew she'd upset him—it was crystal clear—but there was still something about the way he looked at her that made her feel like it was more him getting it off his chest than it was actually calling her out. He wasn't angry, she thought; he was defensive. She could work with defensive.

Carrie walked over to his desk and sat down across from him. Cautiously, she said, "I know you work hard to provide for your children. But you have to show them sometimes that what *they* need is important. If you don't, they'll grow up thinking you don't value them. It's vital to show Olivia how important ice skating is to you— even if you have to fake it—because to her, it's the most important thing." He looked up at her, his face still hard and tense. "They need more than your money."

"I don't have time for this right now."

"You're a busy man. I don't know if you ever have time for this conversation," she said, her voice gentle and empathetic. She could feel how raw his emotions were at that moment, and she hoped by being honest with him that she wouldn't cause him to close up. Telling Adam what he needed to hear hadn't been nearly as hard as she'd expected. "Let them see who you really are. I can help you, and, I promise, it won't take but a few minutes of your time. Show them today how important they are."

He took in a breath and stared at her for a moment, clearly thinking. Was she asking more than she realized? "If I miss this call, I will have to wait for the figures I need to finalize the purchase of a chain of stores that stretches across the entire East Coast."

Carrie leaned toward him. "Forgive me, because I don't know the business, but can't you just call him back?" she asked gently. "What will five minutes change? We've just spent two talking."

"I'm trying to get him while he's with his team and before he flies out to New York. I don't know when I'll get him again."

"Three minutes."

"What?"

"It's been three minutes. We could be done by now."

He blew out a loud breath through his nose. She could tell she was pushing it. She didn't want to upset him. That was actually the very last thing she wanted. The truth was, she didn't think that Adam avoided his kids and his family on purpose.

"I have an idea. I'll bring the craft to you. If you get the call, we'll leave. Deal?"

With another quiet exhale, Adam looked up at the ceiling before settling his gaze back on her. He stared at her, pensive, as if he were questioning his own thoughts. It was the same look he'd given her at the table the other night when she'd pressed him to go to the Christmas tree lot. When he looked at her like that it made her thoughts all run into each other. There was something so lovable about him, even though he hardly gave her reason to think so.

"If the phone rings, I have to go," he said, his tone direct.

"Done. I'll be right back with the children."

In minutes, she'd left Joyce in the hallway as she took the kids, the canvas, and an armful of paint supplies to Adam's office. "Is Daddy going to be mad that we're interrupting him?" Olivia worried aloud.

"No," Carrie said tenderly. "I asked him if he wanted to do some art with us, and he said yes, but we have to do it in his office because he's waiting for a call. Wasn't that nice of him to let us work with him in his office?"

"We aren't allowed in his office," David said, his face unsure.

"Well, today you are."

They walked in, and Adam smiled at them over his computer, giving Carrie a burst of hope. She set the canvas onto his desk. "We're gonna need Daddy to roll up his sleeves," she said to the children. Adam unbuttoned the cuff of his sleeve on each wrist and rolled his shirtsleeves up to his elbows. Then, to him, she said, "Now, we need your hands. Hold them out, please." When he did, she noticed the strength in his hands, the width of them, the stillness of his fingers as if nothing frazzled him. They were so different than her own small, thin fingers that trembled just being near him. She handed a paintbrush to each child and squirted a puddle of red paint onto a paper plate. "David, you paint Daddy's right hand. Do you know which one to paint?" David nodded. "Olivia, you paint his left hand. Not the back of his hand, just the front. Okay?"

Olivia was the first to dip her brush into the color. She dragged the paint-filled bristles down his ring finger to the palm of his hand. Adam's fingers wiggled a little with the sensation, warming Carrie. He looked over at her and smiled, and she almost exploded with happiness. She watched the faces of the children dipping their brushes into the paint and then painting their father's hands—they were focused, happy. Adam was now watching them too, that curious expression playing around his eyes. *See how great it can be?* she wanted to ask him.

As they painted Adam's palms, she thought about her own father's hands, how she'd held on to them as they crossed crowded streets, how they'd felt when he brushed the hair out of her eyes at bedtime, how they looked holding books as they read together on the sofa on weekends. Nothing could replace the memory of that. Carrie was glad that the children would have a moment with their father when they could take in his kindness and create a memory.

Once his hands were covered in paint, she put the canvas in front of Adam. "Kids, if you'll set your brushes down on that plate there, I'm going to let your daddy have a turn doing some of the work." The children obeyed and stepped back. "Carefully," she told him, "press your hands on the canvas to make two handprints." Adam lowered his hands onto the white fabric, pressing down and then releasing. When he took his hands away, he'd left two perfect, red handprints. "Thank you." She smiled. "Now we can clean him up," she said to the kids.

The office phone rang.

Adam held his paint-filled hands out, clearly deliberating.

Another ring.

"Do you mind hitting that speaker button?" he asked. She expected him to be irritated, but he wasn't. He nodded toward the phone as it rang a third time. Carrie hit the button. "Adam Fletcher," he said before putting a finger to his lips to remind the children to be quiet. When he did, it put a smudge of red paint above his lip. Olivia giggled.

A man's voice came over the speaker. "Hi, Adam. It's Robert. I've got the numbers for you."

Carrie ushered the children to the door. "I'll be right back," she mouthed to Adam. Then she took the kids downstairs to the kitchen to get some more towels so Adam could clean his hands.

When they got there, Joyce was having a cup of coffee at the table next to Bruce, who was reading the paper. "You are a brave woman," she said as Carrie neared her. Olivia went around the other side and crawled onto Bruce's lap, rustling his paper. "I saw you and the children with Adam. I don't think anyone's ever pulled him away from his work before."

Carrie scooted a chair out for David, and he sat down, his feet dangling above the ground. He was watching Carrie, and she wondered if he thought the same thing. At four, did he realize the moment he'd just had with his father, or did he think that they were intruding? "I just wanted him to do an art project with the kids. It didn't take very long. I hope I didn't bother him too much."

"I think he needs to be bothered sometimes."

"Do you mind if I go and clean up? The kids can go into the playroom if you're busy." She grabbed a few towels and ran them under the water, ringing them out.

"They'll be fine here with us. Sharon's just getting a shower, and they'll be down in a few. Then maybe we can all play." She smiled at the children.

"Thank you."

Carrie walked back up to the office and had to hold back her grin as she saw Adam writing, the pen and paper smeared with red paint. He had a little more on his forehead, and the smudge on his top lip was still there. Seeing him like that made her want to laugh with joy. He needed to loosen up, she felt, and that made it seem like he had. She imagined that content look of his, what it felt like when it was directed at her, but she quickly pushed the thought away when she heard him mention Andy's name. Every time she heard it, it brought her crashing down to reality. She was willing to bet that they had conversations in which she'd never be able to participate because she didn't know his business—the business that he loved so much.

Carrie walked over to the desk and held up a towel to gesture for him to wipe his hands. He set down the pen, still talking, and reached out for it. He wiped to get the paint off the creases where his knuckles bent, and she thought about what those hands would feel like on her face or stroking down her arm. He looked over at her, startling her and making her knees wobbly.

The only sound in the room was the unfamiliar voice on the speakerphone and the pulse in her ears. She was so clearly not practiced with relationships. The problem was, even though she knew it was crazy, she liked the way it felt to be near him.

He spun around in his chair, away from her, talking about some sort of report Andy had prepared. His smudged paper and the painted pen made her smile. Carrie piled the art supplies into her hands and carried them out of the room.

As she walked down the hallway to the playroom to put the supplies away, she wondered what it would be like to know him better. With a shake of her head, she went into the playroom and put the art project items away.

When she returned to the office to check that Adam had everything he needed to clean up, one of the wet rags he'd been using was in a heap on the floor by the desk. He lifted his gaze to greet her, the receiver now pressed against his ear. The red paint was still on his face. She took a tissue from the box on his desk and motioned for him to wipe it off.

"You have paint on your forehead," she mouthed. His brows creased, he looked down, wrote something else, and then looked back at her. She pointed to her head. "You have paint on your forehead," she mouthed again, tapping her own head. He took the tissue and rubbed, but he kept missing, the red mark remaining. She couldn't help it, a little huff of amusement escaped, and he scolded her playfully with his eyes. It didn't matter; she realized what she'd accomplished. He wasn't angry, she could tell. He'd enjoyed being with the kids. She left the office and retrieved her mirror from her room. When she returned, she handed it to him.

"What would be the last possible date to get it through?" he asked the man on the other end of the line as he peered in the mirror, his eyebrows going up in surprise at the sight of his reflection. "How soon would you know?" He wiped at his upper lip, but the paint had dried and wasn't coming off. He licked his finger and rubbed. "Mm hmm…" The mark finally came off, and he started working on the one on his forehead when Carrie realized that she was standing there for no reason. He could clearly clean his own face, and he had everything he needed. So, with a wave, she left him in the office and went to check on the children, but as she left, she couldn't stop the thrill from rising up, knowing that they'd just had another of their little moments.

Chapter Twelve

Surround yourself with people who make you feel secure.

That line had resonated with her when she'd read it this morning. How was she supposed to do that? David started toward the door when the doorbell rang, so Carrie followed. She knew who was on the other side of it, and it made her legs feel like spaghetti. She'd been talking to Walter about nothing in particular when the bell had sounded. With a shuffling sound, he followed behind David and Carrie. David grabbed the knob and opened the door, sending a burst of cold air toward them.

On the landing outside stood a beautiful redhead, her hair so long that it fell well past her shoulders, each perfectly trimmed layer like an ocean wave, shiny and soft. Large sunglasses covered her flawlessly blushed cheeks. The frames had a logo on the side that Carrie recognized but couldn't place. The woman's trousers were pressed, and her coat was so fitted that it didn't look like a coat at all but a fashion piece, some sort of giant accessory designed to show off the color of an oversized beaded necklace and her tiny waist. Her feet wobbled just slightly in the snow, and Carrie realized that the woman had managed to get through the wintery slush in heels that probably gave her an extra six inches of height. She looked first at

Carrie and Walter and then down at David and smiled, her berry-colored lips revealing straight, white teeth.

"Hello," she said, holding a gloved hand out to David. "I'm Andy."

David reached out and shook her hand, his shoulders squared. Carrie smiled despite her nervousness as she watched him trying to be a big boy in Andy's presence. He stepped aside to allow her to enter. Once Andy got inside the door, Carrie realized that Andy was quite tall, nearly as tall as Adam, towering over Carrie's petite frame.

"Hi," she said, holding out her hand in greeting to Carrie and offering a warm smile. "I'm Andy. I work with Adam."

"Hello," Carrie said, nodding politely and returning her handshake. "I'm Carrie, the nanny. Adam's in the office. I'll just go and get him for you. Can I get your coat first?"

"Hi, Andy," she heard Adam say from behind her just as Andy was handing her coat over. "I see you've met Carrie," he said, his face pleasant and calm just like one would be with someone they knew quite well. "Carrie is our new nanny."

Adam had moved on, introducing Walter and talking to David.

"I've got the latest offer back from Robert on Building C, and I'd like to go over our options," he said, walking with her toward the office and leaving Carrie behind. She wanted to say something more, something relevant, intelligent, but as she looked at the two of them walking down the hallway, Andy tipping her head back and producing a laugh at something he'd said, she'd lost her chance.

David had run off, leaving Walter and Carrie alone in the entryway. "Andy's quite nice," Walter said, grabbing her arm and leading her toward the living room. Carrie nodded, feeling out of sorts.

"And very pretty," Walter added. They sat down on the sofa together. "But I wonder how well she can throw a football?" he said with a devious smile. Carrie laughed. Walter had a way of making things funny, no matter what the circumstance. The mental picture of Andy with a football in her manicured hands was amusing. Leave it to Walter to find the one thing, without even realizing it, that Carrie knew she could probably do better than Andy.

"The snow has started to subside finally," Bruce said as he peered out the kitchen window. "The roads look like they've finally been plowed." Carrie nodded. It was still cold outside, but the atmosphere in the kitchen couldn't be warmer, the buttery smells coming from the oven filling the room. It was interesting to her how Adam's parents felt so much at home in this giant house—they cooked, played games, talked for hours... The way his parents behaved seemed so relaxed and easy, yet Adam had done nothing—that she'd seen—to make them that comfortable. He was so different than his family.

If she had to choose one person who she thought was most like Adam, it would be his sister, Sharon. She was quiet like him, and seemed to enjoy being alone. She'd spent a lot of time in her room upstairs, and, even during the card games, she seemed content being silent.

Sharon was sitting at the table with Olivia and David, drawing a picture. Carrie sat down beside them. When Sharon reached across the table for a game piece, Carrie noticed how thin she was, almost boney, and she always seemed to close in on herself—her arms crossed, her shoulders hunching slightly forward, as if she wanted to crawl into a ball and hide. Sharon had a different look in her eyes that Carrie couldn't quite place. Disappointment, maybe? Carrie couldn't tell.

Sharon's husband, Eric, came in and sat down beside her. At supper the other night, he'd participated in the conversations, smiled, played cards, but he seemed to always have his eye on Sharon as if protecting her from something. Whenever she'd stood, Eric would give a tiny lurch forward as if he wanted to be ready to catch her. Eric had stayed downstairs after supper last night, but Sharon had gone up early, and today was the first time Carrie had had a chance to really be with her. She wondered if perhaps Sharon could be suffering from some sort of illness, but her skin was rosy, her hair healthy—there was no outward sign, except for her weary eyes and thin frame.

"Can you make a dress for her?" Olivia asked Sharon, pointing to a drawing of a circle with legs. For the first time since she'd seen her, Sharon's eyes had life in response to Olivia. She smiled, affection for her niece seeping out from every bit of her face, taking Carrie completely by surprise. Then, as Sharon looked back down at the paper, her face fell into its neutral position, the withdrawn look returning. It was the oddest thing.

"So, Carrie, did Adam say if he was coming out of the office today?" Bruce asked.

Carrie shook her head. Andy had left after a few hours, and Adam had been in the office ever since. The coffeepot beeped and Bruce got up to get a cup. Olivia offered David a brown crayon.

"I don't know why he can't take a few minutes and be with us," Bruce said under his breath. He poured a cup of coffee and looked back out the window.

As good a man as Adam seemed to be, and as lovely as his family was, she found his absence baffling. She understood that it took a lot to run a business, but why, as smart as he clearly was, couldn't he figure out a way to balance it all? Was there some reason he didn't want to?

Bruce and Eric left the room to join Walter, and Carrie heard the click of the widescreen television. Sports highlights, it sounded like. The three women and the children were left in the kitchen. As Carrie watched Sharon with the kids and Joyce chopping apples at the island, she wondered why she was even there. Why had Adam hired her when he clearly had an entire family who was willing to watch them?

Just as she was pondering the question, Adam came into the kitchen. He'd changed and had on jeans and a navy blue sweater, giving her hope that he'd join them.

"I heard the snowplow, and Andy said it's been down the main roads. I'm going to go into work," he said. "I shouldn't be too late, but don't feel like you have to save me a spot at the table." He walked over to David and Olivia, who were watching him with interest. "Bye, kids. See you…in the morning."

A pinch took hold of Carrie's chest as she watched the exchange. He didn't plan to be home until after their bedtime, and the kids wouldn't see their daddy until the next day. She wanted to grab him by the shoulders and look straight into his eyes. *It's been snowing like crazy! Take one little day off! Don't go to work*, she wanted to say. As she was mentally pleading with him not to go, she caught sight of Sharon, whose eyes were on Adam, her gaze like daggers.

Carrie understood that look. She had only known Adam a short time, but her irritation with him was quite strong, so she could only imagine what Sharon felt if she'd been dealing with this for years.

"I wish we could paint some more, Daddy," Olivia said, coloring haphazard streaks across her paper with a purple crayon.

Carrie could feel the tension in the air. Joyce's artificial smile, Olivia's request, Sharon's look—it all put a heaviness in the room. The only one who hadn't added to the moment was David, but even he was looking down at his paper, a disappointed look on his face. He colored slowly back and forth, and she wondered what was going through his little mind. The anger was nearly boiling under her skin. This was so much bigger than her wish for him to spend more time with his kids. This was clearly a family that had dealt with it for much longer than she had. It wasn't just his kids he was letting down but his grandfather, his parents, and his sister. What concerned her most was Sharon's look of disapproval—it wasn't hurt or disappointment, it was anger. What was going on between those two?

"Andy's waiting at the office. We have some things that have to get done. I have to go," he said, his focus on Sharon as he said it. That look Carrie had seen in his eyes before—that moment of consideration, of deliberation—she saw it just then. He knew he needed to stay, she was nearly certain, but he wasn't going to. He was choosing work.

Without any further discussion, Adam walked out of the room. A second later, she heard the door to the garage shut. As the children continued to color, Joyce wiping the counters, and Sharon twisting her fingers in her lap, the rumble of the car engine cut through the silence. The sound hit her like a smack, and she could feel an ache in her chest. Carrie looked at Sharon protectively, wanting to ease whatever was going on in her head. She stopped breathing for a second at the sight of her. Sharon was sitting at the table, turned away from the children, tears sheeting down her face. She was chewing her lip as if it would help stop the tears, but the rims of her eyes were blood red and her face was crumpling under the weight of whatever had caused her sadness. She got up and left the room.

"I'll be right back…" Joyce said, her words trailing behind her as she lumped the rag on the counter and rushed off after Sharon.

The whole situation made Carrie uneasy, her stomach burning with apprehension. She sat down next to the children while they colored, but her mind was elsewhere.

"Was Aunt Sharon mad at Daddy?" Olivia asked, still looking down at her paper. She'd drawn a rainbow in the corner of her page, each color one single arched line.

"I'm not sure," she answered honestly.

Children, she believed, were no different than adults in understanding emotions and social situations. They were just less experienced with the world. They knew when things weren't right, and they could tell when adults spoke over them, so Carrie was always careful about that. It was clear that Olivia sensed the tension in the air, even if she hadn't seen Sharon's tears. She knew that Joyce's quick exit after Sharon wasn't a normal response. Little Olivia just needed help processing what the meaning behind it was, and Carrie couldn't help her with that.

Just then, Eric came into the kitchen. "Where's Sharon?" he asked.

"She went upstairs, I think. With Joyce." Then from behind the children, she mouthed, "She was crying," while dragging her finger down her cheek.

Confusion clouded his face, and he nodded. Whatever the reason for his visit to the kitchen, she wouldn't know because he left the room and headed upstairs after his wife.

"It looks like the other grown-ups in the house have some things to work out," she said carefully to Olivia. "I'm nearly sure that your daddy's handprints are dry on the canvas. We need to finish that project. Why don't we head over to the playroom and we can do a little more painting?"

The children climbed off their chairs and ran down the hallway. When they entered the playroom, Carrie retrieved the canvas from the spot on the shelf where she'd put it to dry and set it onto the art table. Two big, red handprints were the only color against the stark white background. Carrie tapped one of the hands to see if the paint was dry, and her finger came back empty of paint. She tapped a few more places—all dry. She recalled the confidence in Adam's hands when he'd made those prints, how still they'd been when he'd pressed his fingers down, the happiness on his face. Carefully, she put her hand on top of his, noting how his handprint almost swallowed her own.

"Is it dry?" David asked.

Carrie pulled her hand from Adam's print. "Yep. All dry. Here's what we need to do," she said, refocusing on the task at hand. "I'm going to get a teal blue color for you, David, and I'm going to paint your left hand. Then, I want you to let me guide it onto your daddy's left hand, so your print will be inside his." David held out his hand as Olivia clacked around on the hardwoods in her princess high heels. Carrie dipped the brush into the teal paint. "I'm going to paint your hand just like you painted your daddy's, okay?"

"It's cold," David said, smiling, as she brushed his fingers with the paint. "It tickles."

When it was sufficiently painted, she took David's hand, gently placed it inside his father's print, pressed, and then pulled it off. It was a perfect fit, like when she used to put her hand up to her own father's to see how much bigger his was than hers.

"Is it my turn?" Olivia asked. She had picked up one of David's toy train cars, and she was spinning the wheels with her fingers.

Carrie picked up the damp towel that she'd rinsed and hung over the back of the chair after Adam had finished his handprints, and handed it to David. "I can help you if you can't get the paint off," she said, reaching out for Olivia's hand and grabbing the purple paint. She popped the top up on the paint and dipped a new brush into the deep purple color. Then she painted Olivia's right hand.

"I had fun painting with Daddy," Olivia said, looking up just before she squeezed her hand into a fist to watch the paint squirt through her fingers.

Satisfaction tickled Carrie's chest as she realized that she'd done it. She'd made a moment for them. As she looked down at those tiny handprints the kids had just made nestled in the palms of Adam's, she felt hope that she could make more moments like that, and suddenly, she couldn't wait—no matter what Adam said or did.

Chapter Thirteen

Seek out those who support you.

Carrie considered that line as she pulled a casserole from the oven.

"Sorry I had to dart off like I did earlier today," Joyce said. "Sharon is…dealing with some things." She craned her neck to peer into the living room as if she didn't want the others to hear. Walter and Bruce were watching football. "Would you help me wash the lettuce, please?"

Carrie was glad to help. Joyce had actually come to find her in her room tonight after the children were in bed and asked if she'd help prepare supper. Since her arrival, Carrie had made late suppers to accommodate Adam's work schedule. She didn't like that they didn't eat as a family, but the children needed to go to bed. It made for great leftovers the next day, but Carrie wondered if Joyce, too, was secretly waiting for Adam.

Carrie ran the lettuce leaves under the stream of water at the tap. "Is she okay?" she asked. Sharon's response to Adam had worried Carrie all day.

"I honestly can't say if she's okay," Joyce said while chopping cucumbers into thin slices. Just like her own mother, Joyce spent a lot of time and effort on the preparation of her suppers. They were made with the utmost care and attention to detail. It all caused Carrie to feel a little homesick.

She missed seeing the porch light all the way down the road as soon as she turned the corner onto her street, she missed the way her mother opened the door to greet her before her car had come to a complete stop in the driveway, and she missed her dad's smile from his favorite chair when she dropped her bags at the front door. She enjoyed being with the Fletchers, but it didn't ease the weight she felt because she wasn't celebrating Christmas with the people she loved.

Carrie had thought about what Christmas would be like this year, and she had many questions after the way Adam had behaved last night. Would she spend Christmas morning in her room while the entire family opened gifts? Certainly she shouldn't impose by being there. Not to mention she had no gifts to share. Maybe she could go somewhere. Were coffee shops open on Christmas Day? Probably not. Which brought her back to her original question: Why did Adam even want her there on Christmas when his entire family would be with the children? He'd taken time off, but was he actually going to be present?

"It smells fantastic in here," Walter said, coming into the room behind his walker and changing the course of the conversation. "What's for supper?" Walter smiled at Carrie, setting her mind at ease a little.

"Beef and cheddar casserole and salad," Joyce said. She opened a drawer, studied the contents and shut it again. Then she opened another. "Where does Adam keep his serving spoons?" she asked herself out loud.

"Oh, here." Carrie batted at a drawer pull with her elbow, her hands wet and full of lettuce. She dropped the leaves into a large bowl and flicked the water off her hands into the sink. "How's Sharon?" Walter asked. Carrie was glad to get back to the topic of Sharon's well-being. "She was resting when I left her." Joyce dug the serving spoon into the casserole. "I thought bringing her here would get her mind off it all." The worry on Joyce's face was striking. Her thin lips, which were usually turned up into a friendly grin, were pressed together, turned down, the skin between her eyes creased in a way that made it seem like those creases came easily—they'd been there before this moment.

Carrie considered leaving the room to give them privacy, but Joyce handed her a cutting board and a tomato, so she walked to an area of the counter where she could have her back to them and pretend not to listen.

"It's not like when the kids were little," Joyce said. "If we'd had a tough week, Bruce and I would pile Adam and Sharon into the car, and we'd go on a trip somewhere, just the four of us—all our worries gone for the weekend." She added the cucumber to the lettuce by scraping her knife along the cucumber-filled plate in short strokes, each slice sliding down until it dropped into the bowl. "It's different now. Sharon's experiencing adult problems, not kid ones, and a trip away won't solve them. As a mother, I want to fix it, and I can't," she said, her voice breaking.

Almost as a reflex, Carrie turned around to console her but caught herself, not wanting to interfere in a clearly personal matter. Joyce had noticed and she smiled weakly, her eyes showing thanks.

"Hello-o," Adam's voice called from the hallway, changing the mood. It was barely eight o'clock—early by Adam's standards. Carrie was glad to see him because the snow that was melting during the day had frozen into patches of black ice on the roads. Why he had to go into work in those conditions was beyond her. She understood that as the owner of such a large brewery and restaurant, he would have a lot of work to do, but couldn't he find some way to divvy that work out to allow himself more of a life?

"Hey, honey!" Joyce called from her spot at the counter where she was getting glasses from the cupboard and filling them all with ice. "How was work?"

"Good," he said, emerging and clapping Walter on the back. "How are you, Gramps?"

"Not too bad. My knees have seen better days, but I can't complain."

There it was: that grin that completely wrecked her nerves. Nervous energy washed over her, and she busied her hands by cutting more tomatoes. She hoped he didn't mind having her at supper. She wished there were some way that she could tell him that Joyce had invited her, but whenever he let down his guard, she couldn't focus enough to start a general conversation, let alone weave in something like that. Last time she'd tried, she'd critiqued his beer labels. As she chopped, she wondered if she still had blush on her cheeks and if her hair looked nice. She glanced down at her shirt just to be sure it didn't have anything on it from cooking. A tiny spot of tomato juice had splashed on her chest and made a mark. She should've worn an apron.

"My goodness, child!" Joyce laughed. "That's a lot of tomatoes! You don't need to cut any more. Thank you for doing it." Carrie had converted her energy into chopping, and only then did she realize that she'd just chopped enough tomatoes for a small army.

"How were the kids today?" Adam asked, and his proximity startled her.

She swallowed. "They were fine."

She knew he was fatigued by the way he blinked his eyes, but his face was friendly and alive despite how tired he was. That all-too-familiar curiosity was there in his expression as he looked at her. He was finally here again, in the moment. She drank it up like a warm mug of hot chocolate on an icy day—savoring every minute.

He pulled a glass from the counter beside her and filled it with tea from a pitcher. "Want some?" he asked, holding the jug up in offering.

She didn't know what to do. He was asking her if she wanted iced tea. That seemed simple enough. But the way he'd acted yesterday had made her feel like she shouldn't be there, so she didn't know how to answer. Was he just offering to be polite, but she was supposed to decline? Or did he really want to know if she'd like iced tea? She put her hands in her pockets as a nervous gesture, feeling unsure.

"Would you like something else?" he asked, the skin between his eyes wrinkling the way it did when he was reading at his desk.

She shook her head.

"So...you want tea?"

Carrie watched for any indication that he wasn't legitimately asking her what she wanted to drink, but she couldn't find anything there. "Tea would be nice," she finally said. "As long as it's okay with you." She drew out the word "you," her gaze on him in a direct way.

He pulled back as if trying to focus on her, a grin playing at his lips. "I'm perfectly fine if you have tea." His amusement was clear, causing a tickling inside her stomach. "We have an entire pitcher of it here, and I have more tea bags in the pantry." Carrie pulled her eyes away from him to try and calm her beating heart, and she happened to glance at Joyce. The look on her face was completely unexpected. She was watching them, her lower back against the counter, her arms crossed in a relaxed way, her eyes warm, and her lips set in a smile. She looked positively happy.

"Sharon and Eric are in the living room with your dad. Supper's ready," Joyce said. "I'll just call them in." Walter, who hadn't moved from the table, had a game of solitaire spread out in front of him. He flipped a card and looked up.

Adam handed Carrie the glass of iced tea. It was so full that she worried her unsteady hands would spill it. He was ruffling her tonight.

She took it just as he said, "Sorry to have to go so quickly, but I have a few things to work on that I have to get done if I'm going to take time off at Christmas. I'm gonna eat my supper in the office."

The look on Joyce's face—that loving smile she'd seen—withered into disappointment, her mouth turning down, her hands dropping by her sides. Joyce's chest rose as she took in a slow, deep breath. Adam didn't seem to have a response at all, even though he'd clearly let Joyce down. His face was empty of emotion, unaffected.

"We've come a long way to see you, Adam," Joyce said. "I would appreciate it if you would eat supper with us at least."

"I told you not to come before the twenty-first. I'm not trying to be rude, I just don't have the time..."

"I know that's what you told us." She walked closer, looking up at him to make eye contact. "I just thought you may feel differently once we were all here."

Carrie took a step back, leaving the two of them still facing each other, their expressions set, their eyes on one another like some sort of standoff. Carrie was glad that Joyce was finally bringing to light all the thoughts Carrie herself had had regarding his absence.

"Do you think I can just *not* work?" he said. "That it's something I can put down any time that I choose? There's no one else to run the brewery but me. I can barely take the four days off that I have. Do you know how busy this time of year is?"

"You don't *want* to stop working. The brewery has been very successful for you, and you love the success, even more than your family. That's what I think."

Irritation was written on Adam's face. "What do you know, Mom," he snapped, but then he shrunk back, realizing the tone he'd just displayed. Carrie's family had one golden rule, which was never to talk back to one's mother. It was clear by the way he recoiled that the rule was engrained in Adam as well. So for him to go against his mannerly inclination and say such a thing showed that Joyce had hit a nerve.

"What do *I* know?" Joyce's head was turned to the side, her eyes clapped on him, steadfast. "I know that your marriage was a disaster. I know that you have no relationship with your own children. I know that you can't relate to any of us anymore because the only people you ever socialize with are from work. We all represent your failures—your marriage was a mess and you got hurt unbelievably in the process; your connection with your children is a failure because you work so much you don't know how to communicate with them; and your relationship with your family has failed—I think that's why you threw yourself into your work; you barely spend time with any of us. Especially Sharon." Joyce blinked to clear tears that were forming. Then, more softly, she said, "I know you're great at work and I'm proud of you for what you've achieved. But you have to try to be better with everything else, including the things that don't come as easily for you."

"You don't understand," he said, his face like stone. Carrie had never seen him so closed off before. What his mother had just said had bothered him, she could tell, and this ruthless, stubborn Adam was quite intimidating, a stark contrast to the gentle person she'd seen. "I have worked my entire life for what I have," he said, his voice now more controlled. "I'm not going to give this up. I've worked too hard for it, and—that's right—it's what I love to do."

"Do you love it enough to sacrifice your family?" a quiet voice said from the doorway. Sharon was standing with her arms folded, her face blank. She looked as though she were too tired to emote.

Unease was swimming around inside Carrie as she stood witness to this family and its issues. She felt terrible for being there. Clearly there was something going on, and she shouldn't be a part of it, but the door to the hallway was across the room and she wouldn't be able to inch her way over to it without everyone noticing. She was pinned in the corner of the kitchen, her heart drumming with anxiety from the disagreement. They were all saying what she knew to be true about Adam, and he was getting upset. There was a tiny part of her that wanted to walk over to him, tell him it would be okay, and that she would love to help him figure it all out. She'd seen how lovely he could be with the kids if he'd just give himself enough time to bond with them. His family would certainly embrace him—she'd seen it when they'd arrived. It could be fixed if he'd just try.

"I'm not sacrificing anything," he said through clenched teeth. "This is the way it is. Gwen has the kids most of the time, and when they're here, I make as much time as I can for them, but in the end, I'm the sole breadwinner, and I don't see any other way to look at it. They are provided for, cared for, and safe."

"But they aren't loved," Sharon said. She had that look in her eyes like she'd had earlier—daggers.

"How dare you insinuate that I don't love my kids."

"You show them every day how much you don't love them. Some of us would do *anything* to have those kids. Anything." Her voice broke as she said the word. The way she'd ended that statement, it seemed Sharon may have had something else to say, but, clearly, her emotions had gotten in the way. Once she'd centered herself, she asked quietly, "Why didn't you fight Gwen to have the kids more? They're your kids too, Adam."

"Never mind," Adam said, turning away from them. "I'm not hungry anymore." He left the room, never answering Sharon, and Carrie stood there just like the others: mentally trying to pick up the pieces that had shattered tonight.

Chapter Fourteen

Identify what triggers your stress and eliminate it.

Carrie thought how this suggestion had no relevance at all. The tension in the air was so thick she could almost see it, and there was no way to get rid of it.

Walter, who had been sitting silently during the argument, stood up and dragged his fingers across the table, piling his cards into the center. He picked them up, tapped the pile until it resembled a deck again, and put the cards back into their box. As he did so, he nodded toward the seat beside him, his gaze on Sharon. Her face was flushed, her eyes on the brink of tears again, but this time, instead of running out of the room, she sat down beside Walter and put her head on his shoulder. He patted her arm.

"He doesn't get it," she said, her tears revealing her pain. The tears seemed to come easily, like they'd been waiting there to be released, as if she had stored them up over the years and now just being around Adam could make them surface from that deep place where she'd pushed them down. She'd looked thin to Carrie before, but only now did she notice the darkness under her eyes and the way she carried her body as if every movement required more energy than she had.

Carrie knew that she couldn't dare ask the family what Sharon was battling, but she wondered if she needed to know at all. The point was that Adam's sister felt that he wasn't showing love to his children, and she thought it too. She didn't need to know the family drama, but she did want to find out what Adam thought of it. She wanted to check on him anyway after his exit, to be sure he was okay. The whole thing made her feel anxious and upset, and seeing Adam could either worsen that or ease it—she wasn't sure. She didn't know what mood he'd be in if she tried to talk to him right now, but something made her want to go. She was a neutral party, so perhaps he'd open up. Would he listen to her? Could she be his voice of reason? She decided to try.

"I'll be back," she said, but she looked right at Joyce, hoping his mother could read her mind. Joyce took a long look at her, her eyes unstill with thought. Then Joyce nodded, and Carrie knew she understood. Carrie left the kitchen and headed to the office.

The door was cracked open when she got there, and she could see Adam, his elbows on his desk, his hands on his forehead like someone does when shielding the light from their eyes. He was reading something. He slid his fingers down his cheeks and rubbed his face. *How can he enjoy something so much that exhausts him like it does?* she wondered. She pushed the door open and he looked up, his face pink from rubbing it.

"Hi," she said, standing in the doorway.

"Hi," he returned. The friendliness that was usually behind his eyes and the grin that hid around the edges of his lips were both absent. He watched her enter the room, following her with his eyes only, a cautious look on his face.

"I was just checking on you," she said, using all her energy to make the words come out softly. She was still annoyed but worried, all at the same time. He was an adult; he should see what he was doing, but he either didn't see it or he didn't *want* to see it. He was being so selfish by working so much, and his family was clearly suffering. Yelling at him, however, wouldn't make things any better. It would just make him angry, and he'd probably close up more than he already had. "If you want some supper, I'd be happy to bring you some." Then, in a whisper, she said, "I can sneak it up. They'll never know."

Against his will, a smile emerged. He tried to straighten it out. When he looked up at her again, the friendliness had returned to his face. She'd managed to make him feel like she was on his side, and happiness bubbled up. She felt a little like they were a team just now. It made no sense. She barely knew him, and she had no idea of the depth of his family drama, but when he looked at her, it was as if none of that were true.

"Look." She sat down on the chair opposite his desk. "I'm not here to get involved in your family's matters. I don't want to do anything except make sure you're okay and that you've eaten."

"I'd love some supper, actually," he said, leaning on his fist, his elbow propped on the desk. The way the lamplight hit him, she could see lines of exhaustion etched on his face.

She nodded, not wanting to talk for fear that her words would come out a jumbled mess, like her thoughts suddenly were. As much as she didn't want to admit it, as annoyed as he made her sometimes, she was smitten with him and she felt protective of him. While his family's concerns were quite valid, she was nearly sure that he felt they'd ganged up on him. Her growing feelings for him made no sense. He was her boss! He lived a state away from her. He wasn't even the kind of person she knew she'd want to be with—he was never home, he ate by himself, he didn't know how to relate to children. He pawned off major emotional moments on others, not even wanting to buy his children their Christmas presents! On paper, everything was wrong, but she couldn't stop herself from feeling something for him.

"I can bring you supper in your office," she finally said. "Want some company?" She knew Joyce and the others would understand and not take her gesture as rudeness. She was almost certain that they would want her to try and talk to Adam as much as she wanted to talk to him.

"I can't deal with my family's issues right now. I just want to eat and do my work."

"I was hoping that I wouldn't have to eat alone. They'll probably all be finished downstairs by the time I make a plate." She knew it was a feeble excuse. He understood his family better than she did, and they would all stay with her at the table while she ate, she was sure of it. She also knew that by putting him in this position, it would be rude of him to leave her to eat alone in his own house, and he'd be forced to say yes.

He looked at her for a long time without speaking. There was a grudging surrender in his eyes and he finally nodded. Barely. It was good enough for Carrie.

She smiled, trying to maintain the businesslike demeanor she knew she should have, but her insides were exploding with happiness. "Be right back." As she left the room, her back to him, she finally let the big, silly grin emerge on her face, and went down to make them two plates.

When she got to the kitchen, the whole family stopped talking like a jury waiting for a verdict. "I'm just going to make Adam a plate," she said with a little smile.

"You eat first," Joyce said.

"He doesn't want to come down. I'm eating with him in the office." Carrie looked over at the table for their reaction.

Joyce didn't say anything. She just got up and pulled two plates from the cabinet. "I'll help you make your suppers," she said, moving quickly as if she couldn't wait to get their plates made. She had a sort of electric energy—like excitement, which surprised Carrie. "If he won't eat with his family, I'm glad he'll eat with you."

You'd better not get too excited, she wanted to tell her. Joyce seemed overjoyed at the idea that Carrie was eating with Adam, but there was a real possibility that he was going to tell her to butt out, and then he'd be eating by himself in the office for the foreseeable future if he wanted.

Once the plates were made, Carrie wedged two half-full cups of tea between her arms and her body, and Joyce offered her the plates—one in each hand. Carefully, she made her way to the office. As she entered, Adam rushed over and relieved her aching arms.

"Sorry," he said, setting their glasses on the desk and stacking his papers. "I didn't think about you having to carry it all here."

"It's fine," she said, still worried the time alone would let him have the moment he needed to scold her for her actions. She hoped that if he were going to reprimand her for butting into his personal business, he would just come out with whatever it was he wanted to tell her. If he didn't want her there, fine. But sitting across from him and trying to eat when she knew something could be coming would give her heartburn. Why had she pressed him to eat with her? She'd only wanted to make him see that his children might be able to make him happier than his job. She wanted him to delight in finding that perfect present for each of them instead of passing it off to her like an insignificant chore. And she wondered again if he was going to go to his kids' Christmas play or if he'd miss it like he'd missed supper.

When Carrie was twelve, she'd tried out for a solo in her Christmas pageant and she got it. She could still remember the wood grains of the floor on the stage and the black barrel lights above her, with blue and green bulbs shining in her eyes. She remembered the thick velvet curtain separating her from the quiet hum of the crowd. She took her spot at the microphone. It was a little too high for her, so she tipped it down, making a hollow pop register on the speakers. The curtains opened. In the darkness created by the spotlight, she could hear shifting in seats and gentle coughs in the crowd. That one moment when there was silence and blinding light, she wished that she could see her mother and father because the nerves were starting to eat at her, and she needed friendly faces to calm herself. The music started and she opened her mouth to sing, the first few notes coming out jagged like a lamb's bleat. She cleared her throat and started to sing again, and as she did, she saw her mother's face come into focus at the edge of the darkness, tears in her eyes and a smile on her face, and Carrie sang. She sang so well. She sang for her parents. Would Adam's children be looking for him in the darkness? And what would they feel when they couldn't find him?

"You don't mind eating in here?" he asked.

"Not at all or I wouldn't have asked." She scooted a chair over to the desk and sat down. Her plate was resting half on the surface and half on a legal pad, so she carefully pulled the paper out from under her supper and set it on the corner of the desk. The lamplight was soft, creating a cozy atmosphere. She wondered how he could get any work done with so little light. It was enough, though, to show off the blue of his eyes and the serious expression on his face.

"So," he said, clearly trying to fill the silence. "Tell me about Olivia wanting me to take her ice skating. Did she really ask for *me* to take her?"

"Yes. She said she wanted you in particular. And Snow White." She smiled.

"Snow White?"

Carrie nodded. "At this age, it's perfectly feasible to Olivia for her daddy and Snow White to take her skating. And it's important to make her feel like her requests are valid even when they aren't because one day she'll come to you with something serious. And if you listened to her as a child and took her seriously, she'll trust you with the major stuff."

He sat for a long time without talking, but Carrie could tell he was taking it all in. "It's hard for me to figure out what they like, sometimes," he admitted. "When my ex-wife, Gwen, and I divorced, honestly, I allowed her to have whatever she asked for, including custody of the kids, because I just wanted it all to be over quickly, with as little disruption as possible. Now, it's…" His last word trailed off, a hush settling between them. His confession was so honest and so unexpected. Carrie let the quiet linger so that he could be alone with his thoughts.

Then, after a long while, when the silence was finally wearing out its welcome, he said, "You seem to be getting along well with my family. They treating you okay?"

Here it comes, she thought. He was going to tell her she'd overstepped her bounds by spending time with his family. She'd orchestrated this little supper, thought she was getting somewhere, and it was about to backfire. She picked up her glass of tea and took a swallow to alleviate her drying mouth. "They're wonderful," she said.

Adam nodded and her worries about a reprimand lightened a little. "My family wants the best for everyone, but they don't always know what's best." He pushed around some casserole on his plate. "They don't understand me."

Carrie couldn't believe it. In his usual quiet way, Adam hadn't said much, but he'd just admitted yet another very personal thing to her. She hadn't expected him to be so honest. The fact that he told her what he was feeling caused a tiny flicker of hope. She set down her fork and looked him straight in the eye. She asked gently, "What don't they understand?"

"They don't know how hard it is to run a business. If something has to get done, it's me who has to do it—no one else can. They don't get that."

"I think they get it."

His mouth opened as if he were going to say something, but nothing came out. Instead, the skin between his eyes wrinkled, and he looked at her with utter confusion on his face.

"They know how hard you work and what you have to do, I think. What they don't understand is how you can let it get in the way of your family. Think about when we painted your hands. You got your work done, but you got something else done too—you had a bonding moment with your children. You shouldn't miss those moments because, once they're gone, you can't get them back. *That's* what your parents don't understand."

"It's not that easy."

"Why do you say that?"

"I'm building a business here. It takes a lot of work. I don't want to screw it up by messing around."

Carrie's pulse quickened at his comment, but then she relaxed a little when she realized that obviously he didn't understand how his words could be misconstrued. It was the same principle that she used to comprehend why children said things like, "I don't like your sweater. The stripes are funny." They don't know enough about the world to grasp how that would hurt a person's feelings. They had to be taught. Even though Adam was a very bright man, he, too, had to be taught. He clearly didn't realize what he'd implied by his words. Playing with his children and eating meals with his family certainly wasn't "messing around." By spending those moments with his children, he'd be creating the people they would become by giving them moments, memories, a picture of what life should be.

"Do you want your children to believe that you don't have time to love and that they aren't worth love?"

"Of course not." He was looking at her as if she'd just said the most preposterous thing in the world, which made her feel better still. He wasn't heartless; he just didn't understand this part of his life the way she did. She felt a calmness about being there, across from him, that she hadn't felt before. Talking to him was easier than she'd imagined, and, every time she did it, she felt better.

"I want to help you show them what you're like as a person, what life with you is like," she said. "I know you're busy, but would there be any way that you could work from home at least a few more days so you can be with the children? It would give them a chance to get to know you."

The uncertainty was there in his face, but it was as if the feeling made him uneasy. He clenched his jaw and he drew in a deep breath through his nose. He was out of his comfort zone. "I'm not trying to be combative, but I do have work to do. That's why I've employed *you*. I'd prefer to stick to the work schedule I have because, at the moment, things are a bit busy."

"But David and Olivia need you."

"Look, I'm heading up a major business expansion. No one else knows the answers that are needed to carry the project through. However, when it comes to watching the children, there is someone else who can, so I'd like you to do what you do best and stop worrying about me."

Did he just imply that she was asking him to *watch* the children?

"I don't want you to watch the children, Adam. I want you to be a father to them." She knew that statement was daring, and she knew quite well what she meant by it. The last thing she wanted to do was to criticize him, because she knew that he felt he'd been attacked by his family downstairs. She'd just wanted to help.

"I don't like what you're suggesting," he said quietly, his irritation evident in the way he said the words—each one enunciated perfectly.

"I'm not suggesting anything. I'm telling you. I think the children need you to make some different decisions in your life."

"Look, I didn't get where I am by exercising poor judgment. You've been with our family a matter of days. *Days*. I think it would be best if you leave my life choices to me and you stick to what you really *do* know well, which is how to care for my children."

"I'm trying to care for them, Adam," she pushed, "but it's not just about finger paints and bedtimes. It's about teaching them to be healthy, well-rounded adults. Some children don't have the luxury of having a family, but yours do, and I'm just trying to let them see what a great father they have."

He didn't answer. In the silence, Carrie wondered if she'd gotten through to him at all.

Finally he spoke. "You sound like Sharon."

"I'm sure she feels the same as I do."

"I thought it was just her being irrational," he said, slightly more calmly. "I thought it was because of her...problems."

Carrie didn't want to meddle in Sharon's business but she could feel herself asking him to explain with her eyes, even though she tried not to. Her concern for Sharon was overwhelming her reasoning.

"It's a bit of a touchy subject..." He seemed to read her, and she'd never had anyone else who could do that, but she ignored the thought because she needed to hear about Sharon. "She's had a very hard time getting pregnant. When she finally did, she miscarried, and getting pregnant had taken a ton of time, money, and effort. They'd tried to go through the doctors, hoping that would increase their success. It didn't work. Sharon and Eric used every single bit of their savings."

How terrible, Carrie thought. All the pieces were starting to gel, and she was getting a picture now of Sharon and why she broke down like she did.

"But why is she so angry at *you*?" she asked, her thoughts coming out more easily due to Adam's openness.

"She and I had a disagreement."

"About?"

"She battles depression, and the baby issue isn't helping things. One night she and I really went at it because she told me that I didn't deserve my own children. She said that David and Olivia ought to have parents who spend—what did she say?—every moment with them without regard to anything else." He looked at a spot on the wall as if something were there. "I shouldn't have given in to the argument, knowing her state, but I did, and it got heated."

"I'm sorry," Carrie said. And she was. She was so sorry to hear about Sharon, and she was sorry that their disagreement had escalated into something that still lingered between them.

"I thought she was just unleashing her anger at not having success with getting pregnant. I thought she was being irrational, and I hired you because I worried that Sharon's depression would require a lot of Mom's attention, pulling her away from the kids. My mother spent many nights over at their house helping Eric—especially right after they'd miscarried. It took a lot of her energy. When she said that Sharon would be coming, I didn't want to take any chances with the kids' needs being neglected." Adam's shoulders were tense, his forearms resting uneasily on the desk. "What I hadn't anticipated was hearing the same thing basically from you." He leaned back and pushed his food around on his plate with his fork.

Her first inclination was to feel saddened by his statement. Here she was, a stranger, able to pinpoint the issue after only a few days' time. Certainly, that would make him feel awful. But, the more she contemplated it, the less guilty she became, because she realized right then that she knew not just what the children needed, but what Adam needed, and the fact that his own family felt the same only made her feel stronger in her intuition.

"You, Sharon, my parents—it's frustrating to me to have to repeat my reasoning every time I'm hit with this. I don't have any answers for you. I have to work."

It occurred to her that he felt helpless in the situation. "Help me to understand your side," she said. He didn't answer, but he seemed to be thinking about it, so she left it at that.

Chapter Fifteen

Happiness is achieved by doing what you love.

Carrie knew exactly what she loved, so she decided to focus on that today.

Carrie gathered all the kids' sheets and blankets and lumped them in a pile in the playroom. "Why are our blankets in here?" David asked as they entered.

"We're going to build a fort," Carrie explained.

"How?" Olivia picked up a sheet and tried to fluff it out, but her body was too close to the ground and the sheet fell with a plop.

"Well, let's get all the chairs first, and I'm going to drag the art table into the middle of the room."

David's eyes widened. "Are you allowed to do that?"

"Yes, I think it's fine as long as I put it back."

Olivia grabbed the ends of a sheet and started running around the room, holding her hands over her head. The sheet—pink with tiny, green katydids on it—trailed behind her. She ran as fast as she could, as if she were trying to fly a kite on a day with no wind. "I'm a flying princess," she said with a giggle.

"Princesses don't fly," David corrected her.

"Well, I am a princess, and I'm flying right now!" Olivia ran one more lap around the room before tiring out and dropping the sheet. By that time, Carrie had managed to get the art table into the center of the room. She draped one of the sheets on top of it, the fabric cascading over each side and puddling at the ground. Olivia crawled inside.

David scooted one of the chairs next to the table and pulled the corresponding side of the sheet over the chair, extending the length of the fort. Carrie helped, moving chairs over, stacking bins, anchoring sheets and blankets onto the shelves with heavy items, until they had constructed an enormous fort.

"Come in, David!" Olivia called, peeking her head out from one of the blankets.

David grabbed his flashlight and spy goggles from the toy box and headed inside. "Whoa!" he said, once he'd seen under the blankets.

As Carrie crawled in after him, Olivia laughed. "Carrie! What are *you* doing coming into the fort?" Olivia was sitting cross-legged, her hands on her knees, her tiny pink fingernails like candy sprinkles.

"Am I not allowed in?" Carrie asked.

"You're a grown-up! Grown-ups don't get in. They do grown-up things."

"Well, I don't. I get into forts because I like to play just as much as you do."

"Why do you like to play with us?" Olivia asked, getting down on her hands and knees and pushing a piece of blanket farther out to allow more space inside. She turned around and sat back down, her head cocked to the side, waiting for an answer. "Most grown-ups don't like to play," she added.

"I like to play with you because I have so much fun with you and you have the most amazing ideas. I only put the sheet on the table, but it was David who thought to add the blankets to the chairs. Look how much bigger the fort is now. And! What would I do if I sat outside the fort?"

"I suppose you could do some work. Do you have anything to do on the computer? That's what Daddy does," David said. He was always matter-of-fact with his answers, and she wondered if Adam, too, had been like that.

"Shall we show your daddy this fort?"

Olivia grabbed the sheet and ripped it up to allow herself a space to exit. When she did, it jostled the other blankets.

"Careful, Olivia!" David scolded. "We want Daddy to see!"

"I know!" she said in return. "That's why I'm getting out. Let's show him! And Grandma Joyce and Grandpa Bruce! Let's show everyone!"

"Shall we round them up?" Carrie said.

As David carefully crawled out from under the sheets and blankets, Olivia grabbed Carrie's hand. The first child Carrie ever cared for as a nanny had been only a little older than Olivia and David. Her name was Claire. She was six. Claire held Carrie's hand everywhere she went. She was a wisp of a girl with long, brown hair and bright blue eyes. Carrie had completely fallen for that little girl—she did everything for her. She even went to their house some evenings to watch Claire free of charge after Claire's mother had decided to stay home full-time with her.

This year, Claire had turned sixteen. She was in high school now, she drove a car. The last time Carrie spoke to her, Claire was telling her about the courses she was taking to prepare her for college admissions. That little girl with the bright eyes and brown hair wasn't little anymore, yet Carrie didn't feel a bit older than she had when she'd watched Claire. As she looked down at Olivia, her tiny pink fingernails and her petite fingers, she thought about how fast time goes, and, suddenly, she couldn't get to Adam's office quickly enough. She felt as if time were speeding up, as if there were a clock ticking behind her. She couldn't wait to get Adam involved with the children again. She just hoped that he was at a place where he could stop working for a minute. Gingerly, she pushed the office door open, the hinges making a creaking sound.

"No, no, no. I wouldn't do that," he said into the phone. He looked up, his eyebrows raised, an expectant expression on his face. Olivia hid behind the door.

"Can you come with us?" she mouthed while waving her hand toward herself in the come-here gesture. To her surprise, he leaned forward like he was about to stand up. But just as she felt the excitement rise, her hopes slammed back down when his face became serious and he shook his head "no."

She held up her hand in the number five and mouthed, "Five minutes?"

He put out his hand and shook his head as if to say, *I don't know*. His jaw was starting to clench like it had the other night, and she feared that she'd come at a bad time. She was interrupting him, and he clearly wasn't in the mood.

Olivia, who had been peeking around the corner, shrank back, her shoulders slumped.

"Olivia," she whispered. "You and David go get your grandma and everyone. I'll get your daddy once he's off the phone."

"He won't come," she whispered.

"Yes, he will." Carrie was cognizant of the fact that she'd just made a promise to Olivia, and she never went back on her promises.

She wasn't sure how, but she was going to get Adam off that phone, no matter what. "Go get them. I'll meet you in the playroom with your dad."

As Olivia ran off to find the others, grabbing David by his arm and whisking him down the hallway, Carrie turned back toward the door. She took in a breath to steady herself. She'd been about to press him when he was in the middle of something clearly very important. There he was, talking heatedly to someone, and she was about to interrupt him to show him a fort made of blankets. It sounded ridiculous even to her, but she knew better. It wasn't about the fort. She tiptoed in and sat in the chair opposite the desk.

He kept talking, but his eyes were on her, a crease forming between his brows. "Get me the figures. I can't make a decision until I can see it on paper," he said, a curious expression on his face as he watched her. The sight of it made her stomach flutter. "Once I have the report, I'll send it to Andy." The strangest question entered her mind as she took in the seriousness of his face: Could Andy make him laugh? Carrie thought back to the time she'd made him laugh in the garage when she'd asked for the beer that she'd offered his family. The way his eyes creased at the edges, how he'd grinned at her once the laugh had dissipated; it was like the feeling she got sleeping in her own bed after being away. He made her feel comforted, protected.

She mouthed, "The kids need to show you something." He shrugged his shoulders as if to say there was nothing he could do. She pursed her lips, thinking, and then whispered, "Call him back?"

He took in a breath and let it out. "Mm hm," he said, his gaze moving away from her. He was looking down at the paperwork in front of him, but it was clear that he wasn't processing what he was seeing. She could feel the invisible clock ticking. Olivia had probably gotten the whole family together already, and she was still sitting there with Adam. *Come on, Adam*, she thought. She leaned into his line of vision and mouthed, "Please?"

"Chuck, I'm so sorry," he said suddenly, and she felt light-headed. "I think I'm going to have to call you back. When's your flight?" She tried to decipher his expression, and she couldn't. She waited the agonizingly long time for Adam to talk again. "I'm aware of that. If I don't catch you before you leave, I'll see if I can't get you first thing in the morning." More silence. "Thanks." He hung up the phone.

"You have no idea what kind of pressure I'm under," he said, turning toward Carrie. His lips were pressed together, his head turned slightly to the side. He hardly had to move to make his expression intimidating. At that moment, she realized what it must feel like to be on the opposite side of Adam Fletcher in business. It wasn't a good place to be. "This *has* to be a priority. *Why* do you need me right now?"

It seemed ridiculous even saying it now. She felt like she'd overstepped the line more than she ever had. She'd just interrupted a very important call. "The kids made a fort," she said.

He stared at her, his eyes confirming all of her fears.

"But I don't want you to see the fort," she said quickly before he could throw her out. "I want you to show David and Olivia that, just like your business, what they've made using their time and their hands is important and a *priority*."

His shoulders fell just a little, and she could see that contemplative look pushing out the irritation. He stood up and walked around the desk, his gaze on her in a reluctant but surrendering way. Carrie wanted to yelp and clap her hands, throw her arms around him and tell him what a great thing it was for him to do this, but she kept her composure.

"I need you to trust me. When you get to the playroom, I want you to crawl into the fort and play with them. No questions," she said. He shook his head as if he were annoyed, but she could tell by the set of his lips that he was lightening up. As they neared the door, she looked up at him. "Adam. This is very important for your kids. They made a fort, and they don't believe that you'll get in. I'm nearly certain of it. So, please, do it for them."

"I'll get in," he said. She wanted *him* to want to, but she knew that it would take many baby steps to get him to understand. He was getting in. Right now, that's all that mattered.

He pushed the playroom door open and stopped. The entire family was there—they'd even helped Walter up the stairs. For a second that felt longer than an hour, no one spoke. The kids were inside, and Carrie could see the beam from David's flashlight. Sharon looked at Carrie first and then at Adam, her face neutral of any emotion. Adam raised a hand in greeting. Then, without prompting, he walked past the family and got down on his hands and knees. He lifted the sheet up and put his head in. Olivia let out a squeal so loud it startled Carrie. The squeal transformed into a bunch of giggles.

"May I come in?" Adam asked her.

Carrie couldn't see the exchange, but the sheets began to move, and she heard David say, "Scoot over, Olivia, and give him room."

Adam wriggled his way inside the fort. Under the beam of light from David's flashlight, she could make out Adam's shadow. He was sitting cross-legged, his shoulders hunched over to help him fit under the art table. Joyce was standing beside Carrie as she watched, her hand covering the smile on her face. Adam's movement seemed gentler from what she could make out, and he was listening to the kids as they told him about their fort. To see him change before her eyes into this tender, soothing person made her heart patter. Joyce motioned to the others to follow her out of the room, and as Carrie complied with them, Joyce put up her hand as if to tell her to stay. "Help him," she whispered, nodding toward the fort.

Carrie continued to watch his shadow, wondering what the kids would ask him, how he would talk to them. She wondered if David would ask him to help build something like he always asked Carrie to do, or if Olivia would dress him up in her dress-up accessories. The thought warmed her. This part would be easy. Now that she'd gotten him here, even if it was only fifteen minutes, she could easily show him what to do. He was going to play with the kids, and they would never forget it, she was certain. Spending time with them would tell them how much he thought of them, how much he cared.

They were all turning to go, and Joyce was assisting Walter with his walker, as Olivia's voice came from inside the fort. "Will you stay and play with us, Daddy?"

"I can't," she heard him say gently. "I have to finish my work. But you two have fun, okay?"

Carrie's heart fell. She knew what kind of pressure he was under, but she'd hoped, watching him, that he'd stay and play, seize the moment.

"Okay," Olivia said quietly.

"Bye, Daddy," David called as Adam lifted the sheet and crawled out. Sharon shook her head at him. She spun around and darted out of the room. Eric and Joyce followed her.

Carrie's hopes for that moment had just come tumbling down around her. She wondered which was worse: him just not being there at all, or being there and then letting them down. The kids were disappointed; she could tell by their voices. And it had been all her fault. She should have left him in his office. The kids had been so excited about the fort—she should have left well enough alone. Adam approached her.

Walter stopped and hobbled over to Adam. He grabbed Adam's arm and went with him to the door. Unprompted, Walter guided him just out of earshot of the children, put his quivering hand on Adam's shoulder, and said with a smile, "Do you know what I used to love to watch you do?" Adam shook his head. "When you were seven, and you came to visit me and your grandma"—he looked up at the ceiling and smiled again, his bushy eyebrows going up, creating long creases on his forehead—"you used to make forts like that"—he pointed toward the children—"in my back woods. You'd stay out there all day until dark. You've always been a builder of things. You built the model train village with your dad at twelve, you built your first home brewery using that kit in college, and now you're building a business. I'm proud of ya, son. I just wish you'd work on building one more thing for me." That pensive look sheeted over Adam's face, the skin between his eyes wrinkling. "Build your family," Walter said. "The fort's gone now. So's the home brewery and the village. It will all go. But family stays."

Walter's words had caused a storm of thoughts to flood Carrie's mind: she considered how right he was. Certainly, Adam needed some help taking care of his kids, but he *had* a family. Carrie had never married, she had no children, nothing to build. Was she wasting her skills on others when she should just quit and focus on herself awhile?

The buzz of a rev-up car came from inside the fort. Adam was standing quietly as he took in Walter's suggestion. His only movement was when he slid his hands into the pockets of his jeans. He seemed to be thinking—it always showed on his face. Finally, he said, "The deal I'm working on will more than triple our distribution on the East Coast. It's a game-changer. I know that sounds heartless by pushing everyone away, but I am up against a wall here."

The edges of Walter's lips turned upward into a knowing grin, his eyes showing wisdom beyond any Carrie could imagine. "No one's doubting that you can make it happen. But more isn't always better, young man. Now, I'm going down to your lovely, gigantic kitchen so that I can sit at the table and play solitaire the same way I do in my kitchenette at home. Bruce, do you mind walking with me?" After they left, Carrie caught Adam take one last glance at the fort before departing himself, leaving her feeling sad for him and his children, lonely for herself, and altogether confused about how she could possibly fix it all. It seemed no matter what she did, she just couldn't get through to Adam, and as her time with the Fletcher family slipped away, she knew she wouldn't be staying longer to help him figure it all out. In a month's time, she'd be applying to the university back home, taking classes. Her stomach churned with the thought of it.

Chapter Sixteen

Make every moment count.

After the kids had been put to bed, Carrie walked into the playroom to clean up. They'd spent hours in the fort. David had added a few more sections and Olivia had decorated the inside. It was mostly empty now—just sheets, blankets, and toys—but she could almost still hear the laughter and the voices of the kids as they'd played. David had been a pirate on his ship at sea and Olivia had been a mommy, taking care of her baby. The doll was still inside the fort, covered in a small toy blanket. Instead of cleaning up, Carrie crawled inside.

The blankets were thick enough and the room dark enough that the light from the room barely penetrated the space, so she clicked on David's flashlight. As she sat cross-legged, her head at an odd angle because of the height of the art table she was under, she felt the irritation and frustration coming back. Adam had real demands of his work, but he had a family too. The children were only with him a short time, and then they'd be back with their mother. It all made her feel helpless.

Carrie realized now that Adam's problem wasn't an issue of choice, it was an issue of time. He only had twenty-four hours in the day, and that wasn't enough to get it all done. He seemed like he wanted to be able to do it all, but he just couldn't. What bothered her was that he didn't realize that having children who didn't know their father was worse than anything that could happen at work. She'd never faced an obstacle like this one.

The side of the sheet went up beside her, startling her. When Carrie saw who it was, she took in a sharp breath, her heart beating wildly. Carrie hadn't expected to see anyone in the playroom—the family was all downstairs and Adam had been in his office until this very minute when his head poked through the opening in the fort. To her surprise, he crawled in beside her. On a regular day, he had such an authoritative presence that it was almost intimidating, but when he let down his guard, there was a realness to him that she loved. She ached for him to talk in a soft voice like he had with the children, to see that curiosity in his eyes, that smile on his lips. She wondered what he looked like asleep with his eyes closed, when he was the most vulnerable, when there was nothing pulling on him, nothing consuming his time.

The beam from the flashlight hit his face in a harsh way, showing the exhaustion on his forehead and under his eyes. He had on a sweater that made his eyes more blue, jeans, and socks—one was inside out, and Carrie had to swallow her smile. Even though his inattention to his family made her crazy, something as simple as that could make her smile. She tried to hide it, but she knew that her emotions were showing on her face. Her pulse was up in her ears, and she couldn't get a breath.

He looked at her curiously, his eyebrows furrowing just a little, and in a different way than they did when he was working, as if he were responding to her smile, which he hadn't ever done before. It was clear that he was thinking something, a specific thought was registering, but he wouldn't let it show.

"What are you doing in here?" he asked.

His gaze roamed around her face fondly. It made her feel nervous. She didn't know how to be charming and flirty, but when he looked at her like he was now, she wanted to know how. She'd have to go with her gut, and it scared her. She worried that she was misreading him, but he had definitely responded to her smile, and it was clear by the softness in his eyes that he was trying to ease her nerves. What he didn't realize was that by looking at her like that, he was making them worse.

"I was…" What should she say? She was thinking about him. How could she explain herself? "I was…" *Ugh!* she thought. He got her so flustered that she couldn't even get a lie right! She could be doing anything: picking up the toys, looking for an earring, getting the flashlight…But she couldn't get a coherent string of words together.

"You were what?" he asked, his voice kind, his face too close to hers. As she scrambled for an answer to his question, she heard that little huff of laughter, and, when she finally made eye contact, he was grinning at her. She felt woozy. Maybe it was the dark or the long day. She didn't know. Suddenly, she couldn't get anything at all to come out of her mouth. She was staring at him, to her horror. *Say something!* she scolded herself, but all she heard was silence. It was like that nightmare where she would scream and nothing would come out. All she could think about was how much she wanted him to be with his kids and to be with her, spend time with *her*. She knew that was a crazy thought but she felt something that she'd never felt before.

"You're not going to answer?" he asked, and she realized that she still hadn't responded to his question.

"I was thinking about you," she answered honestly and then nearly fell over face-first once she realized she'd said it out loud.

He showed a look of shock but then hid it, his eyes blinking just a little too much, giving him away. It was quick—barely recognizable except for the fact that she'd been so in tune to his expressions lately. In business he had to be on his game, pokerfaced. Even if someone threw him a curveball, he had to maintain composure— that was what made a good businessman, Carrie could imagine. She'd just thrown one of those curveballs. While the surprise was gone, it had been replaced by a crooked grin. It made her feel tingly.

She knew she'd have to explain herself, and she didn't want to harp on the whole you-don't-spend-time-with-your-family issue because she was almost sure that he'd heard enough of that today. But the alternative to telling him that was to tell him what she'd actually been thinking about just now—how he made her feel. She wouldn't dare admit it; she knew how ridiculous it would sound having only just met him, but there was something there on her end, and she couldn't explain why.

"I just wish you had more hours in the day," she finally said. Carrie shifted in the small space to scoot away from him, their body heat under the blankets making her warm in her sweater. He changed positions too as if getting comfortable, but it moved him closer to her, and they were back where they'd started in proximity. She wondered why he'd crawled into the fort anyway. "*I'm* in the fort because I was thinking. Why are you in the fort?" she asked, glad that she'd mustered up enough courage to say something articulate.

"Mom said you weren't at supper, and I was checking on you." His voice was kind and quiet, the type of voice she imagined he'd have in the dark after everyone had gone to sleep and it was just the two of them. She knew better than to let herself think things like that, and the uneasiness it created caused her to feel claustrophobic, the heat becoming too much, making her face feel like it was on fire. She pushed her way out from under the blankets, resisting the urge to gulp the cool air. Adam crawled out after her.

"So you were downstairs at supper?" It was forward of her to even inquire, but she couldn't help it. She knew better by this point than to hope, but she did just the same.

"I wanted to make sure Sharon was okay," he said, insecurity on his face.

"And was she?"

"No, she was upset." He took in a deep breath and let it out. "She thinks I'm taking the kids for granted. I see them once a month and most holidays. Sharon doesn't realize that I've lost a lot, too. I've lost my wife, the life that I'd tried to build with her, and a huge amount of time with my kids. Don't you think it makes me feel guilty?" His voice was almost pleading, as if he *wanted* her to help him fix it. "Gwen broke my trust. She ran off with someone else, and I felt broken. Work made me stronger. It helped me to refocus. Do you know what it's like to see my own children so infrequently that they barely respond when I enter a room? It feels terrible. I didn't just lose Gwen; I lost them too. It breaks my heart to see them stand there and look at me the way they do. The brewery is my outlet. What am I supposed to do?" he asked, exasperated.

He was on edge, his face crumpled in a scowl, his lips pressed together, his body tense—but for some unknown reason, Adam was letting his guard down. Maybe he was just falling apart, she wasn't sure, but he was opening up to her. His candidness made her feel warm despite the icy cold outside. Everything she'd tried to get him closer to his family hadn't worked, and she had absolutely no idea how she was going to help him, but she wanted to. More than anything.

She hadn't said anything, but it was as if he could read her mind. His shoulders relaxed, and his head tilted to the side just slightly, his eyes fixed on her. It was the oddest thing: they looked at each other, and for the first time, she felt like he was on her side. Like he was going to try. Carrie knew he'd still have to leave to run the business, but he seemed to have a different perspective now. He understood what the people around him were feeling, but just like her, he didn't know how to make it any better. Everything inside her wanted to help him. It wasn't because she had a crush on him or because he was very wealthy or kind. It was because it was the first thing in a long time that she wanted to do as much as she wanted to be with children. His happiness made her feel something.

Even though Carrie had never answered him—and maybe he'd meant his question to be rhetorical—he turned toward the door, opened it wider and gestured for Carrie to exit with him. She still hadn't cleaned up the fort, but he didn't seem bothered, so she followed.

They entered the hallway together, side by side. She pondered what it would be like to be by his side in more ways than just professionally. They walked silently as she thought about her predicament: she was getting too invested in this family and she only had a few weeks left.

A look of wonder registered on Joyce's face as the two of them entered the kitchen together. She scanned the both of them from top to bottom like she tended to do when she was processing the situation at hand, a small smile twitching at the corners of her lips.

She was holding a glass of wine, the pile of supper dishes stacked on the counter behind her. The whole family was around the table, all their eyes on Carrie and Adam. Bruce was holding a cup of dice, some sort of marble game on the table in between them all.

"You're a bad influence on Carrie," Joyce said with amusement behind her words. "Now you've got *her* missing meals."

She felt Adam look at her out of the corner of his eye as he laughed gently. She was not only happy that he hadn't taken offense at Joyce's comment, but also that Joyce had expected her at supper. She didn't want to look up at Adam because she knew that if she saw that smile on his face, it would make focusing on the family much more difficult. She had to remember that she was the outsider in this scenario. *Would someone like Andy fit better?* she wondered.

Sharon stood up and put her napkin on the table, causing a marble to roll across it and knock into the game board. It was the only sound in that big kitchen. "I'm finished," she said as she scooted her chair under, standing behind it. "I'm going up to bed." She glanced over at Adam, but this time, it wasn't an angry glance; it was a tired look, as if she were *too exhausted to get upset.* Bruce and Eric both stood, supportively. Carrie didn't know. "It's okay," she said. "I'm just tired." She looked at Adam again.

As she walked out of the room, Carrie remembered the desperate way that Adam had spoken in the playroom. He knew what Sharon wanted from him, but he didn't know how to give her what she wanted or mend what was wrong between them. The tension in the room was thicker than the snow outside.

"Come on over, son, and have a seat. But grab us some beers on your way," Walter said, patting the back of the empty chair next to him. "You too, Carrie." Walter's warm eyes, knowing smile, and gentle nature made it feel like he always knew the outcome of every argument, he was just waiting for everyone else to figure it out.

Adam grabbed three beers and set one in front of Carrie. He hadn't asked if she wanted one, but she was glad for the gesture. She was pleased to see Adam was sitting down with a Salty Shockoe in his hand. Their moment in the fort had brought them closer, she felt. Perhaps he would enjoy himself tonight.

"This snow is nice," Walter said, "but I wish it would clear up so we could see Adam at his best. It's been a long time since you've been in the yard with me."

Carrie looked over at Adam for clarification, but he just took a swig of his beer, a smile playing on his lips.

"Adam chose to go away to a big, fancy university instead of attending one around home, but if he had stayed, he'd have played football. He was offered a scholarship to play, and he was a damn fine quarterback in high school. He could hit a target from the next town over on a pass. You'd better have a ball somewhere in this fancy house, young man."

"There's one in the garage," he said, playfulness in his eyes.

"I'd better not let go of my walker. You might be in trouble."

Adam laughed. Carrie's heart started beating like a snare drum at Adam's amusement. His laugh dissipated into those adorable breathy chuckles that he did whenever something struck him as funny. Fondness showed on his face as he looked at his grandfather, and she couldn't keep her eyes off him.

"You see, Carrie," Walter said. She tore her gaze from Adam and turned to acknowledge Walter. "I chose the school near home. I chose the scholarship. I was a quarterback. I only wish I could have been at my peak when Adam was at his. I would have loved to see who was quicker on his feet. I'm sure Adam begs to differ, but it would have been me."

"Good thing we couldn't have had that competition," Adam said, his lips still set in a grin as he took another swig off his bottle of beer. "Where would my ego be today if you had outrun me?"

"I loved to play catch with my dad," Carrie said, and both men turned to look at her, Walter's eyebrows going up in surprise. She took a sip from her bottle. "He always said I could put a mean spin on the ball."

"Really?" Adam said. It was clear by the light in his eyes that she'd tapped into something good just now.

"I loved watching football with my dad. I was an only child; he never had a little boy to play with, so he taught me. After every game, I'd be inspired by the players and want to go out back and throw balls with him. I can still remember how he'd say, 'Get your fingers on the laces.'"

Just like it had said to do in her book—*find something familiar*—this was the most relaxed she'd been in a long time. And in that moment, she realized that she didn't need the book to teach her how to be happy as long as she was around people with whom she could relate.

She made eye contact with Adam again, and when she did, he was smiling at her, his eyes unstill, that curiosity showing behind them, but this time, it was directed at her and not something she'd said about the kids, which caused a plume of excitement inside her. Without even trying, she'd found familiar ground. It made her wonder what more they might share in common.

"Are you hungry?" Joyce said, washing her hands at the sink. "Let me fix you a plate of food. I made chicken." Before they'd even answered, Joyce began making Carrie a plate anyway.

This moment with Adam had been so nice. Carrie wished that Sharon had given him a chance tonight. Carrie hadn't spent time in Sharon's shoes, but she did know what it felt like to contemplate a future without a family of her own. She knew how frustrating it was to see Adam taking what he had for granted. But ultimately it wasn't Adam's fault Sharon was having trouble getting pregnant. Did Sharon realize Adam's feelings on the matter? He wanted to do more, he just didn't know how.

"Need anything to drink?" Joyce pulled a glass from the cupboard.

"I have my beer, thank you," Carrie said.

Adam had that inquisitive expression still, as if he were trying to figure her out. Little did he know there wasn't much to figure out when it came to Carrie. She was an open book. On the phone interview, he'd asked her all kinds of questions about herself to determine whether she was a good fit for his children. She wished that she could ask *him* some questions now. There was so much she wanted to know about him, but she didn't dare ask. After all, *she* was working for *him*.

Chapter Seventeen

To ease stress, consciously take time to relax.

The moon was hidden behind the snow-filled clouds, making the view from the living room windows a velvety black. The only light outside was the lamplight on the walk, illuminating a patch of snow. Inside, however, the living room was aglow with the warmth of the Christmas season. The tree lights glistened against the green of the Christmas tree, the crystal and glass ornaments sparkling in their light. The stockings Carrie had made with the children had dried and she'd hung them on the mantel amidst the greenery and berries. Carrie sat down on the sofa and folded her feet under her. Most of the time she did that to keep warm, but tonight the fire in the fireplace sent a wave of heat toward her.

They'd finished supper, and she was glad to see Adam joining them for some family time. Walter was still in the kitchen, playing the last round of his marble game. Joyce had shooed everyone else away from cleaning up, telling them she really didn't mind, and it would go faster with fewer people underfoot. She sent them all back to the table to finish the game, and Adam and Carrie had decided to head into the living room to wait for the others. Adam set her mug of coffee onto the table and then positioned his cell phone next to his own mug. It was out of place there, screaming out its imposition.

She didn't want it to be in view because she knew that if given the choice between being there and work, he'd choose work.

Adam lowered himself down beside her, causing the cushion to slant, and she could feel the pull of her body toward him. She fought it, shifting in her seat.

"The house looks very nice," he said, looking around the room. "I haven't had a chance to really enjoy it, but I've noticed."

A fizz of happiness swelled in her chest. He'd noticed. When he'd originally said she could decorate, she'd thought he didn't care, but now she wondered if he was just too busy to manage it. He sat beside her, his cheeks rosy from the heat of the fire, a slight stubble showing on his face. He pulled his mug from the table and balanced it on his lap.

"I wish Joyce would've let us help clean up," she said, feeling festive and suddenly wanting the whole family to gather together to enjoy the atmosphere.

"She's like that." He smiled.

Walter laughed in the kitchen, making her consider the fact that Adam wasn't playing the game with his family. Did he feel obligated to keep her company?

"What's the matter?" he asked.

"What do you mean?" She couldn't think of anything better to say, but she knew he'd noticed something cross her mind. He waited as if giving her more time to formulate a better answer. "Do you want me to let you have a little family time?" she asked.

"No, why? It's nice to have some company over coffee."

"I like being with you too," she said, looking down at her mug, but inside she wanted to squeeze her eyes shut and shake her head. He'd said he liked having a cup of coffee, and she'd just said she liked being with him in general. She pressed her lips together to keep any more of her thoughts from slipping out. His quiet laughter caused her to look up, and when she did, she realized he was smiling at her—a big, happy smile. She'd not seen his face light up like that before.

"What?" she asked, her heart thumping.

His phone lit up on the table, and right there on the screen—clear as day—was the name Andy Simpson. *Andy Simpson.* She said the name in her head. Andy Simpson was the name that could pull the rug right out from under her. She willed Adam to ignore it, but she knew he wouldn't.

Adam looked at the phone, clearly deliberating. It rang again. "I can call her back," he said, nodding toward the table where it sat.

"You can get it if you need to. Really." She was lying. She was telling him to get it, but hoping that he'd refuse. She was wishing with everything she had that he would let the call go to voicemail, because once he spoke to Andy, he could be wrapped up in work for hours. Work colleague or not, she knew that when it came down to it, Andy was more glamorous, wiser about the things in Adam's world, and more of a friend to him than Carrie was. Given the time they spent together, Andy could possibly be even more than a friend.

Adam reached out and took the phone off the table. "Excuse me just a sec," he said before he tapped his phone to accept the call. "Hey," he answered, setting his mug onto the coffee table and standing up.

Carrie had never heard him say *"hey"* like that before. It was so casual, so relaxed. Her admission to him that she liked being with him came flooding back to her, and she felt the throb of mortification in her temples. She was someone with whom he could make light conversation and fill his time when he wasn't working—that was all. Tonight's supper swelled in her stomach as she realized what a fool she'd made of herself. No wonder he'd laughed at her. Thank God she hadn't said any more than that.

When she finally swam out of her thoughts, she realized that Adam had left the room, his mug still sitting on the coffee table. It only served to make her assumption more clear. When it came down to it, Andy was the person he wanted to talk to, and she would win his attention every time. As much as it bothered Carrie to think about it, she knew that, really, that's how it probably should be. From everything she'd seen, someone like Andy would be a catch for Adam. She was poised, polite, confident, pretty. Carrie took in a deep breath and tried to rub the stress from her eyes as she let it out.

"You okay?" she heard, her eyes still shut as she rubbed them. When she looked up, Joyce was standing next to the coffee table.

"Yes. I'm fine, thank you."

"Where's Adam? Did he run off on ya?"

Carrie nodded.

Joyce shook her head just slightly and sat down on the sofa. "I don't know what to do with that boy." She leaned back, folding her arms. "He hasn't been the same since Gwen left him."

Carrie set her mug onto the coffee table. She couldn't drink any more anyway with the state of her stomach. "How so?" she asked.

"After Gwen left, he threw himself into his work," she said. "He's never failed at anything before. I don't think he knew what to do when his marriage fell apart."

The fire cracked, sending red-hot sparks up the chimney. Carrie was on the edge of her seat, holding her breath, waiting for more explanation from Joyce.

"You know what I think?" Joyce wriggled around on the sofa, getting comfortable. Carrie turned in her direction and folded her leg underneath her to face Joyce. "I think that working is his way of being a father because he knows how to be a good provider. I think he's terrified to actually be with the kids because he may fail again. He's very sensitive, you know." Joyce stood up and grabbed Adam's mug from the coffee table. "Why don't you come in the kitchen. Sharon's upstairs. Walter suckered the guys into a second game. It'd be nice to have another woman in the room."

Carrie stood up to follow Joyce, grabbing her mug. She was about to take it into the kitchen when she stopped, facing Adam. His gaze immediately went to the empty coffee table and then back up to her face. Joyce took the mug from Carrie. "I'll take the cups in," she said, but Carrie was still looking at Adam.

"I'm sorry I left you." He looked straight into her eyes, barely blinking. "Again." His face showed remorse, his eyes gentle, his lips turned down slightly.

She wanted to say "It's okay," but she knew that really it wasn't okay. Why was he having coffee with her? Why did he crawl into the fort after her earlier? Why was he bothering to be so chatty if he could drop it in a second when Andy called? It was messing with her mind, making her feel things for him when really she shouldn't. He was making her care about him. For what? She didn't know what to say to him because the truth was that the more she learned about him, the more she didn't want to stay away from him for one second, and she knew that she'd be the one getting hurt in the long run.

"What are you thinking about?" he said, a small line forming between his eyebrows in the most adorable way. She wanted to put her hands on his face and tell him, but she'd never dare, and the fact that she even wanted to made her more aggravated.

She could feel the frustration piling up like the snow on the sidewalk outside: each moment a tiny flake, but added up it was too much to plow through, too much to sweep away. She'd never before felt anything like what she was feeling now. Her emotions were overwhelming her, suddenly. "If you're sorry, then change something," she heard herself say.

This was her boss. What was she doing? She'd never been this direct about anything other than children before.

Adam's face didn't change, but his eyes showed his surprise as he processed her direct comment. He recovered, but it took him a minute. Carrie felt the flush to her cheeks, the heaviness from guilt as she looked at his face. He shouldn't just walk out of rooms mid-conversation whenever he felt like it—even if it was his own house. She felt so many emotions—sadness, anxiety—but what she didn't want to admit to herself was that she was also jealous. Jealous of his work, jealous of Andy, anything that pulled him away from her because not once had he put her or the children first.

He'd offered her attention only to wrench it away at the first opportunity. It made her feel like she wasn't worth his time, she wasn't as important as Andy. And maybe she wasn't, but it didn't stop her feelings from getting hurt.

Adam's chest visibly rose underneath his sweater as he took in a steadying breath. He let it out slowly. Was he thinking about what she'd said? It didn't matter; Carrie had a sinking feeling that nothing would change.

"What do you want me to do?" he asked, his voice soft.

She had a million things she wanted him to do, and they were all flying through her head at the same time. She needed to start small and make tiny changes to make it manageable.

"I want you to go shopping for the kids. Take your mom with you; she'll help you pick out the right toys," she said.

"What?" Clearly, he hadn't expected that request.

"Go shopping." She smiled. His face had lightened considerably, and her heart went into overdrive. Carrie couldn't hide her affection for him. She tried to straighten out her smile, but it kept coming back against her will. It was time she admitted it to herself: she had fallen for Adam Fletcher. She couldn't deny it anymore.

The corners of his mouth turned up in that lovable way, and she wondered if he felt anything at all in that moment. When he was with her and nothing else was pulling on his attention, she felt like she was the only person in his world. He made her feel so assured, so happy. She felt like she could tell him anything.

"Tomorrow, I want you to ask your mother to go," she said. "It's your first day off, and we only have four days until Christmas. You have no work and the kids have no presents." She felt the confidence soaring through her.

"I'll ask her to go tomorrow morning."

"You will?" she said, unable to conceal her smile.

"Yes," he said, smiling down at her. Did she see affection in his eyes?

"Thank you," she said, using all her self-control to keep her feet planted where they were and her arms by her sides.

"You're welcome." His eyes moved around her face. "We have to go in the morning, though, because we have the kids' Christmas play tomorrow night."

He'd remembered. And he'd said "we," which meant he planned to go! The thrill of having him there swelled within her. "Yes," she said. "The morning would be great."

Chapter Eighteen

To ease anxiety, it can be quite helpful to find healthy distractions.

Carrie smiled to herself as she thought about how fitting that line was now. Originally, she'd worried about having Adam as a distraction, but today, she celebrated it. The engine of Adam's silver Five Series BMW barely made a sound as he opened the car door to let her in. When Carrie sat down on the passenger seat, she could feel the warmth from the heater that he'd had running while they'd gotten ready to leave.

When Adam had asked Joyce to go shopping, she'd suggested that Carrie go instead since she was probably up on all the latest in children's toys. They'd tried to convince Joyce further, but she'd flat refused, saying she hadn't bought toys in decades, and she'd rather spend time with the children. Joyce and the children were at the front door, Olivia waving with one hand, her baby doll in the other. David stood behind them, peeking around his grandmother and waving goodbye intermittently. They backed inside and shut the door just as Carrie shut herself into the car.

The seats of his car were black leather, soft to the touch, and perfectly clean—not a speck of dust. Her shoes dropped snow on the floor mats, and she worried that it would make a spot when it melted. She let her eyes roam around the sleek dashboard, thinking about how different this vehicle was to hers. Adam got in and latched his seatbelt. His hands wrapped around the steering wheel, his shiny Rolex peeking out from under his coat, reminding her of the time that was ticking away, the tiny number of hours she had before she'd have to leave this family.

As he drove through the neighborhood streets, she indulged in imagining Andy in her seat. She was willing to bet that Ms. Simpson would look a lot more comfortable in it than she did. Pushing the thought away, she focused on Adam. His hand was resting on the stick shift between them. Why had he surrounded himself with so many pricey things when he never gave himself time to enjoy them? He shifted as they merged onto the highway, and she thought to herself how even his hands were familiar to her now, the curve of his knuckles, the movement of his fingers. She wondered what his touch would feel like.

"I thought we'd go to the mall. Would that be okay?" he said, breaking the silence.

"That's fine." She didn't care where they went. She enjoyed being with him.

When they finally arrived, Carrie was more than surprised by what she saw. In the center of the massive expanse of outdoor shops was a Christmas tree that was as tall as the mall itself, its lights twinkling like stars against the gray sky. The shops were all two stories, the iron railings on the second floor draped with swags of evergreen. Christmas music poured through the loudspeakers as the whistle from a children's train blew when it passed by them. She pulled the collar of her coat together to keep out the cold, but the sight in front of her kept her warm.

"It's cold," Adam said, lightly placing his hand on her back, making it hard for her to breathe. She looked over at him and smiled, the thrill of being with him settling upon her.

There were chocolate shops, perfume shops, clothing stores, anything and everything—their store signs bright against the dull sky. Each one had wreaths in the windows, snow piled in corners, people bustling in and out with their holiday bags swinging from their arms. There was too much to take in; there were too many choices. Then, down the cobbled walk, she saw the glow of primary colors in the shop window—the toy store. "Let's start there." She pointed.

"Okay," he said as he smiled down at her.

The excitement of the season, the ambiance of the shops, and being with him made her feel like she was creating a memory that she wouldn't soon forget.

Adam opened the door to the toy shop and allowed her to enter first. "Shall we shop for Olivia since I see all that pink over there?"

She nodded. He was right. Olivia would definitely love that section of the store. There were fairy costumes, pink unicorn stuffed animals, purple strollers with silver, sparkly wheels. It was perfect.

Carrie picked up a fat white and black stuffed kitty cat doll with a pink rhinestone collar and stroked its fur. "What do you think?" she asked, cradling it like a baby. "It could be her new pet."

Adam shook his head, and she set it back down.

"Or these?" She took a gigantic pair of pink heart glasses from the shelf and put them on. "She may like them."

He huffed out a laugh and shook his head again.

Then it caught her eye from the shelf above, glistening in the light of the shop window. Carrie put the glasses back and pulled a diamond crown the size of Miss America's from the shelf and placed it on her head. The faux metal and stones were light, but the crown itself was substantial, causing her hair to fall into her face as she pressed it down onto her head.

Adam raised his hand and, for an instant, she thought he was going to push her hair behind her ear, but he pulled his hand back as quickly as he'd raised it and smiled instead. It was only half of a gesture—barely enough for her to even know its intent—but enough to make her hands tingle with nervousness. It seemed as if he were seeing her in a new light, making her heart pound in her chest. She took the crown off and ran her fingers through her hair.

"I think she'd like it," he said.

Olivia *would* like it. And the fact that he knew filled her with emotion. Did he feel what she was feeling? He gestured for her to enter the aisle leading to the toy trains and trucks, so she went first, glad that she could focus on something other than his face to settle her nerves.

They stopped in front of the toy construction trucks. Adam's expression was the same as the one he had when he was concentrating at his desk. He scanned the toys in front of him. "David doesn't really play with these types of trucks, does he?"

"You're right," she said, happy that he knew his children better than she thought he did.

They walked to the next aisle. The shelves were lined with blocks of different types. Adam stopped and took a box of bristle blocks off the shelf, read the label, and put it back. Then he pulled a larger box of stacking blocks down and inspected the picture on the front. He turned it around for Carrie to view. "I think he'd like these," he said. "And he mentioned a race car set." It was true: David had mentioned that he wanted a race car set on the day they'd gotten the Christmas tree with Adam. She had thought he wasn't listening.

"How many gifts should we buy? I noticed Mom had put some presents under the tree."

"Maybe we could get two or three each, and then there's always Santa's loot. Anything planned for that?" She knew it probably hadn't occurred to him until that moment, but she wanted to give him the benefit of the doubt. When he considered her question, his face was serious, and she could see David's resemblance to him.

"Hmm," he said, looking around. "We may need something to carry all this. I'll be right back." He disappeared around the corner and returned, pushing a small shopping cart. She placed the crown and the blocks in the basket and headed toward the jungle animals section.

There were stuffed monkeys, trees with bright flowers strung around them, toucans, and frogs with orange feet. An enormous animatronic panda growled in her direction, causing her to jump in surprise. She heard that all-too-familiar laugh beside her, and her hopes went soaring. He was clearly enjoying himself. Could he have these kinds of experiences with someone like Andy? She didn't want to think about it and she scolded herself for the fact it had popped into her mind at all.

"What is this?" Adam said, pointing to a picture of a life-sized indoor jungle-themed play set with a tube slide.

"It looks like a jungle gym," she said, trying to mask her surprise. She remembered the last nanny, Natalie—her quiet demeanor, her strict rules—and she couldn't believe he was even considering purchasing such a thing. The playroom, with its dark wood shelves and burgundy and green rug, was like a toy museum. The toy bins were color-coordinated and labeled, the art table perfectly organized. This orange and yellow contraption would stick out like a sore thumb in that décor.

"Do you think they'd play on it if I bought it for them? Gwen's getting them each a Big Wheels for her house. This would give them something active that they could do at mine."

She didn't want to have seen it, but she'd caught a glimpse of the price tag: one thousand, two hundred ninety-nine dollars. "I think they'd love it," she said, but before she could discuss the cost of it, Adam's face lit up.

"Do you think this could be their gift from Santa?"

She thought back to her gifts from Santa. Her biggest gift had been a bike, and she'd wondered how he'd fit it in the sleigh. How would they explain this? It was okay, though. She'd leave them to wonder. Their daddy had just picked out a gift for them that they'd absolutely love, and he had the money to do it, so she kept quiet.

They paid for the jungle gym and a few other smaller gifts, and walked out into the frigid cold of winter. The tinkling of jingle bells sailed toward her and she saw Santa—all decked out in the most elegant deep red outfit with furry white cuffs and lapels, thick black leather boots and belt, with gorgeous white hair and beard, perfectly combed. She led Adam over to the white picket fence that separated the crowd. Even at her age, there was something magical about Santa Claus, drawing her to him and giving her hope that dreams could come true. If only the kids could see this.

Santa let out a "Ho ho ho," from his golden throne, a line of excited children waiting to sit on his knee and give him their lists. A little boy with a bright red and green sweater and white oxford shirt collar peeking out at the neck climbed onto Santa's lap, his mother holding his coat and smiling affectionately.

"What would you like for Christmas?" Santa called out in his bellowing voice. As he did, he caught Carrie's eye as if he were asking her the question. She felt a little embarrassed, realizing she'd been staring at him, thinking about the magic of Christmas and how much she wished she could have David and Olivia with her. What *would* she like for Christmas? She wished for more days just like this one. As she allowed the thought to come through, Santa winked at her and then went back to the little boy who was unfolding a piece of notebook paper and reading his list. She turned to talk to Adam, but, to her surprise, he wasn't beside her anymore. She scanned the crowd, her eyes moving from storefront to storefront. Where had he gone? Fear took over as she worried that he'd taken a work call. Maybe even one from Andy. She shivered in the cold, putting her hands in the pockets of her coat to keep her fingers from going numb.

Before she could ponder Adam's absence too long, she was relieved to see him walking toward her from the chocolate shop with two steaming cups in his hands, unaware that she was watching him. She noticed his stride, the square of his shoulders under his coat, the confidence in his face as he made his way through the gathering around Santa. Then he locked eyes with her, and smiled, and she could hardly manage the happiness that she felt. If only she could have more time with him like this. It was probably the only chance she'd get with just him.

"I thought hot chocolate might warm us up," he said, handing her a cup.

"Thank you." She took the cup from his hand carefully.

When they both turned back to Santa, he already had a different child on his lap, the camera snapping a pose before the child pulled out her list. Carrie felt self-conscious about her Christmas wish to be with Adam more.

As if he could read her mind, he said, "I know what you're thinking," and she nearly choked on her hot chocolate.

"You do?" she said after swallowing a blazing gulp of the liquid. She let out a tiny cough.

"We should bring the kids to see Santa."

"Oh! Yes. We should." She'd answered without thinking about it, but once she processed his words, she realized that he'd said *we* should bring the kids to see Santa. *We.* That little word sure packed a punch. He could have said, "Why don't you bring the kids…" or "Feel free to bring the kids…" but he hadn't. Did he even realize what he'd said? Or was she reading into things, letting the magical night get the best of her? With the Christmas music, the decorations, Santa—it was easy to do.

"Do you mind, since we're out already, if I get some presents for my family as well? I was hoping you'd help me pick them out. I'm not practiced at present-buying."

"You seem very good at it to me," she said, taking another sip of her hot chocolate. They'd started walking the brick walkway toward the fountain that was full of pennies, each one someone's wish. She contemplated throwing one in for good luck.

"I'm better at it when you're with me to give the final 'okay.'"

His comment warmed her. They walked together, peering in to shops and chatting about possible gifts for his parents and his grandfather. With the conversation and the hot chocolate, she barely even noticed the cold.

"The most difficult person is going to be Sharon," he said. "I'm at a loss for what to get her."

"I'm thinking that you know her better than you realize—she's your sister. Just think about her and not her struggles."

"You're right," he said. Adam stopped outside a small restaurant, the smell of the grill filling the air and making her tummy rumble despite having finished the hot chocolate. "It's nearly lunchtime. I'm hungry. Would you mind getting a bite to eat here rather than waiting until we get back home?"

"That's fine with me," she said, trying not to jump up and down, squealing in delight. She was about to share a meal with Adam at a restaurant with no work and no one bothering them at all. She couldn't ask for more. In fact, it was so perfect that she had to wonder if her Christmas wish had already come true somehow.

"Great. Let's get a table. Is this all right?" He gestured toward the restaurant. Past the green wreath on the window with its cascading red velvet ribbon, she could see the roar of a fireplace inside and the shiny brass of a bar. Its interior lighting was so dim it looked like dinnertime rather than lunch.

"Yes." It was more than all right; it was fantastic.

Adam opened the door for Carrie and followed her inside.

Chapter Nineteen

Create a list of what makes you happy.

Carrie didn't need to do anything to find her inner happiness. She was perfectly happy right now, and she hadn't needed any coaching or words of wisdom. She walked through the restaurant beside Adam as they passed a Christmas tree with white lights and gold ornaments and followed the hostess to their table. Adam pulled out a chair for her before moving around to the other side and taking a seat. A very low light filled the room, allowing the candles on the tables to show off their flames. A fire popped and sizzled at one end of the large dining area, and, even though Carrie couldn't feel the heat from it, the entire restaurant was warm and cozy. Adam sat on the other side of the table, where they'd been seated. It was so intimate that when the server brought their menus there wasn't enough room for both of them to lay end to end, so she had to pick hers up to read it.

"Thank you for making me do this today," Adam said over his menu.

"You're welcome. But I didn't make you do anything. I just asked, so thank you for coming."

The server appeared at their table to take their drink order. "What beers do you have?" Adam asked. She rattled off a short list, and at the end of it, she mentioned Salty Shockoe lager. "Hmm," he said. It appeared that he was considering his choices, but now being able to read him a little better, Carrie was suspicious of his motives. He was up to something. "Have you ever had Salty Shockoe?"

The server nodded.

"And what's it like? Is it any good?"

Carrie thought back to her first experience with the beer and their discussion regarding the label, and she was so relieved that he hadn't put her in the position that he was putting this girl in right now. She was almost nervous to hear the answer for fear that the girl would say something negative about it and ruin their meal. Carrie didn't want anything to mess this up. But he seemed to be more playful than actually inquisitive.

"It's delicious, actually. It's one of my favorites."

"Are you just saying that to make a sale?" he asked, grinning.

"No, sir. It really is one of my favorites."

"Good to hear. I trust you. I'll have one of those then. What will you have, Carrie?" he asked. "Have you decided?"

Carrie had been so enthralled in the conversation about Adam's beer that she hadn't really thought of what she wanted for herself.

"Um, I'll have a Salty Shockoe too."

Adam looked at Carrie and winked. "Two bottles of Salty Shockoe, please."

After the server left, Adam set his menu down and said, "You didn't have to get my beer just because it's mine. If you'd wanted a glass of wine or something, you could've gotten it."

It was true that she hadn't given the order much thought, but it had been the right drink for the moment. The memories of having beers with her father were great ones—warm like she felt tonight. It felt as right being with Adam as it felt with her own family, which was a brand new feeling. When Adam looked at her, she felt pretty, and when he listened to her, she felt confident. While her friends would all choose glasses of wine or mixed drinks, that wasn't who she was. She was the girl who had a beer with her dad. And now with Adam. And it felt great.

"I really love..." she heard herself saying the words and her heart raced in her chest. What she wanted to say was that she really loved being with him, no matter what she had to drink, but instead, she said with a smile, "I love your beer."

The huff. The smile. There was something between them—a kind of chemistry that couldn't be forced, it was just there. She'd definitely fallen for Adam Fletcher. Hard. What would she do when her time with him was up, when she had no reason to see him anymore?

Her feelings were speeding faster with every moment they spent together, and there was nothing she could do to stop them. She hadn't meant to fall for him, but she had. Feeling something for Adam was as easy as breathing. It was beyond her control.

"I'm excited to see Olivia and David in their play tonight," he said, to Carrie's surprise.

"I am too. I have Olivia's angel outfit laid out and ready to go. And David's Joseph costume is all set too. I just need to see if I can tighten his belt a little. It keeps slipping when he moves too much."

"They've been practicing their lines with their mother. I know she's been taking them to church for Sunday school, and they've worked on this for quite a while."

"I'm sure the kids will be happy to see you in the audience," she said.

"I'm relieved we have a whole row of family there for them since Gwen couldn't come." The waitress had set the beers down while they were chatting, and Carrie noticed that they were the bottles with the white labels. She felt sentimental about it because that had been the first time she'd had a moment with Adam. They'd come quite a ways since she'd first arrived. "They'll be glad to have *you* there." He took a sip of his beer and set it down slowly, his eyes on the beer mat below it. Without looking up, he said, "I'll be glad to have you there too."

Carrie could feel the hope rising up from the bottom of her stomach, where she'd pushed it down.

Then, he added, "I'm hoping that you being there will help Sharon. I'm sure watching the children is tough, given her situation. You have a calming way about you. Maybe between you and my mom, the two of you can help keep her spirits up."

Carrie was delighted that Adam thought she might be able to help with his sister's emotional state. But she had to admit that she was hoping he'd say that he wanted to have her there because he enjoyed being around her, or that he couldn't imagine spending the evening without her. Was her wish too big for even a Christmas miracle?

"My halo is itchy," Olivia said, tugging on the circle of tinsel that was pinned to her hair. She scratched underneath it, causing her hair to lump up in the middle. Carrie gently pushed it back down and secured the pins.

"You are a beautiful angel!" she said, fluffing out the white cotton dress that Olivia was wearing. With the gold tinsel halo in her hair and the pink on her cheeks that Carrie had brushed on a few minutes earlier, she really did look like a little angel. "Here, David, let me see if I can get that belt tighter." David walked over wearing a brown burlap material that fit him like a sack, with a black belt cinching it all together. He tugged at his belt, his little, somber face showing his worry that it wouldn't stay tight. Carrie pulled it to fit and secured it with a safety pin. While she worked on David's costume, Olivia pranced around the bedroom, jumping and spinning like a ballerina.

When they were finished getting ready, Carrie grabbed the directions to the church and headed downstairs with the children. Joyce and the others had gathered downstairs. They were following in Adam's two cars to the church. She and the kids met Eric at the bottom of the stairs. "You two look great," he said as David and Olivia showed him their costumes. "I can't wait to see you in the play tonight."

"You're gonna like it!" Olivia said in a singsongy voice. "Is Aunt Sharon coming, too?"

"She sure is. She's just finishing up getting ready."

The kids ran off when they heard Joyce and Bruce in the living room, leaving Carrie and Eric alone at the bottom of the stairway. "Is she doing okay today?" Carrie asked, boldly.

Eric didn't seem to mind her question. "This sort of thing is always tough for her because she wants kids so badly." He was quiet for a moment before he added, "And her depression worsens things. It's been hard for both of us."

Carrie struggled for a positive spin on this one. How would Sharon ever enjoy herself tonight while she watched her niece and nephew? Surely she would only think about the fact that she may never see her own children in a Christmas play.

Carrie had helped Adam pick out a present for her, and they'd settled on a blanket. It was white like the snow outside and so soft that she wanted to curl up with it right there in the store. Carrie hoped it would keep her warm on those cold nights, the nights she needed a little extra comfort.

"I'll just go check on her," he said.

Eric was generally quiet, not one to lead a conversation, but there was something about him that was so strong. Maybe it was the way he took care of his wife, the way he kept it all together when she couldn't, or the gentle manner in which he dealt with the situation. He was always there supporting her, helping her, making her feel better. It had to be hard work, yet it never showed on his face. Whenever she saw him, he was pleasant, smiling, helpful. Carrie hoped that Sharon realized how much of a family she had right now. Eric was lovely to her.

She looked up at the top of the staircase, and Adam was standing there looking down, smiling. "Hey," he said, and she felt like she was going to fall over. He hadn't ever said "hey" to her like that before. It was the same "hey" he'd used on the phone with Andy. It was an informal, friendly, relaxed "hey." He was so handsome standing there that she was having trouble getting anything to come out of her mouth.

"Hey," she said back, the word rolling off her tongue like she said it to him all the time.

He started down the stairs, not breaking eye contact. "You look nice," he said when he got to the bottom.

It was the first time she'd had a chance to get a little dressed up, and she had on her favorite sweater and skirt. She was wearing jewelry, which felt a little weird since she didn't wear it much, and she'd spent time on her makeup tonight. It had taken extra time, but she'd curled her hair and styled it as well. She wanted to look nice for the play, but there was also a part of her that wanted to look nice for Adam.

Joyce came around the corner, holding Olivia's hand, Bruce following along with David. Walter hobbled on his cane behind them. Walter moved around the group until he was facing Carrie and Adam.

"You two look fantastic tonight," Adam said. She felt the flush to her cheeks. Sharon and Eric emerged at the top of the stairs. "Are we all ready to go?" Walter asked. The group murmured in agreement as Bruce opened the front door, letting in a blast of icy air. They all went outside, leaving Carrie and Adam in the foyer with the kids.

Adam cleared his throat. "I'll see you there," he said, the sound of the car engine purring in the background outside.

She wished it could be her riding with him, but his car was already full. "See you there," she returned. He grabbed the knob of the door, holding it open for her. As she and the children walked onto the stoop, they shared one more smile, and he closed the door.

Chapter Twenty

Appreciate your unique qualities.

One of Carrie's jobs was to be sure that David and Olivia got to the play. And now, having dropped the kids off with their teacher in the classroom behind the sanctuary of the church, she found herself getting fidgety whenever she thought about seeing Adam. The bulky velvet curtain was still pulled closed on the stage as she got situated in an empty seat in a row with enough chairs for Adam's family, the room around her nearly pitch black because her eyes hadn't adjusted yet. Walter took a while to get in and out of the car, but she hoped for him to be with her soon. His jovial nature would ease her nerves.

She blinked to try and correct her vision, apprehension creeping in even more as she eyed the empty seats beside her. She was struggling to get comfortable in her chair. She shifted her weight, crossing her legs. In mere minutes, Adam's family, Adam, and, according to her tickets, a man named Robert and his wife would fill those seats. She discreetly turned and glanced at the door behind her. It was still closed.

A woman with a floral dress and cardigan walked onto the stage, her heels clicking over the muffled chatter of the crowd. She began speaking into the microphone just as a beam of light crawled along the aisle floor beside her.

Carrie turned to look, and she saw the silhouette of a cane and a man leaning on it—Walter. She wanted to sit by Walter tonight. She didn't want to be caught after the play in a business conversation about the expansion or the figures for the new building Adam was buying, having to smile and nod even though she had no idea what they were talking about.

She focused on the faces of Walter, Joyce, and the others she knew as they walked toward her, but once they'd said their hellos and taken their seats, she saw the two people with Adam. They looked quite refined like him, well dressed—the woman was pregnant, and Carrie immediately worried for Sharon. She glanced over at her face, but she seemed okay. The woman walked ahead of them. Adam's family had crawled over Carrie and filled the seats to her left, leaving the seats to her right open. She was thankful, however, that Walter had ended up beside her.

When they got close enough, Adam made eye contact and smiled, putting his hand in the air to say hello. He eased into the row and sat down next to her.

On stage, the woman with the cardigan finished talking about next Sunday's potluck dinner, dismantled the microphone, setting it just off stage, and walked down the steps at the side of the stage to take a seat in the front row. Then the curtain opened, the lights illuminating the audience. Olivia was standing on a bale of hay, holding a star in one hand and scratching her halo with the other. David was leaning on the manger until his teacher motioned with a smile from the edge of the stage for him to stand up straight. There were other children on the stage, but Carrie hadn't noticed any of them because she was too busy taking in the sight of the Fletcher children.

She'd already become so attached. Olivia's feet were tapping in place, and Carrie smiled, knowing that she wanted to spin circles or dance—she needed movement. And David was so clearly anxious about his part, he had hardly moved other than to take his hand off the manger.

The children began to sing "Away in a Manger," one of them singing too loudly, but Olivia, who had been fidgety the whole time, became still and focused as she sang. Carrie hadn't known that about her, and she thought how she should incorporate more music into her day. David was singing, but his lips were barely moving, his eyes on the floor. Immediately, her mind went to what she would do for David while Olivia was given more time with music. Then it hit her: she wouldn't be with them much longer, yet she was mentally planning as if she were their full-time nanny. David took the hand of a little girl who was dressed like Mary, and walked with her to the center of the stage to greet the Wise Men, and Carrie had to blink to keep the tears at bay. She would definitely miss this family.

"A king is born!" Olivia said while scratching her head again, the halo moving to the side.

Walter chuckled beside her, and Carrie smiled too through her blurring eyes. Refocusing on Olivia and David as they told the story gave her calm, and as they sang, she tried to forget about leaving.

David struggled with his lines a bit, his nerves clearly getting the better of him, while Olivia was a complete ham most of the time. Carrie wished she could be their full-time nanny, but even if she could, they'd be going to kindergarten next year, and they wouldn't need her anymore. She focused on the kids for the rest of the show and tried not to think about it.

At the end of the show, the lights came on, revealing the large, airy sanctuary.

Adam turned to Carrie. "That was fantastic."

She nodded.

He stood up along with the crowd and she followed suit. The other couple congregated with Adam in the aisle while those from the surrounding rows filtered around them easily, Walter working to get through the chairs and Joyce right behind him pushing them all back just a little for him.

Adam placed his hand lightly on Carrie's arm and led her to the couple from his work as the others came up behind to join them. "I'd like to introduce my nanny and friend, Carrie Blake."

They nodded politely.

"This"—Adam tipped his head to the man with the dark hair—"is Robert Marley, my good friend and the man who is helping me greatly with acquiring property for the expansion."

Robert held out his hand in greeting. He had a firm, businesslike handshake, but there was something quite friendly about him as well.

"And I'd like you to meet Robert's wife, Allie. Their daughter, Carolyn, was the angel standing next to Olivia."

It all made sense now. She'd seen Allie leaning forward when Carolyn had said her lines. The look on Allie's face, she'd noticed, was an outward expression of the way Carrie felt watching the Fletcher children. "It's nice to meet you," she said to Allie.

"Likewise." Allie offered a warm, genuine smile. "I was a nanny for years!"

"Really?"

"Yes. I run a preschool now."

Carrie couldn't help but be excited to find someone else who understood her line of work. "That's fantastic," she said. And it really was. Allie had a likeable demeanor. Carrie could almost picture her cross-legged on the floor, making funny voices while she read stories to the children. "Have you been with the Fletchers long?" she asked.

Carrie shook her head, the dread of leaving them flooding her again.

"I'd love to share nanny stories...You should come to our Christmas party!" Allie looked over at Adam.

This was the first Carrie had heard of a Christmas party. Had Adam planned on going?

"Bring her along, Adam. I'd love to have a chance for some good conversation!" she said.

Adam made eye contact with Carrie, uncertainty written on his face. Did he not want her to go? Was he worried she wouldn't fit in?

"It's a Marley tradition. I remember going to my first Christmas party at Ashford before I married Robert," Allie said. "It was not something I'll ever forget. It's so much fun! She'd love it," Allie said to Adam.

"I'd be happy to take you," Adam said, looking at Carrie, a small grin on his lips.

Allie looked positively delighted. "Oh, that's fantastic! I can't wait to see you two!"

One of the Sunday school teachers came up behind them, carrying Carolyn on her hip, with David and Olivia on either side of her. "Hello," she said, handing Carolyn to Robert. Carolyn's white dress fluffed out over Robert's arms, completely obscuring them as he held her. "I think these kiddos belong to you all." She smiled.

Carolyn couldn't have been more than three. She had dark hair like her father and her mother's smile. "Hi, Daddy," she said, putting her hands on Robert's cheeks and pressing her forehead to his.

He kissed her cheek. Carolyn rested her head on his shoulder, her sleepy eyes on Carrie.

Carrie wished the Fletcher children could have that kind of closeness with their father. If only time were on Carrie's side. She had so much she wanted to do with Adam and his children. Not to mention, she wanted more time with Adam himself.

"I'm heating a ham in the oven, y'all," Joyce said, once they were all back at home and settled after the Christmas play. She came up behind Carrie in the hallway and put her arm around her shoulders to offer a little squeeze. Carrie enjoyed Joyce so much.

The other men had already headed into the kitchen, leaving Adam and his mother still standing in the hallway, and Sharon was on the bottom step.

"I think I might have a rest," Sharon said, starting up the staircase. Carrie noticed Joyce's concern, the way her face dropped from her cheery expression to one of worry. Carrie could only speculate how hard tonight must have been for Sharon, given her circumstances.

"Are you okay?" she asked Sharon.

"I'm fine."

Carrie could tell that it was the kind of "fine" that meant, *I'm the same as I've been and nothing can help*, but she wanted to ease whatever it was that Sharon was feeling somehow. Maybe she could just be there for her. Sharon headed upstairs, and Carrie decided that she'd pop in and check on her once she went up herself.

Olivia, who'd become restless as she'd stood by them, joined hands with Joyce and Carrie, trying to swing between them and pulling the two women toward each other while a sleepy David sat on the bottom step, rubbing his eyes.

"I'd like to put the kids to bed tonight, if that's okay," Joyce said to Adam. "I never have a chance to do that, and it's been a long time since I've been able to read bedtime stories. I miss it."

Adam squatted down in front of the children. "That okay with you two?" he asked.

"Yes, Daddy," Olivia said, leaning in to her grandmother.

"I really enjoyed watching you two tonight," Adam told the kids. "David, you did a great job." David's chest puffed out in pride. "And Olivia, your singing was beautiful." Carrie couldn't believe what she was witnessing. Adam's voice soft, his eyes curious as he looked at his children. It had been unprompted, uncoached.

Olivia put her arms around his neck. "Thank you, Daddy," she said.

He smiled again at her, his face so tender, so sweet. When Olivia let go, he turned to David, picked him up, and set him on his knee. "How did you learn all those lines?" he asked. "Did you practice with your mom?"

"A little. I practiced with my teacher."

"Well, you were awesome."

David's smile took over his whole face, the dimple on his cheek emerging, and he hugged his dad. When he did, Adam closed his eyes, taking it in. Carrie felt as though her heart would burst. In this moment, Adam was feeling what it was like to be a father. He'd initiated this moment himself, and the kids responded to his love and attention. It was the best thing she'd seen in a long time.

He stood up. "I suppose I should let you get them to bed," he said to Joyce.

Joyce smiled with pride at her son and took the two children by their hands. "Tell your daddy goodnight," she said, her voice a little broken. The kids both said goodnight as they walked upstairs. She wanted to grab his hands, hold them, kiss his lips. When he let his soft side show, like he had just now with the children, he was so attractive to her that she could hardly keep herself in check. With that tiny gesture—just talking to his children like he had—he'd filled her with hope.

There was a loaded silence between them. Finally, he said, "Want to go into the kitchen with everyone? I think I hear Gramps at the table. He probably has a game going." He smiled, his expression still gentle like it had been with the children. She didn't want to leave him, but she wanted to check on Sharon. Sharon was always apart from them, always isolated.

"I'm just going to change into something comfortable first," she said.

Adam nodded. "I have to pop into my office anyway. I'll be back in a few."

With resolve, she left him and went upstairs to check on Adam's sister. She knocked quietly and peeked into Sharon's room. Sharon gestured for Carrie to come in.

Carrie wasn't sure how to start a conversation with Sharon, and she really didn't even know what she would say. She just wanted to give Sharon a chance to speak her mind and get some of the load off her chest.

"I just wanted to check in and see how you're doing."

There was a long pause as Sharon toyed with her fingers, running her nail along the cuticle of her other hand. "You know, Adam was my best friend growing up," she said without warning.

In that instant, she was glad that she'd come to talk to Sharon tonight. It was clear now that she wanted to talk to someone. Carrie waited until Sharon continued.

"We did everything together. We were inseparable. He's such a gentle soul—he gets hurt so easily. You'd never know it, but beneath that controlled exterior, he's the most kindhearted, mild-mannered person I know."

She didn't have to imagine it. Carrie had seen it right before her eyes tonight.

"When his marriage was over, he was devastated. I felt terrible for him. But instead of turning to us, he turned to work. He pushed all of us away—including his kids. I can't have kids of my own. We've done all we can do, and nothing has worked. Adam *has* the blessing of children. He has an entire family who love him. For God's sake, we all came to his house for Christmas to try to get him to see that, but all he wants to do is work. He's taking everything he has for granted—all for that stupid brewery. I wish he'd see that he has everything *I've* ever wanted, and he's blowing it. When it comes to living life, he's doing it all wrong. And I miss him. I miss him so much."

"I'm trying to make him see it your way," Carrie said. "I think the same thing that you do. And sometimes, Sharon, I think he's getting it, but then he turns right around and does something to the contrary. But"—she held up a finger to drive the point home—"I saw a glimpse of what he was capable of tonight. He talked to the children after you went upstairs. It was a baby step, I know, but it was amazing."

"But will it continue? He's off work tonight, and he doesn't have to choose. I have a sinking feeling that when he has to decide between work and the kids, he'll choose work." Sharon shook her head. "He makes me so mad that I didn't want to be here. It's only for Mom's sake that I ever come out of the room at all. Mom convinced me to come. I tried to tell her that it wouldn't change things, but she's always so optimistic."

"I'm so sorry about what you're going through," Carrie said. "I suppose I'm a little optimistic too. I thought I could change him."

For the first time since she'd arrived, Sharon smiled. It had been a long time since Carrie had had a girlfriend to chat with.

She felt a strange sort of bond with Sharon now. "Would you like to go downstairs with me? We can be a united front." She grinned. Sharon stood up and walked with her to the door. She shook her head knowingly at Carrie. Together, they headed downstairs.

Chapter Twenty-One

Pay attention to every life event and explicitly internalize what you'd choose to remember about that event.

"I'm the only one who can beat Gramps," Adam said, his mouth turning upward into a playful grin that reached his eyes. Adam sat down next to Sharon as Walter dealt Carrie a hand. Carrie fanned out her cards and then concealed them by turning them over on the table.

Adam hadn't checked his phone once during the play, he'd had a heartfelt conversation with his children after, and now he was playing cards. Carrie could hardly contain her excitement.

"*You* can beat Walter?" Carrie asked.

"Well," Walter said, making a bridge with the cards and letting them cascade down into a perfect pile on the table. "Now I finally have a little competition." He winked at Adam.

Bruce stood up. "How many beers do we need?" he asked.

"Carrie?" Bruce said, and she realized that she'd gotten lost in her own thoughts. She was worrying for Adam and Sharon, wishing they could resolve their differences, wondering how long it had been since they'd sat next to each other and shared anything at all.

"Yes, please," she said in response to the encouraging smile she received from Adam.

As Bruce got the beers, Walter continued the game. "Ace is low," he said. Then he set the deck in the center of the table. "We'll start with Adam. Let's give him a running start before I take over for the win."

"You'd better shuffle that deck a little more when I'm at the table," he said, chewing on a smile.

"Oh, here we go," Sharon said with an eye roll. "Do you know how long I've been hearing this sort of competition between these two?" She had loosened up a bit seeing her brother join them at the table. It really seemed like Adam was trying, and maybe Sharon could sense that.

Bruce opened the beers and set them in front of each person as Carrie studied her cards. The game was much more difficult to play with Adam near her. She took in his hands when he reached for his beer, how the bottle set against his lips as he took a swig, the way he leaned back casually in his chair. She wanted to focus, but his presence was making it tricky. Before she knew it, she'd played most of her cards and nearly finished her beer.

Adam, who could easily peek over and view Sharon's cards, allowed his gaze to shift to Sharon's hand as he leaned back in his chair. It was subtle, but Carrie could see him thinking. He set down a run and, as he did, Sharon perked up, her shoulders rising in interest, and Carrie knew by his face what he'd done: Adam had just helped his sister win the game. When her turn came around, Sharon added her two cards to Adam's run, and smiled—a big, happy smile.

Walter tossed his cards onto the table in mock annoyance. Then he pointed to Adam, who had three cards remaining. "Ha! She got you!" he said. But as they were dropping their cards onto the table to clean up, Carrie noticed that Adam's cards were a perfect run. He'd held on to them on purpose. He could've won, but he chose to help Sharon win instead.

Adam caught Carrie looking at the cards, and smiled sheepishly. He locked eyes with her and she couldn't look away. It caused a rush of excitement so strong that the hair on her arms stood up. She wondered if anyone else noticed how long they'd been looking at each other, or the smile twitching around his lips. It was almost like he wanted to tell her something, like someone with a secret that it was almost killing him to keep quiet.

He finally pulled his eyes from her, but only because Olivia was standing in the doorway. She had on the white nightgown with pink roses, her bare ankles and feet peeking out from beneath. Her hair was down with strands puffed out in every direction. She rubbed her eye with the same hand that held her blanket. "I had a bad dream," she said to her daddy. "Can Carrie lie down with me?"

Carrie worried. In front of his whole family, Olivia had asked her father for the nanny to put her back to bed. While in a healthy family situation this may have been a normal occurrence, in this instance she knew what it implied, and it made her concerned for Adam.

"I don't mind if your daddy puts you to bed tonight. It would be okay with me," Carrie offered from her spot at the table, trying to improve the situation.

Olivia padded over to Carrie and crawled up onto her lap, her pink blanket trailing down to the floor. "But I want you to put me to bed. Not Daddy." Carrie knew that even though Adam had given a little of himself tonight, it couldn't change everything right away. Olivia had had a bad dream. She wanted someone she knew could comfort her, and her father had never been that person.

The silence in the room was palpable. Carrie didn't want Adam to pull back after he'd come so far. He'd been positively happy tonight, and she didn't want anything to ruin it. She felt his loss of face in front of his family.

Carrie took in a deep breath to clear her mind. Once again, she had to go with her instincts. "I really like talking to your daddy," she said carefully. "Do you think he could come with us? For me?" She waited on pins and needles, hoping that Olivia would answer favorably. One never knew with children because they weren't interested in the social delicacy of the situation, answering honestly. Carrie was relying on Olivia's natural sociability here.

"Okay," she said, pushing herself off Carrie's lap. She hopped down and took her hand. Then Olivia took Adam's hand as well. Carrie glanced back at the table to get the family's reaction. Had she done the right thing? Everyone seemed pleased, with Joyce and Sharon smiling the biggest of all. Carrie could feel the tension lift right off her shoulders as the two of them walked Olivia upstairs to her room.

Chapter Twenty-Two

Be in the moment.

"What do you like to talk about with Daddy?" Olivia asked Carrie, crawling under her blankets as Adam pulled them up for her.

Adam was quietly listening. Perhaps Carrie's answer was as interesting to him as it was to Olivia. He sat down on the foot of her bed, and Carrie kneeled down beside her.

"Oh, anything, really." She smiled in Adam's direction. "Do you know what he's great at doing?" Carrie asked with mock enthusiasm.

"Making beer!" Olivia said a little too loudly, clearly proud that she knew the answer.

Carrie and Adam both burst out laughing at the same time, and Carrie had to cover her mouth to keep the sound from traveling down the hallway.

Carrie nodded, still grinning. "That's true. But do you know what else he's good at?"

"No." Olivia looked over at her daddy, her eyes droopy from lack of sleep.

"He's great at reading stories." Adam showed his surprise but then contorted his features to a smile for Olivia. Okay, she'd lied just a little, but it was the perfect opportunity to get him involved, really involved, with no work demands. "Can we find a story?"

Olivia extended a tiny finger toward her bookshelf. "How about that one, the princess one?"

Carrie pulled a paperback off the shelf and handed it to Adam. He lay down on top of the covers next to Olivia and opened the book as Carrie sat down on the floor next to him. She was so close to his face that she could see the tiny lines at the corners of his eyes, the slight stubble that revealed itself at the end of every day, the way his chest moved up and down with his breath. He started reading, the words coming out, but Carrie didn't comprehend them. She was too busy thinking about him. She noticed how small the book looked in his strong hands and the way he had to hold his thumbs to the side so they didn't cover the pictures. His words were finally floating into her consciousness, and she realized that he was quite a natural at reading to children. Olivia snuggled into his side.

When he got to the last page, Adam kept his body still, turning only his head as he looked at his daughter. Olivia was asleep. Her head rested on his bicep, and her limbs were wrapped around his arm. Gently, he kissed the top of her head. It was such a small gesture, but the impact of it caused a lump in Carrie's throat. He turned to her, their faces too close. He seemed to be considering something, deliberating. She became woozy from the thrill of the moment.

"How do I get up?" he mouthed.

Carefully, she leaned over Adam and gently unwrapped one of Olivia's arms from him. When she did, she could feel the warmth of his body underneath her, the presence of him assaulting her senses. She tried not to let it get the best of her as she slid her hand between Olivia's cheek and Adam's arm and gently scooted Olivia onto her pillow. Carrie's hair brushed Adam's face by accident, and, with his free hand, he scratched the scruff on his chin and then pushed her hair away. When he did, he held the strands of hair between his two fingers for a moment and she almost couldn't breathe.

Olivia was safely on her pillow and Adam slid off the bed, standing up and facing Carrie. He looked at her differently. She'd never seen that expression before, and it made her feel elated and terrified and relieved all at the same time. It looked to her like he felt something for her, like he might even want to kiss her, which scared her to death. Was she completely off base? If so, what was he trying to tell her?

She made eye contact in an attempt to tell him in their new unspoken language that she welcomed whatever he was thinking. He took a step closer to her, their proximity causing him to look down at her now. He leaned forward an infinitesimal amount, just enough to make the gesture noticeable. It was as if he were testing the waters. She wanted to grab him by the waistband of his trousers and pull him to her, kiss him, but she didn't know what she was supposed to do. What was a first kiss supposed to be like with someone like him? All the thoughts were racing inside her mind, flying back and forth, making it hard to focus on any one thing. She felt her hands begin to tremble; her breath became shallow. Adam reached out and touched her arm, sending shivers right up her spine.

There was a creak of the door hinges, and both of them nearly jumped away from each other. David was standing in the doorway, a groggy look on his face. Carrie rushed forward and ushered him into the hallway, Adam following behind, closing the door to Olivia's room.

"I heard Olivia," he said. "I tried to go back to sleep but then I heard Daddy." They entered his room and David crawled back into bed. "Will you read to me too, Daddy?" David was already closing his eyes, snuggling down into his pillow. Adam pulled a book off his shelf and sat down next to him. David was asleep before the third page, but Adam continued to read until the entire book was finished.

Carrie took in slow, steady breaths to try to calm the emotions that had been stirred up in Olivia's room. If they'd had a moment at all, it had clearly passed when he stood up this time. She mentally scrambled for a way to keep him from going downstairs. She didn't want to have to mingle with his family when she was in this state of mind. She wouldn't be able to think of anything other than the few precious moments she'd just spent with Adam. Then she remembered! When they got to the hallway, she whispered, "We still have to wrap the Christmas presents. While we're upstairs, and we know the kids are asleep, should we wrap some of them?"

It was almost as if he sensed her motives because he responded with a slow nod, his eyes moving around her face. Then he put his hand on the small of her back and led her down the hallway.

"The presents are in the closet in my bedroom," he whispered as they walked.

She had to work to focus on his words because all she could process was the warmth of his hand on her back. She tried to rationalize the moments they'd had tonight, thinking that there must be some explanation for them, something other than what she was feeling, because that wouldn't make any sense.

When they came to a stop, she realized that she was about to enter his bedroom. She'd never been in it before. The cleaning lady always took care of everything in there, so Carrie had no reason to go in at all. There was something so personal about the place where Adam slept, where he closed his eyes and became vulnerable to everything around him.

The bed was king-sized, sleek, stained in a mahogany color, the crisp white duvet and shams standing out like snow against the blue-gray walls surrounding them. Carrie pictured what it would be like under that fluffy cover, her head sinking into the down pillow… She turned away from the bed to rid her mind of the thoughts and found herself directly in front of Adam. He looked down at her, a very slight smile on his lips.

"I set the bags over there," he said, pointing to a leather armchair in the corner. The chair's surface was nearly hidden from the colossal pile of bags. She'd been with Adam as he'd purchased everything in them down to the red wrapping paper and silver ribbons.

"Do we have tape and scissors?" she asked, using all her inner strength to keep her focus on the presents. She wanted to look back at Adam to see what else he had to say in the silent language they'd created tonight. She wanted to feel his eyes on her, to see that smile, but she kept her eyes on the bags, rummaging around inside them and pretending to be interested in them.

"I'll go get some," Adam said.

After he left, she allowed herself to look around the room once more. She thought how the house was so huge, so perfectly decorated that it almost seemed to be in juxtaposition to Adam. He was refined and slightly formal, but underneath that, when she thought about where he'd come from—that small town in North Carolina—the fact that he was a beer maker, how he'd played sports as a kid—it all seemed too laid-back for a place like this.

Carrie pondered the type of house she'd like to have once she'd found her career and settled in one spot. There'd be a long front porch—the kind she'd had as a kid, a place where she could count the imperfections in the wooden steps from all the years of little feet, bikes, and toys hitting them. Her house would have an oak tree with a swing and a patch underneath where the grass wouldn't grow because the children had scraped away the last of the seed, swinging on the warm days until sunset. She'd have a giant wood-burning fireplace inside for roasting marshmallows and warming sock feet, and she'd have an old sofa with her basket of quilts that her grandmother had made nearby for wrapping up on cold days. She wondered if Adam had ever thought about that kind of house before.

"Will these do?" he said, upon return, standing in the doorway. He held out a roll of tape and a small pair of scissors. "They were in my office. I have more in the kitchen if you need it."

"That's fine," she said.

He walked in and sat on the floor next to her as she unrolled a long, wide piece of red wrapping paper. "What were you thinking about just now? You looked very serious."

She sat silently, unsure of what to say. She didn't want to tell him, for obvious reasons. She tried to find a polite way to put her thoughts into words. "I was just wondering what your favorite part of this house is." It wasn't entirely on the mark, but she had been thinking about her own favorite parts of the home she'd like to have one day.

Carrie slid the scissors along the inside of the paper, cutting a perfect line, the paper falling loose from the roll in her hands.

The skin between his eyes wrinkled in thought. "I don't know, honestly. I've never thought about it."

"Surely there was something that made you buy it," she pressed.

"Gwen and I picked it out together."

Carrie reached into one of the bags and pulled out Olivia's crown. She set it in the center of the large rectangle of wrapping paper. "So, if you could build your own house, what would it look like?"

"I don't know."

Carrie gestured for him to put his finger on the present to keep the paper from slipping as she taped it down.

He put his finger on the top, holding it in place. "As long as it has a desk…"

"…that turns into a card table," she said, finishing his sentence.

He huffed out a laugh, his eyes on her. When his laughter had gone, his smile remained. He watched her as she wrapped the presents. Being with him made her happy, content. When she was finally done, she surveyed the pile of red, shiny presents, and she wished suddenly that she had something to give him, but she had no idea what she could possibly give him that he didn't already have.

Chapter Twenty-Three

Life events can't always be planned. Take each one as it comes and keep focus on your inner happiness.

Other than a quick peek or two into his office and during meals, Carrie had barely seen Adam in over a day. Adam, who wasn't supposed to be working, had spent the whole of yesterday in his office while Carrie and the family stayed with the kids. It was a very odd change of events after their present-wrapping. Usually, she would have been annoyed that he wasn't with his family, but there was something different about him as he worked yesterday. When he passed them in the hallways, he smiled, his face pleasant, which was different than other days he'd worked like that. At lunch, he'd taken a long time to sit with them, but then he was off again after.

Today, he'd had some sort of crack-of-dawn emergency call regarding one of the properties in his expansion—he'd said he had to tie up some loose ends very quickly—and Carrie thought it might be a good idea to take the kids outside to keep the house quiet until he was finished. She had a small sled in the trunk of her car that she'd bought for snowy days when they'd run out of things to do. This would be a perfect activity to keep the kids and their noise out of the house while Adam took his call this morning. Carrie worked quickly to bundle the children so they wouldn't disturb Adam and the rest of his sleeping family. With one last mitten, she'd dressed the twins, and she opened the door.

It was eerily quiet outside—no birds, no cars—just the sound of the wind in her ears. Carrie could feel the sting of it on her cheeks as she trudged through the thick, freshly fallen snow with the children in tow. They could barely walk in it, it was so deep, so Carrie asked them to try and walk inside her footsteps to keep them from falling. When she reached her car, she slipped the key in the lock on the trunk and popped it open. Then she grabbed the red and gold sled with two rope handles and a long rope for pulling and dropped it into the snow. When she shut the trunk, the kids were already climbing on.

Both of them could barely fit on it together, their limbs intertwining as they attempted to get comfortable in all their clothes. Carrie surveyed the area. There wasn't a hill in sight, but the road was packed down more than the yard, and with no cars anywhere. She could probably pull them along the street, maybe run in circles, swinging them gently around. With her mittened hands, Carrie grabbed the rope and began to pull. It took all her might to get the kids to the road, and by the time she got there, she was tired. The kids were giggling and scooting, trying to get it to move more as Carrie struggled to pull it. If only a plow would come by and move some of it. Her hair was itching her icy face from under her stocking cap as she tried unsuccessfully to alleviate the itch with her mittens.

"I think you two are too heavy for all this snow," she said. "I can hardly pull you."

"Come on, Carrie!" Olivia said. "We're not *that* heavy."

Carrie pulled with all her might and they moved a few paces before the sled piled up too much snow in front of it and got stuck.

"We need someone stronger," she said. "Perhaps when Eric wakes up, he can pull you," she said, feeling defeated. She didn't want to take them inside, and she didn't want to have to stop sledding. Disappointment was clear on both their faces, so she tugged again with barely any headway. Carrie stood for a minute to catch her breath, new flakes beginning to fall around her.

Then the sound of the front door as it shut made its way through the silence to the street, and she turned around. Adam was on the landing, wearing a dark ski coat, jeans, and boots. He had on a stocking cap and gloves. "Do you need help with that sled?" he asked as he made his way to the street. Carrie watched him, worried that she'd interrupted his work with her ridiculous sledding idea, but he was smiling, which was a good sign. He addressed the children. "May I pull you two? It looks like too much fun not to join in."

"Yay, Daddy!" Olivia was bouncing on her bottom on the sled, David showing his slight irritation at being jostled. "Pull us, Daddy!" Olivia squealed.

Adam grabbed the end of the rope with his gloved hand, and, taking long, wide strides, he began to pull. The sled was difficult at first, but once he got it going, it was sailing along the street. Adam ran all the way down to the end and back, the kids' laughter and the shushing of the sled the only sounds in all that snow. Carrie, who'd started to get cold, didn't notice it anymore. She was warm with the sight of what was in front of her. Surely he was getting tired, but he kept going, as if he were powered by the laughter of his children. As she watched him, Carrie's emotions bubbled up inside, and she blinked to keep the tears from spilling over. He was making a memory for these kids. As adults, one day, the children would tell their own kids about the giant snowstorm in Richmond when their daddy pulled them on the sled all the way down the street and back. She just knew it.

Adam brought the sled to a stop in front of her. "Pull Carrie, Daddy!" Olivia said.

Adam looked over as if waiting for an answer, his cheeks bright red from running and the icy air.

"Oh, I don't think so," Carrie said with a little laugh, "but thank you for offering, Olivia."

"Why not?" Adam asked.

Carrie could hardly conceal her shock. He didn't really want to pull her on the sled, did he? "You're busy, I'm sure. Thank you for pulling the children."

"Get on." He nodded toward the sled, and the flirty look on his face made her hands start to shake. The kids hopped off and stood next to her.

"No, I can't."

"Get on!" Olivia pressed.

"It's for the children," Adam said.

"Go on," David said.

Carrie climbed onto the sled, crossed her legs, and held on to the rope handles. Adam laughed, and she couldn't help it, she laughed too. It was silly being on that sled, but she was so happy to be there at the same time.

Adam wrapped the rope around his gloved hand, getting leverage. Then, with a hard tug, he got her going, and she was flying down the street, the wind fighting against her cap, blowing her hair back over her shoulders, and pushing its way under her scarf. A squeal rose up as she started to turn, the runner of the sled coming off the ground. Adam hadn't pulled the children this fast. The wind was like knives on her cheeks, the snow getting into her eyes, but she hardly noticed. She was too preoccupied with the thought of Adam pulling her on this sled. Then, faster than she could process it—as if it were in slow motion—she saw his foot go down into a snow-covered ditch, and she watched in panic as he started to fall. The sled was going so fast, she couldn't stop it, her legs stretching out in a vain attempt to do something. Before she knew it, she'd slid right into him, toppling over and landing on his stomach. She was face to face with Adam Fletcher.

"Are you okay?" she asked, winded.

"Yeah," he laughed. "That's what I get for trying to show off."

Carrie was glad that her cheeks were already red because she could feel them blushing. Adam was showing off. For her? That couldn't be. Then she realized that he must have meant that he was showing off for the kids. It was the only rational explanation. She wriggled around until she could get enough footing in the snow to stand. When she felt secure enough, she held out her hand to help him up. He had snow all down his back, on his jeans, in his hair.

"Should we all go in and warm up by the fire?" he asked. The kids, clearly worried about their father, nodded.

"Are you okay, Daddy?" David asked.

"I'm fine!" he said, brushing himself off. "That was fun."

Joyce had offered to watch the kids during the afternoon. The Marleys' party was tonight, and Carrie had to have a dress. She slipped on the dark green, floor-length silk gown she'd bought at a boutique in town. The snow from that morning had hardly let up, making her trip to the shop treacherous, but nothing was getting in the way of her evening with Adam. He'd insisted on paying for the dress since Allie had invited her to the Ashford Estate, and she really hadn't had much choice in the matter. What she hadn't told him was that she wasn't doing anyone a favor by going; she was thrilled to go.

She looked at her reflection in the mirror. The lace overlay at the top was more revealing than anything she'd ever worn before, the fabric coming down in a low V on her chest. She'd done her makeup tonight, but she'd kept it simple so as not to overwhelm the dress. With a tiny wobble, she slipped on the green heels she'd found to match.

The memory of Adam sledding surfaced the whole time she was getting ready. He had changed so much in such a short time. Even though he'd worked yesterday when he was supposed to be off, and he'd had a call to make this morning, he'd made sure to get the kids settled in front of the fire, and he'd even gone and gotten them a blanket before he left. He'd spent a little time chatting with his family, and to her joy, Joyce had asked if she could take the children to see Santa, and he'd said that he'd like to go too. She finally felt comfortable talking to him about the children, but tonight, she'd test the limits of her level of security with herself because she was about to spend the evening with just him—no kids. The idea of it made her more nervous than she could mentally manage, so she focused on the task at hand: getting ready.

She had twisted her hair up to highlight her ruby earrings. They were the perfect Christmas complement to her green dress. She'd never worn anything that elegant before, and she wanted to show off Adam's generosity. She'd learned to style hair when she'd nannied for Claire, who had to have her hair up for dance recitals. She was pleasantly surprised at the way the style had turned out. Standing in front of the full-length mirror, the toes of her dark green heels peeking out from under the satin and lace dress that fit her like a glove, she barely recognized herself.

There were three quiet taps at her door. Carrie took one last look in the mirror and walked over to open it. When she did, Adam was standing in the doorway, wearing a tuxedo. She just knew her heartbeat was probably showing through her dress. After she'd scrambled to calm herself enough to focus on his face, she realized that he looked the same way she felt. His lips were parted as if he were going to say something, his eyes taking in the sight of her from her new shoes up to her hair, but he was silent.

Then the smile. "You look positively radiant," he said. She'd never heard anyone call her radiant, but it came off his lips effortlessly, and she could tell he'd meant it. "Shall we head to the party? I've already got the car running."

He held out his arm, and she linked hers in his, ready to see what the night would hold.

"You don't have to be nervous," Adam said, his eyes darting over to her as he drove them through the snow, down the winding roads that stretched out beyond the city. Now she felt like she needed to be nervous just because he'd said that. She folded her hands in her lap as a precaution in case they started to shake. "The Marleys live in a house that is so big it has its own name. It's called the Ashford Estate. But Robert is more down to earth than anyone you'll ever meet."

The party was about twenty minutes' drive out of the city. They'd passed acres of farmland—mostly horse farms and cornfields—and then, out of nowhere, sitting atop a hill, she saw it: the Ashford

Estate. It was a gigantic brick home, with so many windows across the front that she was sure she'd lose count before they'd parked the car. While Adam's home was old—probably built in the nineteen twenties—this was something completely different. It looked like it had been built well before the turn of the last century. It had a sprawling staircase with a half circle drive in front. The drive was full of luxury vehicles—Cadillac, Mercedes, Range Rover—more than she could mentally label. And now there was a BMW. They pulled to a stop and got out.

"They have great parties here," he said. "They used to be on Christmas Eve every year, but since we all have kids, Allie convinced Robert to make it on a different night. Their party favors will blow you away," he said as he held her car door open for her and offered his hand.

Adam helped her out of the car and shut the door. Carrie lifted her dress so as not to let the hem drag on the snowy ground, but once she was around the other side of the car, she saw there was a bright red carpet that stretched from the drive all the way up the stairs and to the front door, where it was anchored by a massive display of poinsettias on each side. They passed tree after tree of white lights; it looked like every tree on the entire property had been decorated with them. When they got to the staircase, she noticed that the railings and the base of all of the windows had been decorated in live greenery with red sashes intertwined.

"What kind of party favors?" she asked, trying to make conversation so she'd feel like this was all normal somehow.

"Last year, we all got a two-hundred-dollar bottle of wine."

When he'd said *party favors*, she was thinking maybe a small bag of chocolates or a noisemaker. Not an incredibly expensive bottle of wine! She let her eyes trace the brick all the way up to the roof and the four chimneys protruding from it. The house, with its giant wings on either side of the main building that stretched the length of the property, had to have an army of a staff to run it. It was absolutely huge. Adam rang the doorbell, and it sounded like musical chimes.

A man in a tuxedo let them in and closed the massive door behind them. Carrie looked around the space, realizing that they weren't in a room but an entranceway the size of a room. An enormous glass chandelier, bigger than one of those fancy cars outside, dangled above them, sending a shimmer of lights across the shiny floor. Everything felt like a dream as the holiday music poured through the speakers, men with silver trays offered champagne and strawberries, others with platters of canapés. Then she saw Allie coming toward her. She looked absolutely glowing, her brown hair swept up, with simple teardrop earrings to match her dress that was the same color as her hazel eyes. It had a low scoop neck, and it gathered in an empire waist above her pregnant belly.

"Hello!" she greeted them, grabbing two flutes of champagne from one of the waiters and handing them to Carrie and Adam. "I'm happy you two could come!" She offered Carrie a big, genuine smile. "I'm so glad I get to see you again," she said. "I'd love to chat nanny stories later on." There was a buzz of an amplifier and then a few chords. "Oh! The band's about to play," she said, leading them into a living room that was the size of a ballroom.

There was a fire going at one end, and the band was setting up in the corner next to it. At the other end of the room, a Christmas tree stretched to the ceiling. It was at least two stories high. The room was full of people dressed in fine clothes, and Carrie was glad to have someone like Allie there, who could make her feel like she belonged.

"I'm just going to find Robert," Allie said over the music. "Make yourselves at home. Dance!"

Carrie looked up at Adam. The stress of work was gone from his face tonight and replaced by affection, the little lines showing around his eyes as they squinted just slightly with his grin when he looked at her. The band had started to play—something quiet and Christmassy. It made her feel festive, like the holiday had finally arrived. With that feeling, however, came one of dread because she didn't want it all to end. Not just the party, the whole experience. This was the most wonderful Christmas she'd had in a long time, and she knew that it would be hard to top it. She didn't want to go back to North Carolina, never seeing Adam again, or the twins, or Walter or Joyce. She didn't want to leave Adam's side at this party or have him drive her home to her quiet room. She wanted it all to last forever. She didn't know what to do because she knew exactly what made her feel whole. She just didn't know how to achieve it.

"Would you like to dance?" Adam asked.

She couldn't believe it. Allie had suggested dancing, but she'd never have guessed that he'd actually consider it. She liked it when he surprised her. The thought of his arms around her, his body close to her, made her feel unsteady in her heels. She took in a deep breath and let it out, trying to keep calm, and nodded. She wasn't sure how to deal with the situation. He was her boss. She'd only come because Allie had offered to have her. She wondered suddenly if he had wanted to bring someone like Andy, and Allie's suggestion had ruined his plan. Andy would've been a more natural fit for something like this. She pushed the thought out of her mind.

Couples had filtered in near the band in an area that had been cleared for dancing, and they walked over to join the crowd. Adam took Carrie's champagne and set it with his on a nearby table. Then he reached for her and put his arm around her waist. She tried to breathe slowly so he couldn't feel how her breath had sped up. She took in the gentle way his fingers wrapped around hers, the feel of his hand, and it felt like a perfect fit. When his arm was around her, it made her feel shielded, protected from all her insecurities. Their feet moved slowly to the music, her dress swaying around her ankles, and she took in this moment, knowing it would be top on her list of favorite moments for a very long time.

Unsure of where to let her gaze fall, she looked up at him, and her breath caught. He was looking right at her. Just like the waves on the beach in the summer, she pulled back, but there was a force beyond her control pulling her toward him. His eyes were unwavering, certain. As the music played around her, she could feel the magnitude of the moment. Was he going to kiss her? Before she could find out, the song ended, and he pulled away.

Carrie followed him off the dance floor over to the fire, the burning embers giving a homey smell to the large room. Had she imagined the chemistry between them? He was turned away from her, still holding her hand, leading her closer to the fire. She didn't need its warmth; being with him warmed her quite enough. She'd definitely crossed over the professional-personal line. Perhaps it was the way she felt in that dress, all made up, as if she belonged with someone like Adam. Perhaps it was the magic in the air at such a lavish party as this. Whatever it was, it had left her feeling like it could all really happen. She tried to ground herself in reality, but it was hard to do that with everything around her. But before she could ponder it any further, Allie and Robert were walking toward them.

"Found him!" Allie said with a smile.

Adam grabbed their drinks from the table and handed Carrie hers. She tipped it back, the bubbly liquid filling her mouth, and set it on the tray nearby. As the waiter walked past, she grabbed another.

A little boy walked up wearing a tuxedo, his hair combed perfectly to one side. "Excuse me, Uncle Robert," he said. "Have you seen Mom?"

Carrie was delighted to see a little face in this crowd of people. He looked to be around six or seven.

"No, Paul, I haven't. Give her a minute, though. She may be checking to see if Sammy can sleep with all this racket going on," Robert said. When the little boy ran off, his actions in juxtaposition with his attire, Robert explained, "That was my nephew. I'd have introduced him, but he doesn't stay still these days, as you can see. His little brother, Sammy, and our Carolyn are both asleep, but we let him stay up since he's the big boy."

"He's adorable," she said.

"Boys are definitely different than girls." Robert placed his hand on his wife's belly. "It will certainly be a change for us when we have our own."

"Boy?" Carrie said, unable to disguise her happiness.

Allie nodded, giving another loving look to her husband.

"One of each! That's fantastic."

Carrie was genuinely happy for these people, even though she barely knew them. Mixed with that happiness, however, was a sense of longing for her own family.

"Cheers to one of each," Adam said, raising his champagne in the air.

*

Robert and Allie were on the other side of the great room when Adam suggested they head home. The kids would be up early, and he said he was worried about Carrie being out so late. The icy air was frigid against Carrie's skin, which had been warmed considerably by the champagne and the fire inside. Being with Adam had been like a dream, and she didn't want to leave. She wished she could have a little longer with Adam all to herself. Before she could think anything else, Adam set the parting gift basket they'd been given at the door onto the runner leading to the half circle of a drive and looked down at her.

They were the only ones outside, the sound of the band still going in the house, the white lights twinkling in the trees. Without warning, he put his hands on her waist, pulled her to him, and, before she could process what was happening, he kissed her. At first, it was as light as a feather, and then all her thoughts were washed away as his mouth moved on hers. The taste of champagne on his lips, the feel of his unstill hands at her back, the way his hair moved through her fingers after she ran them up his neck, it felt like every kiss she'd had before this one had been completely wrong, as if she were made to fit together with him and him only. She didn't notice the cold outside or the darkness. She only felt Adam's presence, and the complete perfection of the moment.

It had all come on so suddenly, both of them lost in the moment. Just as quickly as it had happened, the realization of what was happening set in. He pulled back and looked at her, his face so calm and still that it almost made him look like a different person. She took in that picture of him, adding it to the front of her list of memories, because *that* was what he really looked like. With nothing bothering him. He smiled at her and she felt tingly all over. "We should probably get home," he said. Even though she totally disagreed, she nodded, the night coming to a magical end.

Chapter Twenty-Four

Don't dwell in the past. Every day is a new day.

Carrie hadn't seen much of Adam all morning, and she wondered what he could be doing. She was a little unsure of how to act around him, and the longer he took, the more she second-guessed whether last night had been a good idea. Had he awakened this morning regretting their kiss? She'd thought about it all night into the wee hours of the morning, and her eyes burned from lack of sleep.

All that aside, this was, after all, one of his days off, and with Christmas Eve tonight, she wanted everything to be perfect for the children. *Where could he be?* she wondered. She didn't want him to be busy with anything except his family. So when he didn't show for the big breakfast that Joyce had cooked, it troubled Carrie. Her stomach was in knots the more she waited, and when he came downstairs fully dressed—shoes, ironed clothes, and all—her stomach felt like it was full of cement. This time, however, instead of being sad and resisting the urge to plead with him, she was going to be downright angry if he went into work. He knew better. They'd had enough talk about it. Going into work on Christmas Eve would show blatant disregard for his family, she felt. Carrie consciously relaxed her shoulders, realizing they'd inched up near her ears somewhere.

"Good morning," he said to her first. She was rinsing her plate at the sink. She turned her head to address him, her hands still under the stream of water. She searched his face for any sign of how he felt seeing her, but he just looked like he normally did when he was greeting the whole family. She smiled nervously.

"Did I miss breakfast?"

She nodded.

"Have you eaten?"

She nodded again, too uncertain to speak. She was worried that he was going to let her down, upset her, that he hadn't changed, and what she feared most was that the kiss had been a mistake. She dried her hands and turned around. He was acting weird. He wasn't stressed out, yet everything about his behavior told her he was going to work. He'd spent the morning absent. He'd come downstairs at the time he normally left for work. Carrie was on pins and needles waiting for an explanation.

"Good morning," he said to Joyce and Sharon, who were wiping down the counters. Then he turned back to Carrie. "I'd like to ask you to do something for me."

"What is it?" she said.

"Would you come to the brewery with me? Bring the kids. I want to show you and the family around. Then maybe we could take the kids to see Santa."

"Oh, that would be lovely!" Joyce said from behind Carrie.

Carrie had been too stunned to speak. Adam had said he wanted to show *her* the brewery.

Joyce walked around the island and patted his arm, smiling.

"I haven't ever shown you where I work," he said to his mother, "so I thought it was about time."

"If Carrie can get the little ones around, I'll organize the big ones," Joyce said with a wink. "Have some breakfast, honey," she told Adam. Joyce looked positively thrilled. As she finished clearing the dishes, she was almost bouncing with excitement.

Carrie was still trying to process what had just happened, when Adam came up beside her, standing closer than he should. He looked down at her, warmth in his eyes, giving her a thrill like she'd never felt before. The way he was looking at her was the same way he'd looked at her last night, but there was something more dream-like about it in the daylight. She took in a breath to steady herself. He reached into the cabinet above her head and pulled out a plate.

"What time would you like to go?" she asked, trying to hide her excitement.

"As soon as everyone's ready."

Carrie pulled her car up behind the camper and put it in park. Adam had driven the adults in the camper because Walter had trouble getting in and out of the car, and the snow had piled up significantly on the curbs. She'd followed behind with the children. As she walked around the car to unbuckle the kids, she tried to keep her emotions even.

When she opened David's side, she was taken aback by what she saw. He was working diligently to unbuckle himself, his usual serious expression replaced by a huge grin, causing the dimple on his right cheek to show more than usual.

"Are you doing okay?" she asked as David fumbled with the buckles.

"Yes!" he said. "Can you get this one?"

Carrie unclipped the last buckle and David hopped out onto the icy city street, nearly losing his balance and slipping. She caught him. "Wait there on the sidewalk, please, while I get Olivia," she said, thrilled to see such excitement in David. She walked to the curb as she allowed the traffic to pass so she could open Olivia's door. Adam had parallel parked up the street since he had the large camper and needed more room and now they were all walking down the sidewalk toward Carrie's car.

"You're a very happy boy today," she said.

"I get to see Daddy's work!" David said.

Carrie unbuckled Olivia and carried her across the original cobblestones and over the snowbank to the sidewalk, setting her down easily so she didn't fall. Her tiny pink snow boots provided little traction on the ice. Carrie looked up at Shockoe Brewery. It was nestled in an old, historic area of the city. Spanning two buildings, the exterior was painted a bright white with a dark green awning above the front door. Every window had a spruce wreath with bright red bows and white twinkle lights. An oval lit sign with curly writing, saying "open," was positioned next to the door.

When the Fletchers had caught up with them, Adam walked around to the front of the group and opened the large wooden door for them to enter. The whole place oozed refinement. The hostess perked up at the sight of Adam, smiling nervously in his direction. She started thumbing through menus, but he motioned for her to hold off. The hostess immediately put the menus back and stood at attention, ready to fulfill any request he had.

The wall of glass with the brew kettle was bigger in real life than it had seemed in the pictures. An entire wall behind the hostess, opposite the front, had Salty Shockoe bottles from floor to ceiling, all kinds of different labels and sizes, arranged artistically. The tables were thick, lacquered dark wood with deep pink orchids in the center of each one. The formality of the orchids against the casual beer design was like chocolate and popcorn—sweet and salty—mirroring Adam's own personality in many ways.

David pushed forward and grabbed Adam's hand, clearly surprising Adam. The little boy was still smiling wide, his eyes darting from one side of the restaurant to the other. "Is this your work, Daddy?" he asked. Before Adam could even answer, he asked, "Where's your desk? What phone do you use?"

Adam let out a quiet burst of laughter and scooped David up into his arms. "Would you like to see my desk first?" he asked.

Carrie could barely focus on what Adam was saying because she was too busy dealing with the elation that she felt at seeing him with his little boy. David had always seemed just like his daddy to Carrie, but what she didn't know was that all he needed was to be given time with Adam doing what Adam loved to do. She'd never seen David so happy, and she'd never seen Adam so relaxed with one of his children before. They were both in their element, and no one could have planned it—not even her. Watching the two of them feed off of each other was like magic, something bigger than all the strategies she'd learned being a nanny. Carrie blinked to keep the wetness in her eyes at bay. It hit her right in the heart.

"Why don't you all go up to the bar and have a seat while I show David my desk?" Adam said, still holding David, whose thick winter jacket had caused his cheeks to become bright red in the warmth of the brewery. "Drinks are on me." Then he called to the bartender, "Can you get a pot of coffee going, Tom?"

The bartender nodded, waving them all over.

The bar and tables were still quite empty since it was barely brunch time, so Carrie helped Olivia up onto the tall stool and they all took a seat, filling the bar. Carrie let her eyes wander the substantial bar where she was sitting—its brass accents and beautiful grains. Behind the bartender, she saw more beers displayed like artwork, and she wondered if Adam had chosen the design or someone else. The colors on the labels flowed like a rainbow-colored wave from one side of the display to the other, each placement clearly meticulously thought out. Her eye caught one particular bottle, causing her to smile. It was the Christmas bottle with the holly leaves that Adam had made for her.

While they all drank their coffees and Olivia drank her milk, Tom, the bartender, was teaching her how to spin a quarter on the shiny surface of the bar. He held a quarter up on its side while Olivia flicked it, sending it spinning across the surface.

Adam returned, holding David's hand. "David just met Andy and most of the office staff," Adam said, helping David crawl up onto a bar stool and gesturing to Tom for another cup of milk. There was some sort of excitement in Adam's eyes when he'd said Andy's name, puzzling Carrie. It was a fondness, a thrill of some sort that she couldn't place.

Carrie was almost certain that she hadn't imagined the moment she'd had with Adam when they'd put the kids to bed, and she prayed that his kiss last night had been more than just the champagne and the magic of the evening. But he hadn't made any further moves. And now he had that odd look on his face.

Adam asked everyone to grab their drinks and follow him to an empty table with enough seats to accommodate everyone. They all sat down, Carrie holding her coffee mug with two hands, pretending to keep warm but really hiding the jitters that had come out of the blue just now. Adam sat down in the empty seat beside her.

Olivia crawled onto Adam's lap, facing him, the lights from the enormous tree in the corner casting a golden shine on the waves in her hair. Olivia was so small that she could crisscross her legs and still fit on Adam's lap. Adam seemed less confident with Olivia than he had with David; he looked as though he were worried he'd break her. He gently held her hands as she wriggled herself into a comfortable position.

"I'm going to paint your face," she said, holding one finger in the air with imaginary paint on it. "Close your eyes, Daddy." Adam looked around at the others at the table as if he were asking what to do. Joyce winked at him and smiled, so he closed his eyes. Olivia dragged her finger down his nose. "That is..." She pursed her lips in thought. "Purple. What color would you like the end of your nose to be?"

With his eyes still closed, Adam said, "How about green?"

"Yes! Green would look very nice." Using her make-believe paint, she rubbed the end of his nose with her fingertip. "Now I'm going to put some eyebrows on..." She moved her finger along the bottom of his forehead. "...and I'm going to paint your cheeks pink."

As Carrie watched the exchange between Adam and his daughter, she was overjoyed by how far they'd come. Olivia probably had no idea of the magnitude of this outing. Her daddy had not only taken time off work, but he'd invited his whole family out to see where he spent so much of his time, something he'd never done before. And now he was sitting with Olivia on his lap as if it were a normal, everyday occurrence.

Olivia and David seemed so comfortable with him now, so relaxed. Carrie wondered how it had even happened. With all her other families, she'd always had a set list of strategies to help the children overcome whatever issues or obstacles they had, but this time things had been different. It had taken a ton of tiny moments.

When Olivia had finished "painting" his face, Adam took her tiny hands in his and addressed the family. "I have a celebratory announcement to make," he said, excitement all over his face, "which is why I've brought you all here today. But I can't tell you by myself. I need to get Andy." He lifted Olivia off his lap and stood her on her feet next to Joyce. "Be right back."

Carrie's mind immediately went into overdrive. Why did he need Andy to make an announcement to his family? Had their kiss been some kind of fling, a crazy night before he committed to Andy Simpson? Carrie's mouth had dried out completely, and she couldn't get her breath. She focused on the family to keep her mind from wandering to all the things Adam and Andy might say. Walter was talking to Bruce; Sharon and Eric were helping David get the paper off his straw; and Joyce was coloring with Olivia. Their faces blurred in front of Carrie as she tried to get her emotions in check, her fear over this situation blindsiding her. She tried to tell herself that Adam Fletcher was never hers to have, but there was something undeniably right about the way she felt whenever she was with him. But she couldn't get the idea out of her head: What if he'd slipped? He'd been spooked by the idea of forever with Andy. He hadn't been ready for commitment, but now he was. She sat on the edge of her seat, waiting for Adam to announce whatever news this was.

Carrie's chest tightened when Adam and Andy came out of the office door and walked toward their table, side by side. Andy was beautiful, smiling, her hair falling loose and wavy over her shoulders. They looked like the perfect couple together, Carrie thought against her will.

Andy turned to Adam and smiled wider, and a wave of unease rushed over Carrie. She knew what kind of smile that was. It was an anticipatory smile. Her chest felt hollow, yet she could hardly get a breath as if her lungs were filled with water. She tried to see if they were standing closer to each other than normal. Andy *was* awfully close to him. Carrie was still scrutinizing when, to her horror, she saw Adam's face. He was grinning back at Andy. It was the same kind of grin that happened right after his little laugh he always did. It was a content, almost reflective smile.

"You all remember Andy," he said, his gaze shifting to the table. "She's a consultant with whom I've been working to expand Salty Shockoe across the East Coast." He turned to the staff and beckoned them over. Tom, the hostess, and a few others stood behind the Fletcher family. Carrie had to work to slow down her pounding heart.

He looked directly at Carrie. What was his expression? Was he silently apologizing for kissing her? She wanted to run out of the brewery right then and there, but she couldn't move until she'd heard it out of his own mouth. So many emotions were slamming around inside her head: She was terrified that he loved Andy, angry that he had kissed her if he wasn't available, totally disappointed at the thought of Adam being with someone else, worried for the children—how would they handle someone new in their lives? Despite all her emotions, her face was blank, blank with the weight of them all.

"In life, sometimes, we need a partner..." he said.

Oh, God.

"I've realized I can't do this alone."

Her fears made the hair on the back of her neck stand up. She worked to control her breathing as she looked down at the table, not wanting to face what was being said right in front of her. Maybe because she was curious or because she liked to torture herself, she looked back up at Adam.

"As you all know, I have been very busy with the expansion project. I know my work has consumed far too much of my time, and I need someone I trust to help me with this. That's why I've hired Andy to direct the expansion."

Wait. Was he talking about work?

"I will be overseeing the project, but it will be Andy who will be in charge of managing the whole thing. Her help on this phase of the business will not only be of huge benefit to the brewery, but it will give me more time to spend with you all." He winked in the direction of the twins. "Congratulations, Andy."

Everyone clapped, snapping Carrie out of her haze of confusion. He hadn't said he was marrying Andy. He hadn't even mentioned anything about being with her. Before she could process anything else, an unfamiliar man came forward and kissed Andy on the cheek. "I'm proud of you," he said to her.

"This is my husband, Jack," she introduced him.

Husband.

The entire table had gone on with their conversations, but Carrie still sat there, stunned. Relief flooded her, filling every part of her body. Andy was married. And having Andy to focus on the expansion would allow Adam more time to be with everyone. With her?

He turned and looked at Carrie. She knew that look. This time, she knew without a doubt that it was meant for her. She wasn't misreading it. He was letting her know how he felt. But now, she had so many questions: She was leaving in almost a week to return to North Carolina—what about that? The children would be with their mother again, and Adam wouldn't need her anymore. How did he feel about her? What was he thinking? Did he want her to stay? All the questions were bouncing around her head still as everyone else broke into excited chatter.

Adam walked over to Sharon and sat down next to her. "I'm sorry," she heard him say. "I've been awful and I'll make it better. I promise."

She smiled at him. "You just did." She put her head on his shoulder, and Carrie looked away from them to keep herself from tearing up.

Carrie took in all the familiar faces, and she thought how even if nothing went any further with Adam—she'd have to figure out how to deal with that—she was glad that she could leave knowing she had succeeded in helping this family.

"Look!" Olivia said, her feet moving so fast that Carrie worried she'd take a spill right onto the bricks of the sidewalk. She was pointing and running, David trailing behind her, as they made their way toward the area roped off for Santa. He was sitting on an enormous throne, his beautiful white hair and beard combed perfectly, little curls at the bottom. It was so cold outside that there wasn't even a line, and Carrie wondered if Santa's cheeks were blushed on or if the cold had done it naturally. He waved at Olivia with a white-gloved hand and let out a "Ho, ho, ho!"

"Hi, Santa!" Olivia said, only slowing down to move through the velvet ropes to enter the area. She climbed onto his lap as David walked up cautiously. Once both children were settled, there was a snap and a blinding pulse of light as the camera went off, their images showing on the monitor at the podium. As Santa made small talk with the children, Adam came up behind Carrie and, to her surprise, put his hands on her shoulders. It was a very personal gesture—his body close enough to her back that she could feel the warmth of him. She turned and looked up at him more out of astonishment than anything else. It was as though he'd only just realized what he'd done, his gaze falling on her shoulders where his hands had been. Then there was that little quiet laugh of his and a smile that made her forget all about the cold outside. The rest of the family were all watching the children. Everyone except for Joyce. She was staring straight at Carrie with a smile on her face.

"And what would you like for Christmas?" Santa asked Olivia.

"I'd like my daddy to take me ice skating with Snow White."

Santa Claus made eye contact with Adam and let out a loud chuckle. "Did you hear that, Dad?" Santa called. "That order's on you, not me."

Adam laughed as he acknowledged the old man.

"And how about you, sir?" Santa asked David.

"I'd like to ice skate with Daddy too, but I'd also like a race car set."

"I'll see what I can do. Have you two been good this year?"

"Oh, yes!" Olivia said, and everyone laughed.

When the kids had finished chatting with Santa, and Adam had purchased more photo packages than he'd ever give out in his lifetime, he turned to Carrie. "Mom's going to take the kids for a little while. Would you walk with me to get coffee for everyone?"

"Of course," she said, excitement rushing through her like fireworks.

They walked over to the coffee shop, the heat from inside nearly overwhelming her when Adam opened the door and allowed her to enter. He stood beside her in front of the board with the offerings of various coffees.

"Let me try to guess which coffee you'll get," she said, feeling confident that she knew him well enough now to choose.

He looked down at her curiously, a smile playing at his lips.

"Hmm." She walked closer to the board, her eyes scanning the various drinks. "Dark roast…" She moved over to the flavors. "I don't see you as the sweet-coffee type." She looked him up and down.

He was smiling now, and she tried not to let it distract her.

"Maybe a *little* sweetness…"

She heard him chuckle. It made her stop and look at him, and, when she did, she felt her limbs go numb. He was telling her something in their unspoken language, something she wanted to interpret, but she was worried she was translating it incorrectly. His face exuded so much affection that she dared not think it was her that was causing it. There was no way, she thought, that she could do anything to make a man like Adam look like that.

"Hazelnut dark roast with milk," she said before her nerves clouded her vision completely.

"I usually just get plain coffee. Black. But your suggestion sounds delicious. I think I'll have that. What do you want to drink?" he asked, still looking at her like he had been. She was so jittery, adding caffeine to her body probably wasn't a good idea. "Want me to guess yours?" he asked. She nodded, glad that she didn't have to speak.

"Definitely a sweet-coffee drinker," he said with a grin.

As he studied the board, she allowed herself to take in the sight of him. His thick brown coat was bunched up around his wrists, his hands in the pockets of his jeans as he leaned toward the board to get a better look. His face was focused but light and happy while he searched the flavors of coffee.

"Caramel is in there, I'm sure," he said, looking over at her.

Carrie grinned. He was right!

"And…"

She hung on his every word, hoping he knew her well enough to pick what she liked. She'd feel terrible if he said something like cinnamon, which she'd never get.

"Wait," he said. "I see a drink that is exactly what I think you'd have. Caramel mocha. With light whipped cream."

Perfect.

"You got it, right on the dot," she said, her heart going crazy. She was thrilled that he knew her well enough to know what she liked. How much more about her would he be able to guess? Could he guess how she was feeling right now or how happy she was to be with him?

As they stood in line, she looked around the coffee shop. There wasn't anything special about it. She'd been in hundreds just like it. But, for the first time, she didn't have her nose in a self-help book, and she wasn't alone. She noticed the Christmas coasters, the paper snowmen that hung from the ceiling above the register, the lights nestled in the greenery along the windows. As she stood beside Adam Fletcher, whose face she knew so well now, she thought to herself how, without even meaning to, he was creating memories for her as well. This would be a Christmas that she'd remember for the rest of her life.

Chapter Twenty-Five

Be careful not to spend too much time planning for the future and keep an open mind while in the present.

Olivia took Carrie's hand and pulled her down the hallway.

"Where's David?" Carrie whispered, confused, wondering why Olivia hadn't gotten him first and then come to get her. After all, it was Christmas morning, and certainly she'd want her brother to be ready to go downstairs with them.

"He's getting Daddy," Olivia said just as Adam and David surfaced at the other end of the hallway. Olivia had been so excited, she'd dragged Carrie into the hallway without letting her get ready for the day. She'd barely had a chance to brush her teeth. She still had on her moon and stars flannel pajamas. But the way Adam grinned at her, it seemed that he hadn't even noticed. Adam himself had on a T-shirt and plaid pajama bottoms, his feet bare. He looked so handsome—just like that—his hair pointing in different directions, David holding his hand. Of course that night at Ashford, when they'd been all dressed up, he'd looked fantastic in his tuxedo, but she liked him better like this.

Together, the four of them walked together downstairs to the Christmas tree, and Carrie couldn't wait to see the look on their faces when they saw everything she and Adam had bought. They'd all stayed up working tirelessly to set it all up in the playroom last night.

There was something so perfect about holding Olivia's hand, David and Adam beside her, that she couldn't imagine being anywhere else on Christmas. She'd only been with the Fletcher family a short time, but they'd impacted her life in a big way.

They entered the living room, and David and Olivia ran full speed past the plate with remaining crumbs of the cookies they'd left for Santa, toward the stockings they'd painted with Carrie. They'd not had a chance to fill them at the candy store, so Santa had done it, and wow, had he delivered! Small toys, candy, peppermints—they filled the stockings like Christmas confetti, the fabric bulging under the weight of it all. Carrie looked over at Adam when she saw what was in them, and he smiled. When had he thought to buy candy? She helped the children get the stockings down off the mantel, and then she sat on the sofa next to Adam.

The tree was the only light in the room apart from the gray of morning coming through the windows. When she'd first gotten there, Adam hadn't even planned on that tree. He'd barely been with them when they'd bought it, and he hadn't even taken part in decorating it. But now, it stood as if it were looking over them while Olivia ran over to her daddy to show him a pack of crayons she'd gotten in her stocking. In that moment, Carrie confirmed that she definitely needed change in her life as well. She finally realized that she wanted a life even more than she wanted to work. She wanted this for herself.

"Thank you," Adam said quietly, looking at the children, but she knew he'd meant it for her. He turned and looked right at her. They were so close that normally she'd have worried about their proximity, but this morning, it all seemed so right.

"Thank you for what?" she asked.

"Thank you for showing me what I was missing."

There was a creak on the stairs, and then the sound of footsteps. Joyce came into the living room in her bathrobe and slippers. "Good morning," she greeted Adam and Carrie. Olivia ran to show her the items in her stocking. "Oh, that's lovely, Olivia." After offering Olivia and David attention and seeing all the things they had in their stockings, she said, "I'm going to make a pot of coffee. The others are on their way down."

Only a few minutes after, as the coffee was percolating in the kitchen, the aroma of it seeping into the living room, the others came downstairs. Sharon sat down on the floor with the kids and everyone else made themselves comfortable on the love seat and chairs around the room. Walter was the last to come in, pushing his way across the floor with his walker. He sat down next to Carrie.

"This is an ungodly hour. You know that, right?" he said with a smirk. He looked at the kids and shook his head. "I don't really mind, though. You think the magic of Christmas morning is over once your own kids grow up, but then you get to have it again with your grandkids, and, if you're lucky, your great-grandkids. I guess that makes me one of the lucky ones."

"Coffee's ready," Joyce said from the kitchen. "And I've whipped up some scrambled eggs and toast for everybody. We're gonna need a good base in our bellies for unwrapping all those presents under the tree. Come on in and eat!"

When they all stood up to go into the kitchen, Carrie almost gasped out loud. She didn't, which was a good thing because she didn't want the kids to think it was anything out of the ordinary, but when Adam stood up, for the first time since Carrie had arrived at the Fletcher house, the kids went tearing after him, Olivia almost jumping on his back. "After breakfast, can I show you what I got, Daddy?" David asked. "I haven't had a chance to show you yet."

"Of course you can," he said, smiling down at David. The affection she'd seen in his eyes was present, but what surprised her more than that was the look of complete adoration that David had, gazing up at his daddy. She thought how this was probably what David had wanted all along. Adam turned around and tickled Olivia, making her squeal. Carrie laughed out loud, covering her mouth in surprise.

The kids could barely sit to eat once everyone had taken their coffee, toast, and eggs to the table. Carrie wanted to savor the moment, take in all the wonderful faces around her. Everyone looked so happy. Even Sharon was smiling when David sat next to Adam, telling him about what he hoped was under the tree.

"Is anyone ready to open some presents?" Joyce asked. Both children began bouncing up and down, their hands in the air. "I don't think they can wait much longer, Adam. Do you?" she kidded.

Adam looked down at David, who was sitting beside him. There was that little amused exhale and then a smile, and Carrie could hardly manage the feelings she had for this man. This feeling just happened. Like lightning. And—*boom*—it had definitely struck.

"Leave your plates, and I'll get them later," Joyce said, standing up. Carrie set her empty coffee mug down onto the table and followed the Fletcher family into the living room.

To her surprise, Adam sat down on the floor next to the tree. In the soft glow of morning, the lights on the tree were as bright as stars. He reached under it and pulled out a present, his eyes squinting to read the tag. "For David, with love, Grandma and Grandpa."

David's eyes got big, the excitement showing on his face, as he took the present from Adam. The ribbon that had been taped around the present fell loose, and David dropped it down beside him. Joyce scooped it up and put it into a trash bag she'd brought with her into the living room. With a rip, David pulled the paper off and turned the gift over in his hand to inspect it. He took in a loud breath when he saw what he was holding.

"It's a model race car that you can paint yourself," Bruce said, his adoration for his grandson clear. "What do you think?"

"Can I paint it now?" David asked.

Everyone laughed, and David looked around, his little eyebrows pulling together in concern.

"How about after we finish unwrapping everything?" Bruce said. "I promise I'll help you."

Adam reached under the tree and pulled out another present. "This one is for...me," he said quietly with a slightly surprised look on his face. "It's from 'Everyone,' it says." He made eye contact with those around him, clearly interested. Gently, he pulled off the wrapping, handing it to Joyce as she reached out for it. It was a book. He turned it over in his hands and let out a "Ha!" and then a chuckle that made Carrie's tummy do somersaults. He turned it around for everyone to see. "*100 Useful (and Not Useful) Things to do with Beer.*"

"Just in case it all goes to pot," Walter said with a wink.

David looked slightly relieved when everyone laughed at Walter's comment, and Carrie wondered if he was still thinking about how they'd all giggled at him. He was such a serious little boy, more serious even than his daddy, and Carrie wanted to abandon presents just to paint that car with him. She watched his face as each person unwrapped their gifts, his interest undeniable. He was patient, quiet, focused. Then she looked at Olivia, who was on her knees next to the tree, waiting for her own gift. She kept leaning over toward Adam and whispering, "Is that one mine?" He couldn't hide his smile whenever she asked as he shook his head. Then, finally, one for her.

Carrie recognized it immediately. It was the crown she'd bought with Adam and helped him wrap. Olivia took the gift and ripped wildly until she was holding the crown in her hands. "Oh!" she said with a gasp. "This is so pretty!" She put it on her head and stood up. It was huge, the jeweled faux metal swallowing her forehead, but she didn't care. She held out her nightgown as if it were a dress and danced in circles. "Do I look like a princess?" she asked Walter.

"You *are* a princess," he said, with doting eyes.

"I have one more gift for David and Olivia together," Adam said, pulling a huge box from the back of the tree where it had been hidden by all the other presents. He slid it out and set it down in front of the twins. "Go ahead. Open it," he told them.

Olivia ripped the paper off the front, David pulling at one end. When they finally got all the wrapping off, the box—empty of any wording—didn't offer any more information about what was inside. David lifted the lid and pushed it back, and Olivia pulled the tissue paper from the top. When she did, she let out the loudest cry of joy that Carrie had ever heard her make. She leaned over Olivia to see what it was. Nestled in the tissue were three pairs of ice skates: one large pair and two smaller pairs. There was also an envelope. Adam pulled it from the box and slipped his finger under the flap. "The ice skates are for you, me, and David," Adam said to Olivia. "But do you know what this is?" He waved the envelope. The kids were watching him, waiting just like Carrie was. "In this envelope, I have tickets to Snow White on Ice at the Richmond Coliseum."

"We get to see Snow White?" Olivia said, her eyes round with excitement. She had pulled her skates from the box, and she was hugging them.

"Yes," he said. "And you know what else? A man I work with knows her, and, after the show, he's going to let us skate with her."

Olivia's mouth hung open with that news. She threw her arms around her daddy and buried her head in his neck. "Thank you!" she said in a muffled voice.

"Will you skate with me, Daddy?" David asked.

"Absolutely."

Unexpectedly, Carrie's eyes filled with tears. No one had told him anything. She hadn't pressed him to do it; she'd barely even mentioned that Olivia had said she'd wanted to ice skate with Snow White. He'd just remembered. He'd made it happen. And it was better than she could have dreamed. She blinked away her tears. Eventually, they subsided, but her heart was so full it was about to burst.

Once everyone had opened their gifts, Adam pulled one more small gift bag from under the tree. "This one's for Carrie," he said, handing it to her.

Surprised, she got down on the floor next to Adam. She took the gift and read the tag: *To Carrie, Love, The Fletcher Family*. She felt around inside until her fingers caught something thin and metal. She pulled it out. It was a beautiful bookmark, shiny, with beads on one end. "Thank you," she said to everyone collectively.

"There's more," Adam said, nodding toward the bag.

Carrie reached in and found something else. She pulled out a gift card to the bookstore. Her face registered shock, she was certain, but she couldn't help it. It was a gift card for one hundred dollars' worth of books.

"I know you like to read," Adam said. "I saw your car was full of books when you first arrived and we got your suitcases out. Perhaps you can find a few you haven't read."

Carrie thought about the books she had—all those self-help books. In the past, she'd have spent the whole hundred dollars on those books, but now she thought how she might buy a novel, or something on travel, perhaps. "Thank you so much," she said. She couldn't help it; she put her arms around Adam and hugged him. It had been innocent enough, but, unexpectedly, the scent of him so close hit her, and then he reciprocated, wrapping his arms around her. The hug was quick but just long enough to make it hard for her to breathe. He pulled away slowly, their faces coming inches from each other, and then he smiled. It was meant just for her. Even though his entire family was right there in the room and his kids were making noise beside them, it felt like it was just the two of them. She wanted him to know how much she cared for him, how much she couldn't stand to be away from him, but she didn't know the right time or place to tell him. She didn't even have a present for him.

"I didn't get you anything," she worried aloud as David crawled onto his daddy's lap and sat between them. Olivia scooted closer, her crown still on her head but tilted sideways.

"Yes, you did," he said, peering down at his children.

It was clear that the rest of the family understood the moment that Adam was having because there was a hush in the air; the only sound was the quiet radio in the background playing "Let It Snow." Carrie hadn't even noticed it was playing until that moment. Watching Adam as he talked quietly with his children, their hands on his arm, their faces so animated, she saw that beauty. Whenever she'd been able to help children overcome their issues, she'd always felt pride, but today, she felt different emotions. She felt a slight relief, but she also worried. This was more than something to correct; this had been heavy on her heart, and seeing Adam with his children, watching the way they reacted to him, she hoped she'd had enough time to make it stick.

"Why don't we see what Santa has brought you two," Joyce said. "I'll make us some more coffee and some cinnamon rolls for anyone who didn't get enough to eat."

"What did Santa bring?" Olivia said, bouncing over to Joyce and grabbing her hands.

"Let me get my camera, and we'll show you."

"Where is it?" Olivia asked. She used Joyce's hands as if Joyce were leading her in a dance, pulling her out and in. Olivia let one hand go and did a spin.

The kids were ecstatic when they saw the jungle gym in the playroom. Carrie was especially pleased when Olivia grabbed Sharon and took her over to the playhouse area, explaining all the things she could do with her dolls. She knew what it meant to Sharon to have the children seek her out. She was struck again by how so much had changed since she'd arrived. The playroom certainly looked different. Now it was a place for exploration, for fun, for laughter. Adam was leaning on the side of the slide, talking to David, smiling at his son as he slid down it. Olivia and Sharon were giggling about something—she didn't know, but it didn't matter, they were happy. But the playroom was only the start. Adam had made time for his family, and they were all together on Christmas.

She'd hoped for all of that, but something else had changed as well. Something she hadn't planned on at all. She'd seen a change in herself. She wasn't unsure of herself personally anymore. She felt confident making her own decisions without looking for the answers in one of her books. She wasn't intimidated by success. She knew what she wanted in life, and she knew that she was strong enough to get it. Suddenly, right there in that moment, she realized that she had a lot of her own living to do, and the sky was the limit. Seeing this family figure out their roles with each other made her want to figure herself out. She needed time to decide what she really wanted to do with her life.

It was late. The children had been put to bed and the whole family was asleep. Adam was in the kitchen, gazing out the window. The skies had cleared, and a giant moon in the sky cast a white light on the snow outside. It made the cream color of his sweater look almost yellow against its bright white. She noticed that the peppermint candle she'd bought when she'd first arrived was burning on the island, and she didn't remember anyone lighting it. When she got closer, he turned around.

"Hi," she said.

"Hi."

"Do you like that candle?" she asked.

He smiled. "I know *you* like it." When he said that, their unspoken language was all over his face, and she felt the prickle of excitement on her skin. He walked around the table to meet her. "I was wondering"—he looked down at her—"what you had planned for after New Year's."

"I haven't ironed anything out yet," she said.

He cleared his throat. "How about a drink?" he said abruptly. "We should have a beer."

She suddenly wanted a drink. Was she supposed to be the nanny or the woman he'd taken to the Ashford Christmas party?

"Glass?" he asked. She nodded, and he pulled a pint glass from a cabinet.

As he poured the amber liquid into the glass, she just came right out with it.

"I saw how happy you made your family today…" She trailed off, gathering the strength to ask her big question. "With them all here to help out, will you need me any longer?" she asked.

Adam took a step closer to her and handed her the glass. "I was going to talk to you about that." He set the beer down without drinking it, so she did the same. "I think my mom wants to watch the kids until Gwen returns. I'd be happy to pay you the amount we'd discussed at the beginning so as not to set you back any pay…"

"Okay," she said, ignoring his comment about the pay. She could feel the rush of sadness at the thought of leaving them all, but there really was no need for her to stay. She understood that. This family didn't need her anymore. And suddenly, while she was terribly sad, she knew it was time to get working on herself.

He took a drink of his beer. "But I was wondering if you'd like to go out sometime."

She sat there silently for a moment, contemplating his offer. Carrie felt a pinch in her chest, and she knew why. Her thoughts on the matter were bittersweet. She could hardly believe what she was thinking. She had true feelings for Adam; she couldn't deny them. She wanted to spend every minute with him. She wanted to wake up next to him in the morning, have him be the last person she saw before closing her eyes at night.

But.

She took in a breath as the thoughts entered her mind. Adam had just carved out time for his children. What kind of person would she be if she filled those hours selfishly? He needed time to grow with his kids, to get to know them, to learn how to care for them without anything or anyone getting in the way.

If she stayed in Virginia, she'd find herself constantly waiting. Waiting for Adam to find time for her, waiting for more than what he was able to offer her, waiting for the chance to begin her own life. She was tired of waiting for her happiness. She needed to move on, get up and make something of herself.

All these thoughts came crashing in on her, and she could tell by his face that he saw them in her expression. He'd asked her to go out with him. She'd wanted to hear that almost the entire time she'd known him. The sadness that swelled in her stomach at her answer was almost unbearable. She knew what she wanted in her heart, but she had to go against it in this instance. It just didn't make sense any other way.

"I see," he said, his eyes dropping down from her face in thought.

She hadn't had to say a thing; he'd just been able to read her. Her chest felt tight at the admission as she shook her head, telling him no—the answer he'd already guessed. All she could hope for in life was someone as wonderful as Adam, who could communicate with her so effortlessly, without a single word spoken like he could. In a different time, a different place, they'd be perfect for each other.

"You need to spend time with your family, and I have things pulling me back home," she said. She swallowed to alleviate the lump in her throat. "I'll spend some time with the kids tomorrow morning before I go," she said, suddenly worrying about them. She couldn't just up and leave without saying goodbye and having some sort of transition. She wasn't sure how she'd get through the day without crying, but she had to. For the children.

"Will you come to see me?" Olivia asked the next morning as Carrie tried to fold her evening gown and pack it into her suitcase. That was a tough question without an easy answer. The truth was, she lived a state away, and she probably wouldn't ever see this little girl with her curly hair and unstill feet again.

Carrie felt the prick of tears and cleared her throat. "You never know." She smiled for Olivia's benefit. "I gave your daddy my email address so that he could send me pictures," she said. The truth was, she'd nannied for many children over the years, and she knew that if she was lucky, Adam would remember to send her photos, and she'd marvel at how much they'd grown, but if and when she ever saw them again, their time together would be a distant memory for them, clouded by the million other memories of childhood, and they'd forget her. It would be different for *her*. She never forgot anything about the children she worked with, but this time, this family would be forever in the forefront of her mind, right there at the top. Without even knowing it, the Fletcher family had made this the best Christmas she could have imagined. They'd taught her about the kind of person she wanted to be, and what would make her happy. She would never forget it.

She zipped up her suitcase and stood it on its end. "Here you go," she said, holding out her fist. Olivia opened up her little hand, and Carrie put the small bottles of food coloring in her palm. "You and David can make some more rainbow volcanoes now that you know how."

"Thank you!" she said, and she kissed Carrie's cheek. "I'm going to go show David." She ran out of the room, leaving the door open. Carrie sat on the edge of the bed, holding her suitcase, the room clear of her things. With a deep breath, she stood up and pulled her suitcase to the door.

"I'll get your bags," Adam said from the doorway.

"Oh. Thank you." She dropped the handle and met him at the door.

"I started your car for you," he said. "So you don't have to drive in the freezing cold. The heat's running."

"Thanks."

"Thank you," he said. "For everything." He leaned forward and kissed her on the cheek. His scent, the softness of his lips, the sweetness in his face—it almost made her falter. She closed her eyes and tried to commit this feeling to memory. She never wanted to forget it.

"You're welcome," she said. As she walked down to her car, she couldn't ignore the sinking feeling that this would be the last time she'd see Adam Fletcher.

Chapter Twenty-Six

One year later

Be open to change.

It had been an entire year since Carrie had been in Virginia last with the Fletcher family, and just like she had a year ago, she was heading there for a new job. Her friends back in North Carolina had sent her off this time with a big party. They'd packed her car with all sorts of Christmas candies and chocolates, a novel for her free time, and a gas card for emergencies. She'd spent the last year working at the Children's Museum of Wilmington. The term "museum" had always amused her because this place was far from that. It was an enormous facility, full of rooms for children to play, explore, pretend, build—if a child could think it up, it was there. They offered story time, science discovery, cooking. Carrie was in heaven. She was able to do all the things she loved to do with children, but when the museum closed for the evening, she could go home, cook a meal, have a glass of wine. When the Program Educator position became available at the Children's Museum of Richmond, she had to apply. And to her complete surprise, she got the job.

Parking was tricky with the U-Haul trailer attached to her car, but she managed to find a parallel parking spot. Carrie pulled up along the curb at the coffee shop where she'd gotten a coffee so long ago, on her way to the Fletchers' house. This time, she decided to sit inside and enjoy it. She ordered her coffee and took a seat by the window. The streets were clear, no snow yet, but the sky looked like it could let go at any moment. While she'd made a ton of friends in North Carolina through work, she had only one friend in Virginia—a very good friend whom she'd kept in touch with the whole time she'd been away. She sent him a text: *I'm here! Just getting a cup of coffee.*

Her phone lit up on the table, and she laughed to see *FaceTime: Adam Fletcher* on her screen. She hit the button, and laughed again when she saw Olivia's distorted image come across. "Hi, Carrie!" she said.

"Let me talk," she could hear David saying in the background.

"Wait, David," Olivia said, clearly annoyed, her image jiggling as she batted David away. "When are you coming?"

It had all started with an email. Olivia had missed Carrie, so Adam had let Olivia send her an email just after she'd left last year. Of course, Carrie had emailed right back. Then, every time Olivia missed her— which was all the time—Adam helped her type another email.

As they went back and forth, occasionally she'd ask Olivia about David and Adam, and then Adam finally sent her his own message. From that moment on, they'd kept in touch. Adam was constantly asking her for ideas for rainy days, things they could make together, places he should take the kids. He had come to an agreement with Gwen to have the children more often, and he was really enjoying his time with them. The emails had started out as simply helpful emails back and forth, but as the year went on, they became friendlier, and Adam would drop her a line just to see how she was. She loved waking up in the morning to find that he'd sent her something, and she couldn't wait to send something back to him. So, when she'd gotten the job in Richmond, he was the first person she told.

"I'll be there in a few minutes. I'm just getting a coffee. What are you and David doing?"

"We're waiting!" Her image wobbled in her excitement, and Carrie felt the swell of excitement.

"I can't wait to see you."

"We can't wait to see you too! Daddy's been cleaning all day."

"Oh!" She laughed. "I hope he's not cleaning for me."

"Yes he is! He said he wants everything to be perfect for you. I even had to clean my room!"

"She didn't clean it very well," David said in the background.

"Well, I'll see you two in a few minutes, okay?"

"Okay, Carrie."

"Bye!"

The picture faded to black on her phone, leaving Carrie with a grin as she held her coffee with both hands to warm them up. The mental image of Adam cleaning sent a giggle running through her.

She'd been on a few dates in Wilmington, and she'd had a good time, but no one had affected her like Adam had. They got each other in a way that she hadn't been able to replicate with anyone else. It was strange because they were both very different people, they had different likes, different temperaments, but when it came to understanding each other, their relationship was perfect. She often wondered about him—if he was dating anyone, if he was doing well—and she couldn't believe her luck when the job in Richmond rolled around. She hadn't planned to come back. She'd driven all the way to Richmond to interview, but she didn't tell him she was there because she didn't want to see him only to have to leave again.

Snowflakes had started to fall as she left the coffee shop. It was nothing like that storm last year, but it was nice to see snow again. Barely enough to require her windshield wipers, she put them on intermittently as she pulled the U-Haul down the street toward the Fletchers'. When she arrived, she stopped and stared at the house. Adam had decorated for Christmas. The candles were lit, the greenery hung on the banisters outside, and she could see the lights of the Christmas tree through the window.

She sat for a moment in her car, taking it all in. Excitement tickled its way up her spine with a shiver. She was about to see Adam for the first time since she'd left a year ago. It seemed like yesterday. She'd spent a year getting to know him better over email, which was strange, but being so far apart, they had no other way. Countless times she wished she could just sit across from him like she had in his kitchen and talk until the sun rose. In the last few months, he'd emailed her almost daily. Now, the zinging excitement that she felt at finally getting to be with him, face to face, was making her giddy.

Her phone lit up on the seat in her car. The screen said *Adam,* and she smiled to herself.

"Hello?"

"Is that you sitting outside in your car?"

She laughed. "I'm just admiring your decorating."

"Well, I learned from the best. Come inside. It's freezing out there."

Carrie turned the engine off and got out of the car. For the first time, she could see the green lawn and the perfectly trimmed hedges. The snow was barely falling, and it hadn't covered everything yet. She walked up the steps and before she hit the bell, there he was in the open doorway. Exhilaration shot through her limbs all the way down to her fingertips. She tried to get a deep breath to calm herself without making it too obvious. They both stood still for just a moment. It had been a long time. His hair was a little shorter, but everything else was the same. He was smiling, his eagerness to see her showing in his eyes.

"Hey," she said as if she'd just left him yesterday.

"Hey." He opened the door wider to let her come in.

"The house looks nice," she said, chewing on a smile as she remembered Olivia's comment earlier. "It's very...clean."

"Mm hm." He closed the door. He was looking at her, and she knew instantly—as if she'd never left him—that unspoken language of theirs. It sent flutters through her stomach. "It's so good to see you," he said.

"It's good to see you too."

They fell silent, as if both of them were taking in the fact that they were together again.

"Did you bring a dress?"

"I did."

"Allie will be happy to see you. You can meet Zach, Carolyn's new little brother."

"I can't wait!"

David came in from the kitchen. "Hi, Carrie!" he said with more enthusiasm than she'd ever seen from him.

"Hi, David! You've gotten tall!"

He smiled shyly and then said, "Daddy, can we show her the trains we built?"

Adam nodded. "Let's show her in a few minutes. We'll let her get settled first."

"Okay. I'll go get Olivia." He ran off, leaving the two of them together again. Adam took her coat and hung it in the hall closet.

"I smell peppermint," she noted as he closed the closet door.

"I put your candle on."

She smiled.

"Carrie!" Olivia's high-pitched squeal and the thuds of her feet came sailing down the hardwoods before she could see her. She rounded the corner, nearly skidding on one foot, and threw her arms around Carrie. "Hi!" Her hair was longer now, pulled back with a ribbon at the end, and she'd gotten a few inches taller as well—taller than David even—her limbs thinning out and looking lankier.

"I have missed you," Carrie said, giving her a squeeze.

Olivia bounced over to Adam, grabbing his hands. "Daddy, Daddy! Let's make her some of that hot chocolate we made together yesterday! It was so yummy!"

Adam looked down at his daughter with love in his eyes. "Maybe we can."

"Will you tell me if you do? I want to go play in the playroom with David."

"Of course."

Olivia pulled him down to her level by his hands and kissed his cheek. Then she let go and disappeared down the hallway. Carrie was almost breathless at the sight of it. Their fondness for one another was effortless, as if they'd been that way all the time. She remembered that little girl in the blue dress and tights who barely acknowledged her father when he entered the room that first day she'd come to work for them. Now she could see the relationship Olivia had with her father, the ease with which she talked to him, the comfort she had in grabbing his hands. And he'd built trains with David. It almost brought tears to her eyes. Seeing Adam, watching this new version of his life unfold—the Christmas decorations, the way the kids were with him, the absence of stress lines on his face—she was sentimental.

"How far away is your apartment from here?" he asked, leading her into the kitchen.

"Only about five minutes."

Adam raised his eyebrows, a smile on his face. He looked so happy. Seeing him like that brought all those feelings right back, and she felt a torrent of nervous energy just like she'd had so long ago. She wondered if he felt the same way. Time would only tell.

"Too full from your coffee to have a beer?" he asked.

"Never." She smiled.

Adam opened the refrigerator and pulled out a bottle, but as he did, she got a glimpse of the beers that had been stacked in the door. Not a white label in sight; they all had her green holly and berries in the background. "Nice label," she said as he handed her a beer.

"Thank you. I had an amazing designer." He winked at her, and her nerves went crazy. She put the bottle to her lips and drank quickly to squelch the buzz of excitement that was consuming her. He grabbed his own bottle and took a drink before moving closer to her. He was standing right in front of her, invading her personal space, their bodies too close. She looked up at him. "I'm so glad you're here," he said, looking down at her.

"Me too." She wasn't at a loss for words this time. She could have said more, but he was already reaching for her beer and taking it from her hands. He set it next to his on the counter.

"I've never asked, but I've always wondered what you thought that night after the Marleys' party when we were outside and I kissed you." He was looking right at her, his gaze unwavering. It was a very direct question, but it was a logical step from the emails they'd shared. He was testing her, trying to see if she felt for him what he clearly felt for her. And she did have feelings for him. She had completely fallen for him, and she hadn't found anyone else who could make her feel like he did.

"I thought it was…perfect." She remembered that night—the snow, the cold, and the warmth she felt in his arms. She'd wanted to have his arms around her quite a few times when she was away over the last year. She'd missed him terribly, and seeing him now was almost as perfect as that night because she knew that she didn't have to leave again. It was as if they were picking up right where they'd left off, but it was even better. For a whole year, she'd gotten to know him in writing—he'd made jokes, told her little things about himself, shared his feelings. Getting to know him through email removed the tension that she felt standing opposite him and allowed her to know who he was as a person. Now, armed with all that knowledge, she could give in to his advances easily. She'd fallen for him inside and out.

He was standing in front of her now, their beers beside them. Slowly, he put his hands on her waist, and in one motion, she felt him pull her toward him as he leaned down and kissed her. She wrapped her arms around his neck, and his hands moved to her back before he embraced her. His kiss was familiar and brand new at the same time, and she knew that this was what it was like to love someone. She'd taken a step toward happiness, and she couldn't wait to see what the future held.

Epilogue

"Push me again," Olivia said, her legs crisscrossed on the porch swing at Adam's new house. Carrie grabbed the chain to slow it down so that it wouldn't bump into the whitewashed wooden siding. The house was large like Adam's last home, but this one oozed character. With double chimneys, working wooden shutters, and a front porch that wrapped around the whole bottom floor, it sat like a diamond solitaire on the grounds that surrounded it. On the Richmond historical list, the house had been many things throughout history, but today, it belonged to the Fletcher family.

"Your daddy and David are unpacking without our help. Don't you think we've had a long enough break, and perhaps we should go help? I'm sure you're cold," Carrie said.

When the Fletchers' house sold in three weeks, no one was more surprised than Adam. He'd asked Carrie to go along with him to look at several houses, claiming that she had similar taste to his. When she saw this place, it was like coming home herself. The home had a stately fireplace in the living room that took up the entire wall, an interior central staircase so wide that five people could sit across the steps easily, and shiny hardwoods. But there were also things about it that gave it its own character: It had bubbles in the original glass in each window and a screened-in porch across the back that had a wooden floor made from scrap wood from the first owner's boat business nearly two hundred years ago. The whole thing had been restored to perfection, and it had taken her breath away.

Just like Adam: he, too, could still take her breath away. He was formal, strong, quiet, with years of experience, but what she loved were the things that made him uniquely him—the curiosity on his face whenever he watched her with his children, the way he leaned forward just slightly when he was interested in conversation, that huff of laughter... Carrie had found many other adorable quirks over the two years that she'd dated Adam. He'd chosen to make Wednesday nights his late nights at work, and even though he only worked late once a week now, he always made sure to apologize and give her a kiss, even though she had told him a million times that it was fine. His thick, wavy hair would stick up in the same spots every morning as if he hadn't changed position all night. She loved the way he fought it when his eyes would close in exhaustion. If he'd promised to watch a movie with her, and he was too tired, he always tried to stay awake, his eyes blinking.

Olivia jumped off the swing, and Carrie had to grab the chain again to keep it steady. "When's Aunt Sharon coming?" she asked, hopping with both feet down the three broad steps onto the ground.

"She should be here soon. We only have a few more boxes, and we'll be finished unpacking."

Olivia grabbed Carrie's hand. "I'm glad you get to stay with us," she said.

"Me too," Carrie said.

Adam met them at the door where he'd been folding empty boxes, David by his side. He leaned toward Carrie, stealing a kiss.

"David and I are finished unpacking. We wanted to get it all done before everyone came."

Adam scooped Olivia up into his arms, gave her a squeeze, and set her back down. Then he led them to the living room. They weren't there long before there was a knock at the door. It creaked as it opened. Carrie turned to see Joyce down the hallway, poking her head inside. A gust of cold air seeped in, crawling across the floor and wrapping itself around her legs. Joyce came in followed by Walter and then Bruce.

"Sharon and Eric are coming," Joyce said. "They're just getting the baby out of the car. It's amazing how many things are required for a three-month-old." When she got to the living room, Joyce put her hand on her chest. "Oh, Adam. Your Christmas tree is beautiful!"

"Would you have expected any less from Carrie?" He grinned in her direction.

Sharon and Eric came in, Eric awkwardly hauling a baby carrier, his hand red either from the cold or the weight of the thing. He set it down gently onto the hardwoods as Sharon hugged everyone to say hello. After, she tugged on the blanket that had been draped on the carrier to keep out the cold, and underneath was the most perfect sleeping baby girl. She had a rose-colored dress on, covered mostly by the thick blankets tucked around her, and a matching rose-colored woven band on her head with a yarn flower sewn onto the band. Her tiny lips were pursed and moving in a sucking motion as she slept. "This is Mia," Sharon said.

"She's gorgeous," Carrie said, leaning down to get a better look, the powdery smell of balms and baby lotions wafting toward her.

This Christmas, they could celebrate their own little miracle right there in the flesh. After another miscarriage, it had been quite an ordeal to get her here, but now Mia was safe, and happy, and so was her mother. Sharon, who hadn't stopped smiling since she arrived, took off her coat and draped it on a nearby chair as Eric settled down with Walter and Bruce on the sofa near the fireplace. The flames from the fire licked their way up the chimney, pops and sizzles from the burning embers as festive as holiday music.

With the fire going in the old fireplace that had warmed generations of families for two hundred years, the Fletchers were starting their own life. The painted stockings were hung, the greenery up, the presents wrapped, and, once again, the whole family was there. Adam's cell phone rang in his pocket, and he pulled it out.

"It's the guy I mentioned from work," he said, answering the phone. Adam had warned Carrie that someone would be calling. Adam walked over to the heavy drapes at the front window. "Yep, you found us. I'll see you in a sec." He turned off his phone and opened the door as the truck pulled down the winding drive. "Our beer's here," he said, smiling over at Carrie. "Let's fill up that fridge in the cellar. Carrie, do you mind helping me?" Then he addressed his family, "We'll be right back."

That was the only call Adam took that night as they all settled in to celebrate Christmas. She was no longer the children's nanny, but Carrie was more than happy to watch the kids anytime they were with their father, which was quite a bit these days. Adam's agreement with Gwen was to have them every weekend, and they split holidays.

Carrie went out to get the cases of beer with Adam. Together they carried the large boxes, bottles clinking inside, to the door leading to the cellar. This cellar definitely wasn't the cellar that the original homeowner had envisioned. Adam had it remodeled with wooden floors, diamond-shaped cubbies along the walls for wine, and, at the end of it, an entire wall of retail-grade glass refrigerators where he could store his beer. Carrie wobbled the box onto the floor, the bottles tinkling inside with the jolting movement.

"Do you mind just opening the fridge for me?" he asked. "The middle door."

The heat from the hallway had snuck in with them when they'd opened the door at the top of the stairs. With the cold temperatures in the refrigerator, the glass was foggy, giving the bottles a cloudy look through the door. When she opened the refrigerator door, at first she was confused. She realized the whole thing was already full of beers that had the Christmas label she'd suggested when they'd first met. Trying to make sense of his request, she studied the bottles, looking for an empty spot to fill until her eyes came to rest on the center row. The labels were the same, but they didn't say Salty Shockoe. There was one word in that curly red writing on each bottle. She started at the left and read: *Will. You. Marry. Me?*

Feeling her pulse shooting around inside her, she spun around to find Adam on one knee, a velvet box in his hand.

"Caroline Elizabeth Blake, will you marry me?" With shaky fingers, Adam opened the box to reveal a platinum band with a perfect princess-cut diamond in the center. Like a flash before her, thoughts of all the nights he'd chosen her over work, the times they'd spent under her grandmother's quilt, cuddled up together, reading books, how he'd popped popcorn on movie night because the children were asleep upstairs and they couldn't go out to the theater, the way she could not, no matter how hard she tried, get him to cook a soufflé properly.

Before she could answer, he reached into a box and pulled out two bottles with one hand. Somewhat fumbling them—partly because he had the ring in one hand and because he was shaking quite a bit at this point—he set the two bottles down on the floor beside him. Carrie threw her head back and laughed. One of the bottles had a label that said, "Yes," and the other said in a font so small she had to squint to read it at first, "I have to think about it, but probably yes."

Carrie reached down and picked up the one with "Yes." When she did, Adam let out the breath he'd clearly been holding in the entire time, slipped the ring onto her finger, and pulled her close. He reached down and took her hand, admiring the ring. Then he released another little breath as if to say, "finally," and shook his head. There was no humor in his eyes when they met hers.

He took her face in his hands and kissed her, and she knew that this had been what she'd wanted all along. With the new ring on her finger shining in the lamplight of the cellar, they walked up to see his family together, bringing the "Yes" bottle along with a few more to celebrate.

A Letter from Jenny

Thank you so much for reading *A Christmas to Remember*. I hope that you enjoyed the story and it got you feeling all Christmassy!

If you'd like me to drop you an email when my next book is out, you can sign up here:

www.ItsJennyHale.com/email-signup

I won't share your email with anyone else, and I'll only email you when a new book is released.

If you did enjoy *A Christmas to Remember*, I'd love it if you'd write a review. Getting feedback from readers is amazing, and it also helps to persuade other readers to pick up one of my books for the first time.

If you enjoyed this story and would like to spend a little more time under the mistletoe, do check out my other holiday novels—*It Started with Christmas* and *Christmas Wishes and Mistletoe Kisses*!

Until next time, and happy holidays!

Jenny

Acknowledgments

A big thank you to my wonderful husband, Justin, who picks up all the pieces while I meet my deadlines. He is the rock that keeps it all together.

Thank you to Oliver Rhodes for his guidance, support, and amazing ideas throughout this creative process. I am so lucky to be a part of it.

To my editor, Kate Ahl, who knows how to build me up and challenge me to create the very best version of my story that I can write, I thank you.

About the Author

Jenny Hale is a *USA Today* bestselling author of romantic fiction. Her novels *Coming Home for Christmas* and *Christmas Wishes and Mistletoe Kisses* have been adapted for television on the Hallmark Channel. Her stories are chock-full of feel-good romance and overflowing with warm settings, great friends, and family. Grab a cup of coffee, settle in, and enjoy the fun!